Suddenly, there were eight jet-black spheres hanging motionless in the sky over their heads, forming a perfect circle in the sky over the Parley Pavilion.

Adam checked his wristcomp again, and watched as the last few moments until the designated start time for the meeting melted away. Thirty seconds before zero hour, the eight spheres fell, dropping like stones, but holding their perfect formation.

A scant ten meters off the ground, sun-bright tongues of red fire lashed out from the bases of all eight spheres, retro-rockets that roared with ten times the noise the sonic booms had. Adam felt himself grabbing harder and harder, holding on to Roberto's and Aaron's hands for dear life. He knew that if he had not been holding their hands, he would have turned and run, all the way back up Human Hill. The Devlin ships were all around them, landing ahead of them, to either side, behind them.

The retro-rockets stabbed down into the ground and kicked up a torrent of dirt and debris. Suddenly the air was filled with blinding, billowing clouds of dust. Adam closed his eyes and ducked his head, trying to keep the dust out of his face.

And suddenly it was over. The retro-rockets stopped their thunderous roar, and the world was silent once again.

They were surrounded.

Other Avon Books in
DAVID BRIN'S OUT OF TIME *series*

YANKED!
by Nancy Kress

TIGER IN THE SKY
by Sheila Finch

DAVID BRIN'S
OUT OF TIME
THE GAME OF WORLDS

ROGER MACBRIDE ALLEN

CREATED BY DAVID BRIN

AVON BOOKS  NEW YORK

This is a work of fiction. Names, characters, places, and incidents either are the product of the author's imagination or are used fictitiously. Any resemblance to actual events, locales, organizations, or persons, living or dead, is entirely coincidental and beyond the intent of either the author or the publisher.

AVON BOOKS, INC.
1350 Avenue of the Americas
New York, New York 10019

Copyright © 1999 by Roger MacBride Allen
"Out of Time" is a trademark of David Brin
Library of Congress Catalog Card Number: 98-94860
ISBN: 0-380-79969-3
www.avonbooks.com

First Avon Books Printing: August 1999

AVON BOOKS TRADEMARK REG. U.S. PAT. OFF. AND IN OTHER COUNTRIES, MARCA REGISTRADA, HECHO EN U.S.A.

Printed in the U.S.A.

WCD   10 9 8 7 6 5 4 3 2 1

To
V., M., J., B., A., and A.,
who were there already, and
MATTHEW THOMAS ALLEN
who came along after

ACKNOWLEDGMENTS

I should like to offer my thanks to David Brin, for inviting me into the new world he created, and for his stern editing job on the early drafts of this work.

Thanks also to Sheila Finch and Nancy Kress for their sterling contributions to the series (thus giving me more places from which to steal ideas).

Thanks likewise to my wife, Eleanore Fox, who gave the manuscript the going-over it deserved—and, needless to say, thanks to her for everything else besides.

RMA
Takoma Park, Maryland
December 1998

HOTWIRE

1999 A.D.
Carrboro, North Carolina, USA
Earth

Adam O'Connor slid his hand through the grillwork under the hood of the car and found the hood-release latch on the first try. He pulled on it, and the hood popped up an inch or two. He put his hands under the hood and lifted it up.

It swung up and clear. He took the flashlight out of his jacket pocket, turned it on, and aimed the light into the engine compartment. It was, he knew, a 318 V-8. The car, an ancient 1973 Dodge Dart, belonged to his math teacher, Mrs. Meredith. Half the kids in the car club had worked on it, one time or another. Adam had himself, before the faculty advisor kicked him out of the club for pulling the potato-in-the-exhaust-pipe trick on a fellow student's car. Everyone had gone after him for that one—the club advisor, the guidance counselor, his parents. It didn't seem right for all the adults to gang up and cause so much ruckus over such a little thing. The potato trick hadn't caused *that* much damage. It wasn't fair.

And so Adam had decided to carry out just a little bit of harmless revenge.

He pulled the cherry-bomb rig out of his other pocket and tried to balance the flashlight on top of the car's battery, but the light started to roll off, and he had to grab it before it dropped into the engine compartment. But he'd need both hands to hook up the cherry bomb. He should have thought about that before he headed out, rigged some way to steady the light, with duct tape or something.

That wasn't the only problem. Even with the flashlight, it was hard to see what he was doing. The tight beam cast harsh shadows and dazzled his eyes, making the darkness around the cone of light seem all the darker. And even though he had worked on this very car a half dozen times, he had forgotten one of its most annoying quirks. The counterbalance springs that held the hood up were old and worn, and the hood didn't stay up properly. It tended to drift down slowly, until it hung about a third open. He should have brought a stick or a pole to hold it up. Instead, he was reduced to holding the hood open with one hand while he held the flashlight with the other so he could find the spot where he was going to clip the leads—a procedure that left him a couple of hands short for doing the job.

He had thought it was going to be easy, fast. Pop the hood, hook the alligator clips on electric leads he had rigged to the cherry-bomb fuse *there* and *there*, slam the hood, and get out of there.

He pointed the flashlight at his wristwatch. It was almost 9:00 P.M. The drama club's rehearsal was going to break up any minute. That was why he had chosen this particular evening for the prank. Mrs. Meredith was the drama-club sponsor. Not only would she be here at school tonight, but so, too, would all the drama-club members. A prank needed an audience. It would do no good at all to set off a cherry bomb in Mrs. Meredith's car unless a bunch of kids saw it, and set the school hallways buzzing with the story the next day.

But no one was going to be talking about it at all if he didn't get this thing hooked up before the rehearsal ended and Mrs. Meredith and the club members came out into the parking lot.

The hood was drifting down again. Adam tried to get it to stay up by standing on the driver's side of the car and wedging his body in under the hood, supporting its weight between his shoulders. A sharp corner of metal caught him at the base of his neck, pinching down painfully. At least that got one hand free so he could hook up the leads—but the angle was incredibly awkward. He was practically facedown in the engine compartment. He had to crane his neck around to see even part of what he was doing, and that just seemed to make the piece of metal cut deeper into the back of his neck. Adam was starting to sweat, in spite of the cool night air. He hadn't planned this one well.

Finally he managed to get a clear look at where the first lead went. He squeezed the alligator clip open, shoved it into place, and released it. It looked like a good, solid connection.

Now all he had to do was clip on the second lead, and then—

"Hey! Mrs. Meredith! I think someone's trying to steal your car!"

Adam jerked back at the sound of the voice, and slammed his head into the inside of the Dodge's hood. That sharp bit of metal bit deeper still into his neck, breaking the skin. He felt a flush of warmth on the back of his neck as a small dribble of blood welled up from the cut.

He dropped the second lead and the flashlight and levered his hand around to shove up hard on the car hood, forcing it out of the way. The flashlight bounced and tumbled through the engine compartment, and the beam of light caught him square in the eyes, dazzling him. The flashlight hit the ground hard and went dark. He pulled his head out from under the hood just before it bounced off the top of its springs and came slamming back down. It crashed shut with a tremendous bang.

Suddenly all was quiet. He blinked and turned around, his vision still muddled by the glare of the flashlight. The dim lights from the school showed him nothing but the silhouettes of a half dozen kids, all of them seemingly frozen in place, staring at him in shock. Another silhouette, an adult, came hurrying out of the building. It was a heavyset woman with long dark hair, wearing a dress and carrying a thick sheaf of papers. She was too far off and too dark for Adam to see her face, but it had to be Mrs. Meredith.

"Who is it?" the woman demanded. "Who's that messing with my car?"

He didn't need to see her face. He knew that voice. Mrs. Meredith. Everyone else might be frozen to the spot, but not her. She was moving forward, her shoes clip-clopping loudly on the concrete, straight for him.

His head was throbbing from hitting the car hood. His neck was stinging like crazy. Adam stared at his math teacher in shocked terror. The moment seemed to come to a halt. This was it. She was going to catch him and then—

He got hold of himself. *And then, nothing*, Adam thought. No one was going to catch him. Not tonight.

He turned and ran.

Principal Benton sighed wearily and leaned forward in his chair. He folded his arms on his desk and stared at Adam, waiting. At last he stood and picked up the tangle of wires hooked up to a cherry bomb from his desk. He wrapped one wire and then the other neatly around the firecracker, and clipped the two alligator clamps together. He dropped the gadget onto his desk and looked down at Adam. They had already been through all the accusations and denials more than once. It was a lousy start to the day.

"What's the point of the game anyway?" he asked in a voice that was almost gentle. "We know you did it, and you know we know."

"I didn't do it," Adam said, staring straight ahead at the principal's desk.

"Uh-huh," said the principal. He turned and walked around his desk to stare out the window at the school parking lot.

Adam shifted uncomfortably in his chair. He had been there a while, and he wanted to unbutton his collar, but he didn't dare. The bandage over the cut on his neck was itching like crazy, but he couldn't bring attention to it. The cut on his neck was evidence against him, as much as the cherry bomb sitting on Mr. Benton's desk.

Adam risked a glance up at Principal Benton while his back was turned. Mr. Benton was a pretty nice guy. Medium height, brown hair, going a bit bald, with a kindly, patient face. Adam had always sort of liked him. Except for times like this, when the principal turned out to be the enemy.

"Honest," Adam lied. "It wasn't me." Part of him wanted to admit the truth, admit it and get it over with. But he had denied everything from the first moment, and, somehow, it got harder and harder to turn back from the lie. "It wasn't me."

"It wasn't you," echoed Mr. Benton. "Except we know it was."

"It *wasn't*," Adam said, his voice coming close to a whine.

"If you deny hard enough and long enough, you might even start believing your own lies. In fact, I bet you're starting to feel a nice big gush of self-pity, telling yourself how brave and noble you are for standing up under all the cruel punishment you don't deserve."

Adam looked up in shock. How had he known?

Adam dropped his eyes back down to the desktop as Mr. Benton turned around. "Except you haven't been punished—yet—and you know, deep in your heart, that you *do* deserve it." Mr. Benton turned around and leaned against the window frame as he looked down at Adam. "This one is serious. Very serious."

"But I didn't—"

"Do it. Of course not. The tooth fairy did," Mr. Benton said sourly. "You know, sometimes I think that the worst part of this job is getting insulted all the time by kids like you."

Adam looked up at Mr. Benton in surprise. "Kids insult you?"

"By treating me like I'm really, really, stupid," Mr. Benton said. "They—you—look me right in the eye and tell me the dumbest, most obviously phony story, something a kindergarten kid wouldn't believe, and expect me to buy it. Of course you didn't do it. Of course not."

"Honest, Mr. Benton. I didn't do it," he said again. "Really."

"You didn't?"

"No. Honest. I didn't. Um, ah, I'm missing social-studies class. Can I—can I go now?"

Mr. Benton looked at him hard for a long time. "Yes," he said. "In a minute. After you pretend to hear a speech I'm going to give. First I'll tell you something and you'll pretend to understand it and agree with it, and then you'll rush out of here so fast we'll both know that you didn't listen at all, and don't care what I said. Ready?"

Adam felt a strange little pit at the bottom of his stomach. This kind of sarcasm wasn't like Mr. Benton. "Um, ah—yeah, I guess."

"Then here goes. You could grow up to be a worthwhile person who makes good use of the gifts he has been given. But you're headed down a path, Adam. One that goes straight in the wrong direction.'' He sat down at his desk again and held one hand flat about six inches above the desktop. ''There's a file that thick on all the trouble you've been in over the years, the kids you've beaten up, and the lectures and punishments you've gotten, and the promises you've made to do better. Obviously none of the warnings took, and you didn't mean what you said, because otherwise you wouldn't be here now. That path is going to lead down, Adam, straight down. One day you wake up and notice you're a loser, a punk who threw everything away. You won't even know for sure when it happened. With me so far?''

''Yeah, yeah,'' said Adam. Even as he spoke, he knew his voice was too nervous and edgy to sound the least bit sincere. All he wanted to do was get out of there. He'd agree to anything that would let him escape.

''I bet you are,'' said Mr. Benton. ''So I take that file, and what happened last night, and together they tell me one of two things is going to happen. Either you admit what you did, and tell us what everyone knows. Tell us you did it. You'll be disciplined—no, you'll be *punished*, and you won't get off easy. But it can be handled inside the school, and when it's over, it'll be over.''

Mr. Benton stared straight at Adam in silence for a moment, then spoke again. ''Otherwise, this time, we'll have to call in the police.''

Adam's stomach suddenly tightened into a cold, iron knot. ''The police?'' he asked. ''But—but I didn't do any—''

''I've heard that already,'' Mr. Benton snapped. ''And I don't care.'' He pointed at the M-80. ''Someone rigged up a *bomb*, a small one, but a bomb all the same, to go off in a teacher's car when she turned the ignition. We *can't* let this case go without being officially solved. We *have* to find out who did this, and make sure it never,

ever, happens again. If that's what it takes, we *have* to go to the police. Once the police are involved, it will be a lot harder to control the situation. There have been a lot of vandalism cases recently, and the police are taking them seriously. They won't treat this as a prank. They *might* want to treat it as attempted murder.''

"*Murder*? But—but—'' Adam was on the verge of blurting out *but I didn't mean to hurt anyone*, when he realized just how much of an admission he would be making.

"I know,'' Mr. Benton said, exactly as if Adam had finished his sentence. His voice turned gentle as he went on. "It was just a prank. You didn't mean to hurt anyone. Just a big noise, and a big laugh, and that would be that. But what you mean doesn't count. What you did was put a bomb in a car and try to set it to go off when the car was occupied.''

Attempted murder! Adam felt a flush of shock—and of anger—rising in his face. One little gag with an oversize firecracker, and they want to call it murder! They were out to get him. Old Man Benton got him in here and treated him nice just to trick him, scare him into admitting something.

"I didn't do it,'' Adam said in his most surly and angry voice.

"Right.'' Mr. Benton put his hands behind his head and leaned back in his chair, and suddenly there was no patience left in his voice or his expression. "Of course not. All right, I know when I'm beaten. This one is up to you now. I'll give you until tomorrow. Either you admit what you did, and we punish you for it—or else I pick up the phone and call the police, and see what they can make of it.''

Mr. Benton paused once more, and glared at Adam. "Well, that went pretty much the way I expected. I just hope you surprise me tomorrow. Now get out of here.''

HOT SEAT

The day didn't get any better. No one seemed to want to talk to Adam, but they all seemed eager enough to talk *about* him. Everywhere he went, it seemed as if a cloud of whispers and giggles and shocked looks trailed behind him.

His classes seemed to drag on and on, each leading up to what would be the worst of all: last period in Mrs. Meredith's math class.

Adam was strongly tempted to skip her class, but he realized that it would be a bad tactic. It would just give everyone in class something else to gossip about, and more than likely get him dug in deeper at the same time. He was going to have to face Mrs. Meredith sooner or later. He might as well get it over with.

He slunk into class just as the bell was ringing, to the accompaniment of more whispering and buzzing and giggling than he had heard all day. He took a seat at the back of the room, instead of his normal seat in the second row. He was embarrassed enough by the commotion that he did not notice at first that Mrs. Meredith was not in the room.

9

That *never* happened. She was always there before the bell rang. Adam was just starting to wonder if her absence somehow had something to do with him when Mrs. Meredith swept into the room, moving fast, but not appearing the least bit hurried. "I'm sorry I'm late, class," she said. "I had some matters to attend to in the main office."

That put a chill down Adam's spine. It took no imagination at all to believe the "matters" had something to do with him.

"Let's get started, shall we? Jackie Andrews?"

"Here."

"John Bolton?"

"Present."

Adam found himself staring at Mrs. Meredith as she worked her way through the roll. She was one of the fun teachers, one of the good ones. Whether it was quadratic equations in math class, or working on the blocking of a tricky scene at a drama-club rehearsal, Mrs. Meredith made the subject exciting and interesting. Every other math teacher Adam had ever had treated mathematics as something to be learned by rote, dull formulae and rules to memorize. Mrs. Meredith made it fun, a series of complicated, intriguing puzzles to be solved. Adam liked her. He hadn't even been thinking of her, personally, when he had tried to rig the cherry bomb. He had merely been out to play a trick on a teacher, any teacher.

But today, her usual good cheer was gone, replaced by a cool, crisp efficiency that didn't fool Adam. She was upset. He could read it in the way she drummed her fingers nervously on her desk, in the wary expression on her face—and in the way she didn't look at anyone. She kept her gaze locked down on the roll-call list.

"Adam O'Connor?"

Adam was so focused on Mrs. Meredith's mood and appearance that he didn't notice when his name was called.

"Huh?" he grunted. "What?"

"Adam?" Mrs. Meredith asked. "You are here, aren't you?" There was nothing joking or humorous in her tone.

He was suddenly aware that every eye in the class was on him. "What? Oh. Yeah. I'm here."

"Wonder how you got the nerve to show up, dude," some boy muttered from the middle of the class, setting off a whole new flurry of giggles and whispers.

"That will do," Mrs. Meredith said sharply, glaring around the room until quiet prevailed. The kids in the class quieted down fast, a lot faster than they would have for a teacher they didn't take seriously or respect.

"Very well," said Mrs. Meredith. "Jennifer Parsons?"

"Here," said Jennifer in a subdued tone of voice.

Mrs. Meredith finished the roll and launched directly into the lesson. She kept the class focused and attentive, and somehow treated Adam exactly the way she normally did—while at the same time making it clear she knew perfectly well things were nowhere close to being normal. He tried to do the same. She called on him two or three times, and he answered as best he could, getting the answers more or less right. He found himself admiring the way she was handling the situation.

It dawned on Adam that he knew very little about Mrs. Meredith. He wasn't even sure what her first name was. He had a vague recollection that it was something plain-sounding, and a little bit old-fashioned. Alice or Agnes. Something like that. *Mrs.* Meredith. Not "Miss." Except she didn't act married, somehow. Now that he thought about it, he had a vague recollection of something in the school paper two years before, about her husband dying, and there being lots of bills and no insurance. Maybe she was still paying them off. Maybe that was why she drove such an old car, and was always eager to serve as a chaperone at a school dance or a basketball game. They paid the teachers extra for that work—though, Adam gathered, not very much.

Adam found himself being drawn into her determined show of normality. It was a math class like every other. There was no crisis.

When the bell rang, ending the period and the school day, it seemed as if the sharp clanging rattle popped the balloon. All the make-believe normalness rushed out into the hallway the moment the door opened and the kids started hurrying out through it.

Adam gathered up his stuff and started heading for the door. Maybe he could pretend, just long enough to get through the door.

But Mrs. Meredith was through pretending. "Adam," she said, "I'd like to talk with you a few minutes. There's something I'd like to show you."

Adam felt his stomach tighten up again, and he felt a hot, unreasonable shot of anger wash over him. Man, *everyone* wanted to talk with him. Talk at him, more like. They all wanted to give their little speeches, give him another big moral lesson. Why couldn't they leave him alone? What had he ever done to them?

And then Adam remembered what he had done to them, or at least to Mrs. Meredith. Maybe he had been lying to everyone else, saying he hadn't done it. But he hadn't started lying to himself. Not yet, anyway.

Well, he could worry about that later. But even he had to admit that Mrs. Meredith had a right to talk with him. "Ah, yeah," he said. "Sure."

"It's something on my car I'd like you to look at," she said, in a tone of voice that made it sound like she was asking because he belonged to the car club, and might be able to tell her if there was something wrong with the exhaust system. "Why don't we wait a few minutes to let the buses and cars clear out of the lot?"

"Okay," said Adam. "Ah, I guess I could do a few minutes of my homework here. While we wait, I mean."

"Good," said Mrs. Meredith. "I can do some paper-work, too."

They both sat down again, and both pretended, as hard as they could, that nothing unusual was going on.

The parking lot was just about empty by the time Mrs. Meredith led him out to her car. Adam was glad of that. He didn't want anyone to see—see whatever it was she was going to do.

She stopped in front of her car, then turned around and looked at him. The second Adam saw the expression on his teacher's face, he knew that the pretending was over.

He opened his mouth before she even spoke, ready to defend himself, to deny whatever she said, but Mrs. Meredith held up her hand and gestured for him not to speak.

"Don't talk," she said. "Don't say a single, solitary word. Just look and listen. See and hear."

"But—"

"Just do me the favor, Adam. Do *yourself* the favor. Don't talk."

Adam shrugged and nodded. Mrs. Meredith knelt, popped the hood release, and pulled the hood open. It wobbled a bit, but stayed up. If only it had the night before, then—well, never mind.

She pulled a small bundle out of her pocket. It was nothing but two pieces of string masking-taped to a twist tie that was in turn taped to a lipstick. There were paper clips tied to the free ends of the string. "I made this up myself, in Principal Benton's office, just before last period," said Mrs. Meredith. "I borrowed the real one long enough to get all the dimensions right. Let's pretend this is an M-80 firecracker with a long fuse, and that there are two long electric leads with clips on the end, hooked up to a length of wire that gets hot when electricity runs through it. And we can pretend the heating wire is wrapped around the end of the fuse. The pieces of string

13

on this are exactly the same length as the wires that I found on the real one last night.''

She leaned into the engine compartment and hooked one paper clip to the same place Adam had attached the real electrical clip the night before. She draped the rest of the dummy rig across the top of the engine. ''That's about how I found it when I opened the engine compartment last night. Someone showed me where the other end of this would have to be connected if this thing was going to go off when the car was started.'' She made the second connection with the second paper clip.

The lipstick, dangling down from the twist-tie ''fuse,'' banged up against a narrow metal tube leading into the carburetor. Mrs. Meredith pointed at it. ''That's the fuel intake,'' she said. ''Start the engine, and that's got gasoline pumping into it. Bang! goes this funny little prank, just a little joke. Now that fuel line is a strong metal tube. Maybe it wouldn't have been torn open. *Maybe* nothing would have happened besides a loud noise. But there was at least a small chance of the cherry bomb tearing the fuel line open and igniting the fuel pumping into the engine compartment. It could have blown up the car, with me inside it. Wouldn't *that* have been a funny joke?''

Mrs. Meredith looked up at Adam, stared him straight in the eye.

He didn't say anything. What could he say?

Mrs. Meredith pulled the pretend cherry-bomb rig out of the engine compartment and slammed the hood down. ''But wait, there's more,'' she said. She stepped away from the car and pointed to it. ''That heating wire would have taken a few seconds to ignite the fuse, and that fuse was pretty long. The cherry bomb wouldn't have gone off until the car was started and moving. I parked it today the same way it was parked last night, the way I park it every day. I wanted you to see that, too.''

She pointed at the parking-lot exit. The nose of the

car was aimed straight for it. "I park here so I can make a quick exit. All I have to do is start her up, drive straight ahead, and I'm on the main road—which was pretty busy last night—about five or ten seconds after I start up. Even if it didn't blow up the car and set fire to it with me in it, the cherry bomb would have gone off while I was merging into traffic.

"Rehearsal was just getting out. By the time I got my car started and moving, there would have been other cars coming and going to pick up students, and students walking through the parking lot and crossing the street. I might have hit someone. But even if the car didn't catch fire, even if I missed all the other cars and people on the road, I bet I would have had a one-car accident, and run the car off the side of the road. Wouldn't *that* have been hilarious?"

She looked back at Adam. Still he stood silent.

"Even if I wasn't hurt, and didn't hit someone, my car could have been so badly damaged that it wouldn't be worth repairing. Did you ever wonder *why* I drive a twenty-five-year-old car and let high-school students fix it instead of going to a real mechanic? It's because I can't *afford* another car. I can't even afford to get this one fixed as often as it needs it." She ran her hand through her hair, leaned against the car, and let out a weary sigh.

"I know that this wasn't directed at me. No one hates me that much. This was supposed to be a student playing a prank on a teacher. Nothing more or less. Students play pranks, and teachers are their natural targets. Law of nature. The problem is that none of that *matters*. This could have gotten me killed."

Both of them were silent for a minute. A car horn honked, somewhere off in the distance, and Adam heard the sound of a girl's laughter echoing out of the school's hallways.

"That's all," said Mrs. Meredith. "Think about it. And don't forget Mr. Benton's deadline."

She pulled her keys out of her pocketbook, opened the car door, got in, and pulled the door shut. The latch didn't catch on the first try, and she had to try twice more before it held.

She started the car, and almost immediately had it in drive and was moving forward. Adam couldn't help counting to himself, timing it. Sure enough, she was on the main road, with cars coming and going in both directions, inside of ten seconds.

HOT IDEA

Dinner with his parents and his little sister Molly was as close to stony silence as Adam cared to have it. He had been in trouble enough times to know that they knew something was up. Maybe the gossip had reached his mother from school. Maybe the principal had called his dad at work. But no one said anything.

Adam got through dinner somehow, and was excused from the table the first time he asked. Even as he ran upstairs to his room, slammed the door, and plopped down on his bed, he could see the whole thing coming. If this time was like the other times, one or both of his parents would just happen to wander into his room either late tonight, or, more likely, before breakfast tomorrow morning. Dad, probably. He'd come in and sit on the bed, and work around to the subject by gentle degrees. Adam would tell his father what he wanted to hear, and maybe even mean it as he said it.

But then would come the moment for Adam to act on what he said. He could see that part, too. The part where he chickened out, or convinced himself that the grown-ups had no right to push him around.

It would be easier, so much easier, to do nothing, to let the twenty-four hours run out, rather than work up the courage to march himself into the principal's office voluntarily and confess, admit what he had done, admit that he had lied about it. Anything, maybe even dealing with the police would be easier than that.

Adam thought back to what Mr. Benton had said that afternoon—and not just what he said, but the way he said it. It was far from the first time Adam had heard a speech like that. But something had been different this time. Principal Benton had been serious. And he'd sounded worried.

A small, sensible part of his heart told him that Mr. Benton was right: There was no one else to blame but Adam O'Connor. No one else had rigged the cherry bomb, or lied about it afterward.

But it was easy to push that voice away. What he had done the night before didn't matter so much. It was what they were going to do to him *next* that was important.

And when he started to think about all the things they would do to him, given half a chance, Adam started to get mad. Why did they have to come down on him like a ton of bricks? Sure, okay, maybe something bad *could* have happened—but nothing bad *did*. Why did they all have to make such a big deal out of it?

If only he could make it all go away. Make it all like it had never happened.

Suddenly Adam sat bolt upright in bed. That was it. Make it like it had never happened. Say they called in the police. What would the police do? Look for evidence. Well, suppose there *was* no evidence? Suppose he made it all go away?

What about the witnesses? Probably half a dozen kids had gotten a good look at him—but at night, from a distance, with lots of tricky shadows. And it wasn't like anyone had taken pictures or made a videotape or anything. It would be their word against his—and Adam had brazened out plenty of situations where that had been the case.

All it took was picking a story and sticking to it, no matter what. His story was pretty simple, really—total, complete denial. If he just kept saying he didn't do it, over and over and over again, no matter what, their witnesses wouldn't do any good. The only way he could lose would be if he gave up.

There was the cherry bomb itself. But there was nothing about it that could be linked to him. The wires and the alligator clips had come out of the scrap-parts bin from shop class. Even if the cops could trace the parts back to the shop class, it wouldn't do them any good. Any kid in the school could have filched them. As for fingerprints on the cherry bomb or the wires or the clips, Adam doubted he had anything to worry about. From what he had seen from cop shows on TV, the cherry bomb wouldn't take a print very well. Besides, Mr. Benton and probably Mrs. Meredith, and who knows who else, had handled it. No. He wouldn't have any problem with prints from there.

But what about prints on the car? In the engine compartment? Lots of nice smooth metal surfaces and lots of grease and oil to take up fingerprints. Adam reached up and gingerly touched the deep gouge on the back of his neck. He had probably left bloodstains, or maybe little scraps of skin or hair, on the inside of the car hood where it had caught him in the neck. That was evidence, and plenty of it.

But suppose, Adam thought, *it all just went away?*

It was close to midnight before his parents went to sleep and Adam managed to sneak out of the house. Getting his bike out of the shed in the dark without making any noise wasn't easy, but he managed it.

He stood up on the bike pedals, pumping hard, as he made his way up another hill. This time he was ready, all the tools and supplies he would need tucked into his backpack.

He had another flashlight *and* a roll of duct tape so he could tape the light into position. He had a broken broomstick from the shed that would be just the right length to prop the car hood open. He had his mother's old gardening gloves to wear so he wouldn't leave any fresh prints. He had a bottle of window cleaner and a whole roll of paper towels to wipe down every part of the car he had touched. He had even thought to bring a trash bag to stuff the used towels into.

All he had to do was bike to Mrs. Meredith's house, wipe down the car, inside and out, making very sure to check the inside of the hood for hair and blood and fiber, and that would be that. No evidence at all. It had never happened. Stuff the used towels and the window cleaner and the broomstick and the gloves into a trash bag, toss the bag into some Dumpster in the back of a store in downtown Chapel Hill, and back home to bed. Mission accomplished. Let Mr. Benton bring in all the police he wanted. All they'd have is an engine compartment someone had cleaned—but they wouldn't be able to say who, or why.

It was foolproof. Nothing could go wrong.

He pedaled on through the lovely fall night, down Greensboro Street, over to Franklin, and then cutting over to the bike path that led across the town line from Carrboro into Chapel Hill proper.

He slowed down and stopped when he came to the campus of the University of North Carolina. He hopped down off his bike on Columbia Street and looked at the redbrick-and-concrete buildings of the campus. He couldn't count the number of times his Dad had slowed down the car just to let him get a look at the campus. A generation ago, his father had nearly—nearly—got in. But the money hadn't quite been there, even for in-state tuition, and Dad's grades hadn't quite been good enough to qualify him for a scholarship. Adam had heard his father talk a thousand times about how different, how much better, his life, their lives, would have been, if only he had tried a little harder and made it to college. His father had grown up and raised a family one town over from the dream that hadn't come true. Scrabbling from one job to another, always one payment behind, the chance to get ahead always just a little out of reach.

" 'Don't you pull a Moses, Adam,' " Adam whispered to himself, echoing his father's words. It seemed as if his father had told him that all his life long, every time they had driven the old pickup truck down Franklin Street. " 'Don't pull a Moses. One in the family is enough.' "

Moses had seen the Promised Land, but had never actually set foot in it. It had been there, in front of him— but it was for everyone else, not for him.

It occurred to Adam that, somehow, he himself had never actually set foot on the campus of the University of North Carolina at Chapel Hill. And, thinking on it, he couldn't remember his father ever doing so. There were lots of events on campus, but, somehow, his father never took the family to any of them. Was that just chance? Or was it some sort of unspoken superstition that Adam had picked up unconsciously, that said you didn't set foot on the college grounds until and unless you had earned the right to be there. You didn't enter the Promised Land just for fun.

Don't you pull a Moses, Adam. Well, why should he? What could stop him from going to college? He had pretty good grades. Well, not great, but okay. He had the rest of this year and next to bring them up. His parents were saving up money for the in-state tuition.

That same small sensible part of him had an answer to his question. Making a worse mistake was no way out of the bad mistakes he had made already. He forced the thought down. His heart was pounding in his chest.

Was it just the exertion of the bike ride, or was he scared? Scared of what he was about to do, or scared to admit that all he was doing was digging a deeper hole for himself?

He heard the church clock chime the hour and was startled to realize it was midnight. He blinked and forced himself to focus. Why worry about trouble that hadn't happened yet? There was nothing to stop him. Nothing at all. All he had to do was hop back on his bike, ride to Mrs. Meredith's house, and take care of business.

He started walking his bike along, and was just about to swing his leg over the saddle and mount it when he noticed something odd about the sidewalk in front of him.

There was a strange blue disk the size of a manhole cover in the middle of the walk. It seemed to be glowing faintly. Strange he hadn't noticed it before. Maybe it had something to do with the college basketball team, the Tarheels. Sometimes it seemed as if everything in town was painted the team color, "Carolina blue." Glow-in-the-dark blue manhole covers would be nowhere near the strangest Tarheel tribute.

But manhole covers did not throb brighter and dimmer, or grow larger and larger as you watched.

Adam stopped walking toward the whatever-it-was and stared in astonishment. What was it? What did it mean? His guilty conscience was making him see things. He dropped the handlebars, and his bike toppled over and crashed onto the sidewalk.

The blue thing throbbed brighter and brighter, taking on depth and dimension. It wasn't just a flat disk set into the sidewalk. It was a *tunnel*, dropping down through the sidewalk, down into the ground.

Suddenly, it moved toward him, sliding in under his feet. "Adam O'Connor," a strange, flat-toned voice said. Adam scrambled to keep his feet on a piece of normal sidewalk, but the tunnel moved faster. For half a heartbeat, it seemed as if he were hanging in midair, directly over the tunnel. Then he fell, dropping into impossible depths of the unknown.

ARRIVAL

2345 A.D.
Earth

Ahna Varkan stood in the Yank t-port receiver room of the Central Operations Building. The technicians who ran the t-port were in a separate room, running it by remote. No need to have a whole crowd of people around at arrival, confusing the newcomers even more. The reception room was totally empty, with nothing but a soft carpet on the floor and padding on the walls to soften the impact for those who were moving a bit too fast as they came through.

It made Ahna nervous to have to wait all alone in the chamber. But it wasn't the time-Yanking itself that had her worried. Snatching someone across hundreds of years of time was a delicate business, but the machines were quite reliable. What worried her was the job they would have to do once all the Yank subjects had been collected.

A low throbbing whir came up out of nowhere, and

the receiver platform flared to life. There was a flash of light, and a boy about her own age suddenly appeared in the air just over the platform falling fast. He landed heavily on the deck of the receiver platform and stayed down. He was unconscious. Well, that happened a lot to the Yank subjects. They didn't take long to wake up. This one, Adam, started to come to even before Ahna could cross the room to him.

"Wha—where—what's—what's going on?" the boy on the platform asked as he stood up and looked around. "Where am I?" He spoke, naturally enough, in the language of his home time and place.

Ahna had learned enough twentieth-century English to let her more or less understand, and reply. "Many people faint at Yank." He looked even more confused. "Hard—to—tell," she said, struggling to remember her vocabulary. It had all seemed so easy when she had practiced on her own, but putting words together into useful sentences was much harder than she had expected. "We—take you," she said. "We track you until alone, and *take* you. Yank."

Adam's eyes widened suddenly, and he scrambled to his feet. "You caught me!" he said. "You caught me before I did it and—and arrested me, or something. Is this some kind of jail, or reform school?"

"What?" Ahna understood the words he was saying, but the concepts were utterly foreign to her. "What—you—talk—about?" she asked, struggling a bit with her twentieth-century English.

"Mrs. Meredith's car," he said, talking too fast for her to follow. "You're some special kind of police, and you were tracking me, and you could tell what I was going to do and—and . . . but that doesn't make any sense." He looked around. "And the police can't do anything like this." He looked to Ahna. "What's going on?" he demanded. "Where am I? Did I bang my head? It's killing me."

For a split second, Ahna thought he was talking literally, that something in his head was going to kill him. But then she realized he was exaggerating. She had walked in confident she'd be able to explain it all in English, but she could see that wasn't going to happen. Time to drop back to plan B. "Head—will—feel—better—soon," she said, speaking with exaggerated care. "I—will—tell—more—soon," She pulled a broca amplifier out of her pocket. "Put—on—this. It making—talk—easier."

"Huh?"

"Hold—still." She stepped forward and slipped the amplifier onto his head. It was nothing more than a small, streamlined blob of circuitry encased in shockproof plastic attached to a headband. Once the amplifier was close enough to Broca's area, one of the key speech centers of the human brain, it linked itself, in effect adding temporary pretrained language skills to the subject's brain. Anyone who wore one would be able to understand and speak the twenty-fourth century's dialect of English.

"Listen—to—new—words—I—say—next," said Ahna in twentieth-century English. She took a deep breath and went on, speaking in modern language. "That gadget lets you understand the way I talk. Is it working?"

Adam blinked in surprise and confusion. "Huh? Yes. Yes it is. I can understand you." He frowned and touched the broca-amp. "You're not speaking regular English, but I can understand you. I don't get it."

"I'll explain later," said Ahna. It didn't seem like the time to point out that Adam wasn't speaking "regular" English, either. "It will make more sense to you after I explain the larger situation." She looked around the t-port chamber, and decided it wasn't such a good place to tell it all. They had taught her in diplomacy school just how important it was to choose the appropriate place

26

for a conversation. "Follow me," she said. "We'll go some place better to talk."

See the other being's point of view. The diplomatic training staff had drummed that into Ahna's head, over and over again. It was never possible to do it altogether, of course. The beings they were to meet with were alien, after all, and by definition, aliens were unknown, and unknowable.

This boy Adam, following quietly behind her, was plainly shocked and disoriented. He was by no stretch of the imagination a native of her world and time, but he was far less alien than the beings Ahna had been trained to deal with. If she was expected to deal with non-Humans from other worlds, surely she could get somewhere with her own kind.

She led him down the hallways of the Central Operations Building and into a conference room that had a good view of the city below. The C.O.B. was built in the shape of an inverted four-sided pyramid, wide at the top, coming nearly to a point at the bottom. Its flat base was fifty stories above ground level. They were on one of the upper floors of the C.O.B. One wall of the room was all windows, slanted in from the vertical at about a forty-degree angle. Low couches in the room were arranged to allow for conversation while looking out at the view.

The plaza down below was filled with people enjoying the mild weather. Some relaxed in the shade of the C.O.B. pyramid, while others sunned themselves on the lawn. Slow-moving aircars trolled overhead, dodging the decorative spherical floating aquarium that hung in midair over the park. Two or three Humans were swimming in the floating tank alongside the fish. Robots, both airborne and on the ground, zipped back and forth busily on their myriad errands.

Adam O'Connor walked into the room a step or two

behind her, stopped dead in the doorway, and stared, openmouthed, at the vista before him. Ahna looked not at the view, but at Adam. All of this was absolutely outside his experience. *Make him see it for himself.*

"Come in and sit down," she said.

"Um, ah, okay," said Adam, still plainly quite distracted. Ahna touched the arm of his sleeve and moved him toward one of the couches. He sat down without taking his eyes off the view outside the window.

She sat down next to him and began to speak. "My name is Ahna Varkan."

"Hello," he said. "Look, Anna?"

"Ahna. There's an 'h' sound in it."

"Ahna, then, okay. Could you tell me please, Ahna, what's happened? You seem to know."

Ahna thought for a moment, considering all the things she might say. But still it seemed better to let him work it out for himself. "You had some idea before now," she said. "Something about them catching you before you did something."

"Ah, yeah, right," he said. "That blue hole opened underneath me, and—and I don't know. It's crazy, but I thought, just for a second, that somehow the police knew what I was going to do and decided to stop me." He turned his gaze away from the window for the first time and looked at her. "I know it doesn't make any sense," he said, almost apologizing.

"So if that doesn't make sense, try something else," Ahna suggested.

Adam looked out the window again. "All of that out there is real, but it's all impossible. This thing you put on my head"—he reached up and touched the broca amplifier—"*that's* impossible, too. I'm not even speaking English, am I?"

"No, not the form of English used in your century."

"But I don't know any language other than English,

so that's impossible. But it *can't* be impossible, because it's happening. It's real.''

''If it's real, why do you think it is impossible?'' Ahna asked.

Adam pointed to the floating aquarium. ''Because no one can do that. Or make a gizmo that lets me talk your language. No one knows how to do anything like that.''

''People learn how to do new things,'' she suggested.

''They don't learn how to do that much''—he nodded at the scene outside the window—''in the time it takes for me to fall down a hole.''

''Think about time for a moment,'' Ahna suggested.

Adam frowned for a moment, and turned toward her and stared in shock. ''*Time*?'' he asked. ''What are you saying?''

''You say it,'' she replied. ''You tell me.''

He hesitated again and then shrugged. ''All right,'' he said. ''Best I can see it, there are just two explanations. Either I'm crazy, or else this—this is the future.''

Ahna smiled and patted him on the arm. ''You're probably saner than any of us,'' she said. *After all*, she went on to herself, *you're not the one who came up with this whole crazy plan.* ''Wait there,'' she said. ''Let me get you something for that headache.''

Adam watched the strange girl as she stood up and went back into the hallway of the building. He felt strange, dizzy. But he knew it had nothing to do with anything being physically wrong with him. It was the *world* that had something wrong with it. The *future*? How could that be?

Ahna came back in a moment carrying what looked for all the world like a damp washcloth—and turned out to be just that. She handed it to him and he put the cool cloth on his forehead. Somehow the idea that they still used something as low-tech and old-fashioned as a cool, wet cloth on the forehead for a headache made the future seem a lot more believable.

He looked Ahna over for a minute, trying to think things through. She was slender and athletic-looking, and tall for a girl, Adam's height or just a bit over. She was much darker-skinned than Adam, sort of a coffee-cream color. She was square-faced, with a strong jaw, and a wide-lipped mouth that seemed to fall naturally into a very serious expression. Her eyes were set wide apart, and they were a deep, luminous blue, startlingly so against her dark complexion. Her hair was long and straight and black, and her eyebrows were thick and expressive. There were lots of immigrant kids from all over the world at Adam's school, and all the kids there got pretty good at guessing where people came from, but Ahna would have stumped them all.

Neither of them spoke for a little while, until Adam realized that she was waiting for him to start the conversation. He tried to think of something to say. His head hurt enough to make for a plausible starting place. "If this is the future, shouldn't you have something fancier than this for a throbbing head?" he asked, holding up the damp cloth for a moment.

Ahna smiled. "We do—for most kinds of headaches. But not for the kind you just got. That kind is pretty new to us."

"I don't understand. What's new about headaches?"

"Nothing. What's new is the way you got that one. Space t-port headaches are rough, and time Yanks are even worse."

Adam shook his head. "I'm sorry, but this is all riddle-talk to me. I don't understand what you're saying." But then something else occurred to him. "Wait a second. You know my name. And I heard a voice speak my name just before I went down that hole."

"Yes, that's right. We know who you are."

He thought a moment longer. "Then—you came after

me, in particular. It wasn't just anyone from—from my time that you were after. It was *me*."

"Quite right. We know all about you, and you're the person we wanted. The person we needed."

"But why? I'm nothing special. I'm just an average kid."

"So far," Ahna replied, with something close to a smile playing around her lips. "You might say we know more about you than you do."

Adam looked at her in utter confusion for a moment, but then he got it. This was, unless he was absolutely crazy, the future, and a good long way into the future at that, maybe hundreds of years. Adam only knew about things that had *already* happened in his life. These people—whoever they were—knew about stuff in his life that *hadn't* happened yet. He opened his mouth, about to ask for some of those details, but Ahna shook her head.

"There are rules," she said. "Very, very, strict rules. You can't know anything at all about your future life, beyond the fact that it was of—interest—to our people. That much we can say, because of course you'd figure it out for yourself anyway."

"From the way you're talking, about there being rules and so on—it sounds like I'm not the first one you've pulled out of, of, ah, the past." *The past.* Everything in his world, everything and everyone he had ever known, the street he had been walking his bike down ten minutes before, the trouble he had gotten into the day before, all of it was suddenly in the past. History. Or maybe not even history. Maybe it was all forgotten, unremembered, as if it had never happened. Except—except they knew about him, knew exactly when and where to find him.

"No," she said. "Not the first, and far from the last." Ahna looked at him thoughtfully. "You've figured out a lot on your own," Ahna said. "But there's so much more you couldn't possibly get to by yourself. So let me tell you the big stuff, the main stuff, flash-bang, all at once.''

"Okay," said Adam. "Fine."

"For starters, this is the year two thousand three hundred forty-five—A.D. We still use the same year-numbering system. So we're just under three hundred fifty years into your future." Ahna smiled. "For the most part, they've been very good years. There were hard times, very bad patches, between your era and this one—but we got past them and built a very healthy world for ourselves. By about a hundred years or so ago, we had wiped out just about every kind of disease, eliminated hunger, improved life span, gave everyone a good education, got the Earth's climate and ecology back in balance, explored all the planets of the Solar System, and established all sorts of bases and settlements."

"Sounds great," Adam said. Those were all wonderful things, but none of them had anything to do with him—and they all served to remind him of just how alien a world the future was likely to be.

"It is—was—great. Some of our philosophers have said it was all a little *too* great. Life was too easy—no challenges, no threats, no dangers. Every once in a while there'd be some proposal to create some sort of artificial problem or danger, something that would challenge people—but those ideas never came to anything. A real challenge would be too, well, dangerous, and what use is a pretend challenge that doesn't really matter?''

"The way you're talking makes it sound as if things changed."

"Yes," Ahna said, the word coming out perhaps a bit more emphatically than she had intended. "Things changed a lot, for good and bad, just about fifteen years ago—on the day I was born, as a matter of fact. The Gift Givers came on my birthday."

"The who? Who are the Gift Givers?"

Ahna smiled, tight-lipped. "We've been working on

that one since the day they showed up. They turned everything upside down, and gave us all the challenges we're ever going to need.''

"And that's the gift they gave you?''

Ahna looked surprised. "I'd never really thought of it that way, but in a sense, I suppose it was. But what they really gave us was, well, the stars.''

Adam had been starting to forget how much his head hurt, but that last bit was enough to make him remember. "I think you just lost me again. What do you mean, gave you—us—the stars?''

"A bit of poetry there. Sorry. They gave us the sally ports. And before you can ask 'Sally Who?' I'll tell you that the verb 'to sally' basically means 'to go out on a job.' The sally ports are the way we head out.''

"Head out of what?'' Adam asked.

"The Solar System. Out of our planetary system and into others.''

"So what's the catch?''

"The catch is that you got one devil of a headache coming through the Yank port.''

"Whatever that is,'' Adam said. He felt as if he had been thrown in at the deep end, with too much coming at him from all sides, washing over him, pulling him down.

"That's what we call the ports that yank people from out of the past. Sally ports, t-ports—that's short for tele-ports—and Yank ports are all variations on the same idea. The Gift Givers gave us sally ports, and we learned how to use the same technology to build the shorter-range t-ports, then the Yank ports.''

"And people get headaches when they go through them?'' Adam asked. "That doesn't sound like much of a price to pay for the stars, and for time travel.''

"The price is a lot higher than that,'' said Ahna. "The older you are, and the longer the distance you travel, the worse the headaches and the other effects get. If adults travel by regular teleports once a day over short distances, it won't hurt them. If they travel longer distances on Earth, or more often than once a day, they get the same sort of headache you just got. If an adult t-ports from one planet to another, say, from Earth to Mars, or from the Moon to one of the Edge Stations out past the orbit of Neptune, they are risking their lives. And if an adult goes through a sally port—does an interstellar jump—well, it could be fatal. Even adults who survive are likely to lose their memories or lose their minds. Going through a Yank port, a time-teleport like the one you just made, is even worse—for an adult."

Adam's headache was fading, and somehow he felt as if his brain was working at extra speed all of a sudden, pieces falling into place. "So they need teenagers. The grown-ups, the adults, have to send teenagers if they want to go to another star system." No wonder Ahna looked so adult, so mature—they had taken her childhood away, forced her to be an adult before her time.

"Not 'they,' " Ahna said as she stood up and turned to face the window. "There isn't some big faceless 'they' in all this. *We* need to send teenagers. *We*, the Human race. We don't have any choice at all." She didn't speak for a time, but looked out over the paradise outside the glass wall, the paradise built by Humans— the paradise that had started to fall apart on the day she was born. "Because," she said, "we're not the only ones who got visited by the Gift Givers.

"There are at least a dozen other intelligent races who were visited by the Givers. Some of them pleasant enough. But we have to go up against the Devlin—the ones we know least about. And what we know isn't good."

"I'm sorry to hear that," he said. "But what does that have to do with me?"

She turned around to face Adam, and seemed about to say more, when a—a *something* appeared in the air midway between Ahna and Adam. It was roughly the size and shape of a slightly rounded-off fifty-five-gallon drum, with a smaller, slightly rounded cylinder, the size of a can of paint, sitting centered on top of the larger drum, right where the head would be. It was a painted in gleaming metallic white with a design of vertical blue trim lines here and there, and what looked like closed hatches and ports and doors all over its body. It hovered in midair, with no apparent means of support. And, perhaps most disconcertingly of all, Adam could see right through it, see Ahna on the other side of it. It looked for all the world like the floating ghost of a robot.

"You're needed," it said to Ahna. "Please return to C.O.B. Yank Reception area."

"Very well, Giotto," Ahna said. The apparition vanished as quickly as it had appeared. Adam thought he recognized the voice as the same one that had called out his name when he had been caught in the Yank port.

"I must go," she said. "Your friends will be arriving very soon."

"Friends?" Adam asked. "What are you talking about?"

Ahna had already started moving toward the door, but she stopped and turned to face him. She hesitated, then seemed to reach some sort of decision. "There isn't time," she said. "Our rules say that I'm supposed to promise to return you within one hour, unless you agree to stay and help us, once I've explained things more. But I can't take the time to explain now. There is a great deal I have to do. Will you let me bend the rules a little, and ask you to stay overnight? I'll explain more to you in the morning."

Adam was about to say that he'd be in big trouble if he stayed out all night. What if his parents noticed he was gone and thought he had run away or something? But then he remembered where he was—or, really, when he was. The future. Time travel. If they could pull him out of a particular moment in the past, they ought to be able to send him back. Maybe they could swing it so no time at all had passed.

Besides, he had gotten into trouble for the sake of doing lots of things less worthwhile than seeing the future. How could he not be willing to pay that price?

"Sure," he said. "You've got a deal."

Ahna smiled, and her smile seemed to light up the whole room. "Thank you," she said. "I've got to go now. I'll see you later."

Adam wanted to say something more, but she was already out the door.

- INSPECTION

2345 A.D.
Negotiation Island
The Planet Bogwater

Clearwater swam up out of the underwater entrance of her home and toward the nearby island through the rapidly shallowing waters, using both her hand and foot flippers to propel her through the currents. Not far offshore, her head broke above the waves, and she shifted her eyes from their recessed submerged-focus position to the forward, air-focus position. The tidal flats were shallow enough to stand in, and she did so, enjoying the feel of the smooth, sandy bottom on her flipper-toes.

She stood waist deep in the sea, just off the shore of the island, and watched the alien robots, sent by the Humans, at their work. The Humans had taken to calling the place Negotiation Island. Somehow, the name had stuck, even among the K'lugu in spite of the fact that no Human had ever set eyes on the place. The Humans and the Devlin knew the island, indeed, the whole planet, only from remote imagery, and from what their construction robots could tell them. It had been agreed that no "true" beings of either alien world, no actual Devlin or Humans, would set foot on Bogwater until the conference began. In the meantime, Human and Devlin robots prepared the facilities the aliens would use once they arrived.

The island was a pretty little place, covered in green plants, with white-sand beaches that ran along most of its shore. Giant flightless shorebirds of various sorts bellowed and frolicked on the shore and on the surf, and Clearwater took the time to admire their sport.

But she was not there merely to admire the view. She also had to consider it from a critical, practical point of view. Standing in the waist-deep water, she could confirm what she had suspected: both the completed Parley Pavilion and the half-built Human embassy were plainly visible from the water.

That was to be expected, and endured, but it was not the K'lugu way of things. The K'lugu preferred to build in such a way as to leave the natural world undisturbed as much as possible. Neither Humans nor Devlin seemed much concerned by such matters. But the K'lugu were not fanatics on the point, and, besides, there was a certain advantage to doing things the way the aliens did them. It could well prove useful to keep an eye on their visitors. And the Humans would be in plain view of the shore.

The Devlin were being less cooperative. They had insisted on building their embassy on a neighboring island, and were constructing it well out of sight from the shore. Well, there were other ways to monitor them if it came to that.

Clearwater walked out of the water, and toward the Parley Pavilion. All was in readiness, at least as far as the physical structure was concerned. She was less certain that all mental and emotional preparations were complete. Dealing with one sort of alien was a strain.

Dealing with Humans and Devlin at the same time would be more difficult still.

She walked once around the Pavilion, and satisfied herself that it was done. She spotted her eggmate, Waveripple, coming down the hill from the Human embassy, and walked toward her to engage in conversation.

"Do the Humans' robots object to your watching them work?" she asked, as soon as Waveripple was in earshot. It never entered her thoughts to waste time in offering Waveripple a greeting before they started conversation, any more than she would bother saying hello to her own arm or her flipper-toes. They were eggmates, and shared the closest relationship possible between individuals. Each was herself, but each was also a part of the other.

"Not in the slightest," Waveripple replied. "They are almost alarmingly friendly. Plainly, they have been trained, or programmed, to avoid giving offense, and to make it clear their masters, the Humans, have nothing to hide."

"Perhaps they merely counted on your not being able to see their secrets from any sort of distance," Clearwater joked. The K'lugu scientists believed that Human vision and hearing were far superior to the K'lugu senses, probably because their eyes and ears had not evolved the compromise structures needed to function both above and below water. The Devlin senses, they believed, were better still.

Clearwater bobbed her head up and down a time or two, in the K'lugu equivalent of a laugh. "Perhaps," she said. "But even so, everyone has something to hide." The two of them turned toward the shore and began walking toward it.

"Quite true," Waveripple agreed. "But the Humans wish to hide their secrets by making it seem the secrets do not exist in the first place."

"I believe I prefer that approach to the way the Devlin

39

robots work,'' said Clearwater. ''They wish to hide not some things, but all things. Their construction robots chased me away when I went to inspect them this morning. They were quite aggressive. It is not diplomatic of me to say it, but the Devlin are not the most likable of creatures.''

''While the Humans—or at least the Humans we have been allowed to see, the ones we deal with, are almost too likable. I read a report from our social-science theorists this morning. It put forward the theory that the Humans had succeeded perhaps too well in eliminating stress and competition, violence and danger from their world, prior to the move into interstellar space.''

''So that now they are unequipped to deal with such things, out among the stars?''

''That is the notion, at least.''

''They do seem remarkably trusting,'' Clearwater agreed. ''I could not help but notice, in the reports of our dealing with them, that they seem quite ashamed of much of their own history, perhaps with reason. Their present peacefulness may mask a fierce inner nature. Perhaps they hide their ferocity from themselves as well as other races. But we dare not judge. One must fight, at times. Our own past—well, what race has always done right?''

''True.'' Waveripple peered across the water to the next island in the chain, where the Devlin were building their embassy. ''Who will win out,'' she wondered aloud. ''The overly trusting and gentle Humans, or the too-secretive and violent Devlin?''

''Both are dangerously immoderate,'' Clearwater agreed. Moderation, moderation in all things, was the core value of the K'lugu.

''And I do not believe either side has a full grasp of the other's intentions,'' said Waveripple. ''We may well be facing a time of great interest—and danger.''

Clearwater's silence expressed her agreement more fully than any words might have. Between eggmates, there was always complete understanding.

QUESTIONS

Adam lay back on the fancy bed in the bedroom they had put him in and tried to think things through. It hadn't occurred to him that making him wait until morning meant locking him up for the night. And it hadn't taken long to establish that they had indeed locked him in. The bedroom door had no visible handles or latches or knobs or futuristic controls. He had tried calling out, in hopes that some sort of magical room controls would hear him and obey. That sort of thing worked in the movies sometimes. But if there were any fancy voice-controls in the room, they weren't paying him any attention.

Besides, if he did get out of the room, what would he do? Walk home?

It seemed pretty silly to be yanked hundreds of years into the future and then be forced to wait around. Why not just yank him in the next morning, or a week later, or whenever they'd be ready for him? He gave up worrying about it. The reason didn't matter that much. Maybe the future people had a heavy schedule, or something.

The future! Why in the world did they want him— not just any teenage kid, but Adam O'Connor by name— in the future? What was going on? It seemed as if there was little he could do at the moment to find out. He rolled over onto his side, reached out for the bedside controls, and set the window-wall to clear. He lay there, staring out at the impossible world outside the window-wall. He was still struggling to make sense of it all when he drifted off, to dream of popping the hood on Mrs. Meredith's car and finding a glowing blue tunnel where the engine was supposed to be.

Outskirts of Fortaleza, Ceará State, Northeast Brazil, 1883 A.D.

Roberto Galvão mucked out the last of the fouled straw from the stable and threw it into the middle of the worn square of burlap. The burlap was as big as the sheets on Dom Luis's bed, but as filthy as the Dom's sheets were clean. Roberto gathered up the corners of the burlap, forming it into a sack, then dragged the sack out of the stable and toward the gully several hundred meters away.

The equatorial sun beat down on him as he stumbled, barefooted, toward the gully. Even this late in the day, the heat was punishing, but Roberto ignored the sweat and the discomfort. Disposing of the straw was his last chore of the day. He was supposed to return to the stable at once—but Roberto had timed it all carefully. He glanced toward the west, and the sun as it edged down toward the horizon. He would, if he hurried, just have time to make his way to the fishing village on the shore and get in a quick swim before he was missed.

He knew perfectly well that he was risking a severe

beating at the hands of the chief slave. But Roberto was willing to take the risk, for the sake of a chance to swim, or just to walk through the waves at the water's edge. He loved the water, loved the wide expanse of the ocean, the booming surf, and the clean white sand. There was precious little else clean and expansive in his life.

He got to the gully and dumped the load of foul straw down into it. In the wet season, a stream moved down the gully most days, but in the dry season, only a feeble trickle flowed.

The next rain, which was likely still some weeks away, would wash the straw—and all, or at least most— of the other filth and garbage and debris dumped into the gully down into the sea, well away from the delicate noses of Dom Luis and Dona Flora. In the meantime, the gully was at least more or less downwind and downstream of the nearby slaves' quarters. They would only catch a whiff of it now and then.

Roberto folded up the burlap as carefully as he could and tucked it in under a cleft in a pile of stones, where he could recover it quickly after his swim. As worn and dirty as the burlap was, he did not dare even think of the punishment he would receive if it went missing.

He started northeast, toward the shore, at a rapid dogtrot, keeping to the paths where the *patrões*, the masters, would never go. He slowed to move a bit more cautiously through a nameless seaside village. Even ''village'' was too grand a name for the place. It was nothing more than a small collection of shanties, sheltered from the water by the first line of dunes. It would be blown over in the first good storm of the season—but the people who lived there would build it again the next day, right where it was. It would have been foolish to try and build anything more substantial so close to the ocean.

He slipped through the shadows, and over the dunes. He paused for a moment, and smiled broadly, drinking in the splendid view. The beach itself lay before him, white sand that stretched for miles in either direction. The sun was behind him, close to the horizon. His shadow was as long as a giant's, stretching out before him, reaching for the deep blue water and the frothy whitecaps of the sea. With a whoop of delight, he raced across the beach and into the water.

He dived into the warm, clean water, and swam out a good way from shore, exulting not just in the physical pleasure of swimming, but in the sense of freedom, of liberation. He had escaped from Dom Luis and the stable and the dust and the hopeless future, if only for a moment.

The sun drew ever closer to the horizon, and the stars began to come out over the waters to the east. Roberto trod water for a moment to admire them. They were faint and fogged by the sea mist, but there all the same.

But it was time to go. The full moon was rising over the water as he waded back onto the shore. He felt the cool evening breeze on his body and the wet rags that were all the clothes he had. He turned for one last look at the ocean. The full moon hung over the wide expanse of the sea, her reflection seeming to form a path of silver that stretched over the water, beckoning to him.

He felt as if he could run on that silver path right up to the sky, right up to the Moon. He longed with all his heart to go, to get away, to escape the life of endless toil that was all he knew. But he could not run away. If he did, they would beat his parents and his little sister, and the slave-catchers would go out after him. They would catch him, and beat him, and collect their reward.

He lingered, just a heartbeat longer, drinking in the beauty of the moment. The tide was coming in, and the rising water seemed ready to flood all the world, and wash it all clean. It seemed as if the silver path upon the waters were calling to him. He could almost hear a voice call his name.

And then, with a start, he realized that there *was* a

voice—a flat, serious-sounding voice—and it *was* calling his name!

"Roberto Galvão," it called.

Roberto peered into the glimmering darkness. There, just at the water's edge, right at the start of the magical path of silver that led to the Moon, was a circle of blue light that grew brighter as he watched, and throbbed and pulsed with clean blue light.

Roberto lived in a world full of spirits and portents. It was instantly plain to him that Iemanjá, the goddess of the sea herself, was calling to him. At the start of every new year, the people sent offerings out onto the water for her, but never had he heard of her summoning any of her people in such a way.

His heart pounding with fear, he walked toward the moonlit waters, toward the pulsating blue disk that marked the first step on the path up to the Moon herself.

Berlin, Germany, November 11, 1938 A.D.

Aaron Schwartz turned and ran down the alleyway, half a block ahead of his pursuers. Why, oh why, hadn't he gotten home on time? Especially after last night, and the night before last. *Kristallnacht*, they were already calling it. Crystal Night, a lovely and poetic name for a time of black terror. The Night of the Broken Glass. It seemed as if every window of every synagogue and Jewish shop in Berlin had been smashed. The rumors said that Jews, dozens, maybe hundreds, had been murdered by mobs for no greater crime than being Jewish. The Nazis running the government were doing nothing to stop it. Some said that the Nazis had encouraged the mobs, or even ordered them to action. What further encouragement, beyond such rumors, did the bullyboys need to chase a Jewish boy foolish enough to venture out of the ghetto?

But Aaron had wanted to see for himself, wanted to

know with the proof of his own eyes what had happened. Wild rumors and horrible stories came from all sides, and it was hard to know what to believe. So he had slipped out of the ghetto, to see for himself.

And he had seen it, seen that all the stories, all the very worst of the rumors, were true—and did not even go far enough. The brownshirts and the mobs were still at it. They were everywhere, burning and looting, smashing every Jewish window they could find.

But Aaron had not taken care to watch out for himself. A gang of toughs had found him, and started to chase him through the darkened night. He knew this neighborhood better than his pursuers seemed to, and that had kept him ahead of them—so far.

The alley ended in a T-intersection, and Aaron had entered it at the base of the T's long arm. He ran forward, planning to swing into the left-hand arm of the passage and get away. He made his turn, then stopped dead. The left-hand way was blocked by debris. They had burned out Hyman Goldstein's store, and charred roof timbers and the collapsed remains of the store's rear wall shut off his escape route. Smoke was still eddying up from the ruins. He'd never get through in time.

Footsteps. Close behind him and closing fast. He turned toward the right arm of the alley. It ran for only a block before it opened out into a main street, where the mob was still at it. It was a poor second choice, but it was his only chance. Maybe he could melt away into the crowd before some Nazi thug decided he looked Jewish. He started to run, his pursuers less than a hundred meters behind.

"Aaron Schwartz," a deep voice intoned from somewhere in the alley up ahead. There was a door open, and a strange blue light that seemed to come from the floor of the room behind the door. "Aaron Schwartz," the voice said again.

Aaron looked toward the street up ahead. A torchlit

parade of brown-shirted thugs was marching along. He heard shouts behind him, and knew his pursuers were closing in. He was caught between a rock and a hard place and he had only an instant to decide which way to go. The blue light from the door was growing brighter. An unknown someone who knew his name seemed a far better chance to take than to trust to the tender mercies of Nazi thugs two nights after *Kristallnacht*.

He ran for the open door in the alley and dived in through it, headfirst.

The door slammed shut and locked itself behind him.

LEAST HELP

2345 A.D.
Roanoke Crash Site
Planet UH-A-134 (Devlin Designation)

Least walked down the corridor of the monitor ship that orbited in the far reaches of the star system, turned, and stepped into the t-port.

He instantly transited from the starship, through a t-port link, and into an armored bunker on the surface of a certain nameless planet.

The bunker was a windowless, reinforced-concrete box, and the t-port gate was the only thing in it.

The bunker had only one interior room, a cube, three meters on a side. Aside from the t-port itself, the only way out of the bunker was through a massive steel door that led to the planet's surface. The bunker was a special custom design, meant to ensure that no one outside could get to the t-port, and thus, off the planet and out into the stars—and the Devlin empire.

The bunker was strong, and the risks of anyone attempting such an escape were not great. The elder Humans on this world were too old to survive the trip, and the younger ones were but cubs, not mature enough to be trusted on such a mission.

Least activated the door controls, watched the door swing open, and emerged from the bunker out into the afternoon sunlight.

The Devlin had set their t-port bunker down in the midst of the crash-debris field. A Human ship had come down here, about fourteen Earth years ago—about twelve Devlin years, Least reminded himself. Least had studied Humans for a quite a time, and he was sometimes in the habit of thinking in Human terms.

The crash site, and the wreckage itself, looked a lot more than twelve years old. Least shrugged, a more complicated gesture, given that a Devlin has four arms and two sets of shoulders. Least had picked up several Human mannerisms during his observations. What did it matter how old it looked? That didn't change the essentials of the story, a story it had taken Least a long time to piece together.

Back before the days when Humans understood what the sally port could do to adults, a Human colony ship named *Roanoke* had made a sally port jump, and the jump had killed every adult aboard. The surviving children and adolescent Humans on board had attempted a landing, and done none too well. Only a relative handful lived through the crash.

The *Roanoke* had come in fast on a long, flat trajectory, gouging out a kilometer-long trench that had sliced through the ground, the treetops, and everything else that had come its way.

The impact had been tremendously powerful, but time had long since started to heal the wounds left by the crash. Brambles and vines grew over the torn and shattered fragments of the hull that were scattered everywhere. Moldering cargo containers, smashed bits of electronics, half-buried pieces of the ship's interior were strewn about the landscape, all but hidden by creepers and tall grass.

But even now, so long after the fact, burns and scorch marks were plainly visible on the older trees. Here and there, the exposed faces of the underlying bedrock were still blackened by the flames of that day years before. The fires touched off by the impact had burned for three days.

But those who survived the sally port disaster and the crash and the fire still faced an extremely hostile and dangerous situation. The first winter had killed several of them. But twenty-seven young Humans had, somehow, lived through it all, down to the present day, marooned on this nameless world.

A Devlin survey ship had found the crash, and the survivors, about a half a Devlin year back. The survey team's Prime somehow got her survey group merged into the Contact-with-Humans working group. The survey Prime then made a successful bid for Primacy over the entire Contact Group. Least hadn't paid a great deal of attention until all the politicking was over, and he had little understanding of how his new Prime had caused it all to happen. Nor did he much care. In Least's extremely humble opinion, the endless battles to establish rank, priority, and standing rarely had much to do with getting any work done.

But when it was done, there was a new Prime in charge, one who at least understood that the *Roanoke* survivors could be of great value. The Devlin knew next to nothing about Humans, but what they did know strongly suggested that Humans might well be great rivals in years to come. A captive population of Humans was a precious resource for research.

Once they needed to make contact with the official Earth government, appearances of status before the enemy would require the highest-ranking Devlin available be made the Prime of any such group. But contact with non-Devlins was so inherently distasteful, that until it was absolutely necessary for Prime to deal with Humans herself, such unpleasantness could be left to her lessers.

At present, for example, the Devlin were dealing with a bunch of juvenile castaways for purposes of intelligence gathering. No questions of status or position were involved. No Devlin with any rank or age of consequence had to, or would want to, deal with such grubby and unimportant creatures.

In short, it was inevitable that whoever of the Group was Least, whoever had the lowest age, the lowest status, would be assigned the task of contacting the castaway Humans.

A few months before, a certain very young, very small, male Devlin who had barely survived cubhood, and who had only recently emerged into legal adulthood, was assigned to the Contact-with-Humans Group. By law, right, and tradition, he was the Least of the group. And so he was assigned the Least job—the actual task of Contacting Humans.

Least did not care for the job, but he tried to make the best of it. He trudged wearily toward the Human camp, threading his way around the larger bits of wreckage toward the huts built from salvaged cargo containers.

He did not bother to try and hide his approach. He knew full well that the Humans would have tracked him from the moment he arrived through the t-port. Nor did he even bother to try and find the watchers. Whoever it was they had tracking him would do the job silently, moving stealthily, using every bit of available cover. The first three times he had gone to the Human camp, he had found it utterly deserted, but with the cook fires still burning, food still warm in bowls on the rough-hewn tables. The Humans knew how to fade away.

Prime, Secondary, and the rest of the elder ranks had all wanted to send Least in with infrared trackers, motion detectors, and whatever other advanced tracking equipment was available. Overawe the savages with technology. It would seem like magic to them. Least, they said, should hunt them down, intimidate them, and force their cooperation. But Least had resisted, in part because some intuition told him such stunts would be worse than useless, in part as a small form of rebellion. They had made him take this job. Very well then—but he would do it right, and do it his way.

The Humans here, he reminded his superiors, might be living like primitives—but the eldest of the survivors had been competent adolescents when the crash happened, and had grown up with their memories intact. They knew about technology—they just didn't have very much of it left anymore. They wouldn't be that easy to intimidate.

Prime of the Group, and the other elder ranks, didn't seem to understand that. They were of the opinion that only cowards ever had reason to hide. That the Humans ran away at the mere approach of a Devlin, of a Devlin as insignificant as Least, told them all they wanted to know.

But not, Least feared, as much as they *needed* to know. It would be helpful if Humans were cowards, and pleasant if Prime's logic led to correct conclusions. But Least had his doubts. They assumed so much from so little. Unarmed and isolated survivors of a shipwreck ran away from Devlin. It was proof that no Humans anywhere were possessed of courage! When the shipwreck survivors finally did come out to meet with Least, on his fourth trip, they were cautious and careful. It was proof that all Humans were timid creatures, easily dominated! The ship had crashed. Proof that Humans were inept with technology! Humans even looked like smaller, weaker, deformed Devlin, with two arms instead of the proper four, peculiar-shaped heads and faces and furless bodies, and too much fur growing from the tops of the heads. And these castaways appeared to be malnourished, thinner than they should have been. Weak. Proof they were lesser beings than the Least and most degenerate of the entire Devlin race!

Prime of the Contact-With-Humans Group read meaning into everything, and, worse still, always seemed to find the most optimistic possible meaning. It was a dangerous way to think, but, of course, Least could not possibly tell her any such thing.

Least came to the end of the trail he had walked so many times by now, and into the camp. How often had he visited? Twenty times? Thirty? Enough times that the Humans had come to accept him, to trust him—at least to a certain degree.

Three of the Humans, three of their eldest, came out of the largest hut to greet him. Least bowed to them solemnly.

He knew them well enough by now to connect faces to names. The tallest one, a male named Ethan. Markus, another male, and the most suspicious of their entire group. Markus's female sibling—*sister*, that was their word—his sister, Maurha. They had been mere children at the time of the crash, but fourteen years had changed that. They were fully adult now. The youngest, the least, of the survivors, were now older than these three had been on the day that the *Roanoke* had hit the ground. Least saw a little face peeking out from behind Maurha's skirt. Ah, yes. The youngest, the little one called either Virginia or Ginny, had been born here, on this nameless world.

Maurha spoke in her own language. Least waited for the translation device that he wore on a chain around his neck to convert her words into Elder Speech. "Greetings to you, Least. You are welcome here."

Least bowed his head and spread all four arms out wide, hands empty, the Devlin gesture of peaceful greeting. "And I am honored to be welcome," he said.

At least the "language learning" charade was over.

The translator had been fully programmed to deal with Human speech when Least had first arrived, but the whole idea was to pretend to the castaways that the Devlin had never heard of Humans, other than in vague rumors and stories heard from other races. That way, the castaways would have a greater incentive to speak freely about their race. And so Least had been forced to waste precious weeks, a time convincingly long enough for his translator to "learn" a language it already knew.

"Hello, Least," said the little one, Ginny, in a solemn voice.

"Hello, Ginny," said Least.

"Run along and play with the older ones," said Maurha to her daughter, giving her a little shove to get her moving. The girl slipped away and ran off across the center of the compound.

Least got the very strong impression that she did not want her child getting too friendly with Least. *They don't trust me very much,* he thought. *But then, of course, they shouldn't.*

"Do you bring us any news?" asked Ethan.

Least shook his head back and forth, deliberately imitating the Human gesture that indicated "no." Some of the younger Humans began to appear, coming out of the huts, or out from under the trees, in groups of two or three. They stood, and watched, without making any sound.

"I am sorry," said Least. "Establishing contact with your people is—difficult." He had been lying to these Humans since the first time they had spoken together. Manipulating them, tricking them for his own gain. He did not like it—but the Prime of his Group had ordered it, and so he had no choice.

And, like so many of his lies, this one had its threads of truth woven through it. Yes, it was difficult to arrange a face-to-face meeting with Humans—but it was difficult only because the Devlin chose to make it so, in order to establish status and dominance.

While intricate negotiations might be required to set up the details of a full meeting, it would have been easy for the Devlin to give the Humans the coordinates of this planet and the news that there were crash survivors on it. They could have done it at any time. But Prime of the Group did not want to give up the advantage of learning all she could from the castaways, and so they had told the Human government nothing.

"Space is vast," he said. "We still have not located your home planet. We will continue to search, of course. But there are two things you could do that would be of great help."

"Of course," said Ethan. "We'll do whatever we can."

"Or at least whatever we can do that makes sense," said Markus.

"Excellent," said Least. "Allow me to explain what we need. You have read small portions of your surviving records to me, and they have been of some help. I would ask once again that I be allowed to make full copies of all your records and databases, so that our scientists might be able to study them in greater detail. Somewhere in them there is quite likely a clue that will let us find your home world."

Ethan looked hopefully at Markus, but Markus shook his head no. "I'm sorry," said Markus, "but we can't risk it. The playback machines that could decode certain of our records were all destroyed in the crash. For that reason, we can't read many of our records ourselves any-more. Some data stores were deliberately encrypted so only the captain and the senior officers could read them. Without knowing what's in the data stores, we don't dare hand them over to strangers, no matter how friendly. There could be any number of things in those records that Earth wouldn't want *us* to see, let alone aliens. I'm sorry. I don't mean to be rude, but there it is."

"There must be *some* records we could let them copy," said Ethan. "There must be something that we know doesn't have any classified information in it." He turned toward Least. "You've done so much for us," he said. "It seems to me we have to do *something* to make it easier for you to help us."

"That is most kind of you, Ethan," said Least. *Especially as we have actually done less than nothing*, he told himself. "You would be astonished at the sort of thing that might yield a clue. It need not be anything technical or scientific. The starfaring races exchange folklore of all kinds. It might well be that some tale from an Earth history, or even one of your fictional stories, has traveled from Earth to some other race, and from them to a second race, then to a third, who has forgotten where the tale came from. If we could match such a story to your people, we might well be able to track down this planet Earth of yours." The story sounded more or less plausible in the context of all the other lies he had told. And, of course, the lie served Devlin purposes. Histories, biographies, stories about how Humans dealt with each other might be of tremendous value going into Meeting One.

Markus stared at Least long and hard. "All right," he said at last. "We don't want to seem ungrateful or unhelpful. We ought to be able to come up with something."

"Thank you," said Least. "Whatever help you can provide will be most appreciated."

"It will be our pleasure," said Markus. Even across the gulf between two species, and the filter of the translating machine, it was hard to miss the complete lack of sincerity in the Human's voice. "You said that there were *two* things we could do to help. What's the second?"

Least came to his final, and his greatest, lie. He had

crafted it carefully. He was not sure why, but he wanted it to have at least some resemblance to the truth. Perhaps because telling them something that was a little bit true would ease at least some of his guilt. "We Devlin are about to convene a meeting with another race," he said. "It is a race we do not know much about, but one that has a reputation, not only for gathering a great deal of information on every conceivable subject, but also for being a species of tricksters. Some of our scholars have studied various very subtle clues that make them think it is possible this race has some knowledge of Humans. However, in the past, we have not found this race to be truthful. It is possible they will claim vast knowledge of your people, when they know little or nothing. They have played such games in the past."

"What's that got to do with us?" asked Markus.

"If they falsely claim knowledge of your people, and we bargain with them to get that information, they could cheat us and be on their way before we had any way to know they were lying. That would be to our detriment, and yours, if they send us off to pursue false leads. We would have no defense against their tricks—unless we had you, here, ready to serve as a sort of hidden, living lie detector."

"Go on," said Markus.

Least gestured back the way he had come, toward his t-port bunker. "We will link that t-port, through a series of relay stations, to the place where our meeting with this trickster race is taking place. If we ask about Humans, and they claim to know about you, it is part of their character that they will offer all number of details to demonstrate their knowledge. Things about your history, or what sort of clothes Humans wear, or about your culture. I will be standing by, ready to t-port from the meeting to this planet. If these tricksters say thus and such about Humans, I will t-port here and ask you if it is true."

"So you'll know if they are lying," Maurha said, her voice as flat and careful as her brother's. "So you'll know whether you can trust them in the rest of your dealings."

"Precisely," said Least.

"We'd be glad to help," said Maurha.

"Excellent," said Least. "We would be most grateful."

"We'll need to discuss the other matter," said Markus. "Figure out what we can show you, what would be useful to you. And, of course, we need to retain all our records. We have very little, and we dare not lose any of it. You'll have to make your copies here, in our presence. Come back tomorrow, and bring whatever equipment you'll need to duplicate our records, and we'll have something for you."

Least nodded vigorously. "That is precisely the arrangement I was about to suggest myself."

"Very good," said Markus. "Until tomorrow, then."

"Until tomorrow." Least bowed, very slightly, and the three Humans did the same. "Farewell," he said, and turned back toward the t-port bunker.

Least had many worries, but one worry weighed most heavily on his mind. Prime of the Contact-with-Humans Group had found it useful to keep the *Roanoke* survivors alive so far. But once the official Meeting One was over, their value would drop almost overnight. One way or another, Prime would have endless other sources of information about Humans. And the longer they were alive, the greater the chances were that the Humans would find them, and discover that the Devlin had, in effect, kept the Humans as prisoners, test subjects. Prime would not wish to endure such embarrassment.

The solution was obvious, and Least had no doubt it would be put into effect.

Once Meeting One was over, Prime would order that the *Roanoke* survivors, every last one of them, be eliminated.

ANSWERS

One, two, three. Adam, Roberto, Aaron. It had been a long, grueling day, but all three of the Yank subjects had been successfully pulled out of the past, and Ahna had given all three at least a preliminary welcome and orientation, and assigned all three to quarters for the night. All three had agreed to wait until morning for her explanations.

It had been a struggle indeed, explaining the situation to them. Simply because Adam was from a time where crude computers and technology existed, more or less, she had been able to tell him the most.

Aaron's world was not as advanced, but he did live in a time and place with machines and technology, and where the idea of the future as something different from the present, different from the past, had taken hold. She had been able to get at least some of the basics across to him. And both Adam and Aaron could read information off the data viewers. That would help.

Roberto had been the toughest challenge, through no fault of his own. In his world, yesterday, today, tomorrow, last year, this year, next year, were all very much the same. And a slave in Fortaleza was not likely to have seen much in the way of what passed for technology in 1883. She would have to explain spaceships and sally ports to a boy who had never seen a steamship, who lived before the airplane was invented.

Ahna was exhausted. She wanted desperately to get to bed. Her three new friends had done so, long hours ago. It was hard for Ahna to believe that anyone could drift off after what the three of them had been through—but, incredibly, the monitoring equipment on their rooms showed them all to be fast asleep.

Ahna stood up from her desk, stretched, and looked out the window at the plaza below the dark night beyond the city, and the stars above. "So far, so good, eh, Giotto?" she asked.

"We haven't attempted much of our agenda yet, Ms. Varkan," the robot replied. "We have neither succeeded in much or failed in anything. And we have a great deal more to do."

"Thanks for reminding me," she said.

"It is my pleasure to serve you," the robot replied. Giotto never had been good at picking up on sarcasm. At least he was a more stable model, and didn't lock up under stress the way some other advanced robots did.

Giotto had been nearby, if mostly out of sight, for all three arrivals, ready with sedatives and restraints in the event someone lost control. But though they had all been scared and confused, none of them had panicked.

"One thing did strike me as most unusual about the retrievals," Giotto said. "I wonder if you might be able to explain it. Typically, time-yank subjects flee from the time-access portal, as Adam O'Connor did. But Roberto Galvão and Aaron Schwartz entered willingly, almost eagerly."

"Look what both of them were running *from*," said Ahna. She shuddered to think of what their lives must have been like—would be like, after Operation Hour-

61

glass was done with them and put them back in their own times. To live as a slave, or to be hated, threatened with death, just for being a part of a smaller group in the midst of a larger one. What would it be like to live in such barbaric times, when justice did not exist? How lost and confused would the Yanks be in this world?

For that matter, Ahna was pretty disoriented herself. Up until a few days before, she and her eight-person diplomatic team had been in intensive training for Meeting One with the Devlin. But then three of her team had been pulled off the mission to make room for the Yanks, and she had been assigned to greet and train the Yank team members. The plan was for the Yanks to attend Meeting One in the guise of the trained young diplomats they were replacing.

It was bad enough asking a bunch of teenage kids to serve on a diplomatic mission. Replacing three of them at the last minute with a trio of refugees from the barbaric past made it worse. And yet, she knew there was no better choice. She *had* to do this job—and she needed the three time-Yank subjects to help her.

"Tell me, Giotto," she said. "Is it always like this?"

The robot turned its near-featureless head toward her, so its paired stereo-cameras were looking her straight in the eye. "I am not sure I understand what you mean."

"How does this compare to a typical Op-H mission? Are we doing better or worse than average?"

Giotto paused to consider. "I have been directly involved in four Operation Hourglass missions thus far, and of course have complete data sets from the robotic members of all the other missions. None of them go according to plan. That is quite common. But this one is unusual for having you managing the Yank arrival. It is far more common for an adult to do the initial briefing job you did today."

"They figured it would save time to have me do it," said Ahna. "Using me was faster than bringing one of the adults who know about Meeting One."

As if, she thought sourly, *anyone knew anything at all for certain.*

Roberto opened his eyes and sat up straight in bed, his heart pounding. He had had the most remarkable dream, all about going under the sea to an impossible—

One look around and he realized it was no dream. All his life, he had slept in the same room with all of his family, father, mother, brothers, and sisters. To awaken in a chamber this large, this grand, all by himself, was a thing so impossible as to make him believe all the rest was true as well.

The bed he lay in was far larger and grander than even Dona Flora's bed back home, and the blankets far softer. The sheets—to sleep in a bed with sheets!—were cool and smooth against his skin.

Roberto climbed out of the bed. It was still hard for him to believe in all that he saw, and harder still to believe that it was all the work of people, and not of demons.

He stepped to the far wall of the room, the wall that angled in from ceiling to floor. He pressed the magic button that the girl, Ahna, had shown him. The wall turned into a great window made of the finest and smoothest glass he had ever seen, a window that looked out on the wondrous plaza below.

Light flooded into the room as Roberto gaped once again at the strange world outside. As it did, Roberto realized what had been bothering him about this room, this place. It was too *much* inside, *too* protected from the elements and the weather. In Fortaleza, even the grandest rooms of Dom Luis's house always had the windows open onto the courtyard. One could always hear—and smell—the outside world. Here, all was closed up, as silent as the tomb. Perhaps tonight he would sleep with the wall left as a window. Perhaps there was a way to open up the great window, swing wide the casement and let the night air in.

But whatever this place was, it was full of wonders. Roberto remembered the bathroom that Ahna had shown him the night before. She had showed him how to use the bathtub, how to fill it, what all the sorts of soaps and potions were for. He had reveled half an hour in the tub before climbing into bed. Never in his life had he felt so clean, so purified. A swim in the ocean was the only bath Roberto had ever known. And this soap was far finer stuff than anything Dona Flora had ever used. If it was not the future, perhaps it was paradise.

Would anyone object if he took yet another bath, this morning? Would they punish him, send him back to his old life?

Roberto grinned to himself. Well, if they did, he would be clean when he got back.

He opened the spigots, and watched the tub fill up again.

Aaron woke with a scream, but there was nothing so unusual about that. Not after all he had seen in 1938 Berlin. He climbed out of bed in a cold sweat, his nightmare already fading.

He looked at the strange room, the strange bed, not remembering at first where he was.

And when he was.

When! The year 2345, they had said. It was hard to believe, but he had already seen and heard too much that would not be possible in the twentieth-century. Aaron had read the adventure stories of Jules Verne and H.G. Wells in German translations, before the Nazis had banned them, and the films by Herr Lang, *Metropolis* and *Die Frau im Mond—The Girl In the Moon*. Stories about the future. Just a year ago, he had heard on the BBC broadcasts, the ones you weren't supposed to listen to, about a British film, *Things To Come*, based on a book by Herr Wells. It was all about how there would be another war, a terrible one, but that after it would be a wonderful future.

Maybe that film had got it right. Who could know? It didn't matter. He was here, he was safe, at least for the moment, and besides, there was no way he could get home on his own anyway. Why worry? And what was the hurry, anyway? Maybe those thugs were still waiting in that Berlin alley for the chance to beat him up. Let them wait a while.

At 0800 hours, Ahna sent a trio of service robots to escort the three Yank subjects back to the conference room. The three boys from the past came into the room, one after another, all dressed in the same sort of pale blue coveralls that she wore. If they dressed alike, maybe they would see themselves as being linked together. As a team in this new world.

"Good morning," she said to all of them, as soon as they were seated. "I am Ahna Varkan, of the year 2345. You are Roberto Galvão from Fortaleza in northeast Brazil in the year 1883, Aaron Schwartz from Berlin, Germany, in the year 1938, and Adam O'Connor from Carrboro, North Carolina, the United States, in the year 1999. You'll all get to know each other—and me—very well. You have been brought here, to this time and place, because we need your help."

"Why?" Adam asked.

"I beg your pardon?" Ahna asked.

"Well, you told me last night something about why your people need to send teenagers through these, ah, sally ports, to the other worlds. But why bring us from the past? Wouldn't it make a lot more sense to use teenagers from this time, who know the culture and the situation?"

"You have answered your own question without realizing it," said a voice out of nowhere.

"*Madre de Deus!*" Roberto cried out. "What is that?"

"It's—it's all right, Roberto," said Ahna. "It's just D'Alembert. He is—a colleague of mine. Of ours."

"*Mas onde esta ele*—where is he?" Roberto asked. "I heard the voice, but there is no one here speaking the words."

"I am not exactly anywhere," D'Alembert replied. "Forgive me. *Desculpe-me, Robertinho. Não intendir se assustar.*"

"D'Alembert is—is a friendly spirit, if you will," said Ahna, trying to speak smoothly and calmly. Why hadn't he waited to be introduced? Why speak up out of the blue like that? She was used to him, and it startled *her*. But there was no point in asking D'Alembert such things. He never explained himself. Maybe he just wanted to remind their visitors things were different in 2345. "D'Alembert is what we call a highly advanced artificial personality. I realize that term doesn't mean much to you, but it doesn't matter what we call him. D'Alembert is very definitely part of our group. He will watch, and observe, and advise us, from many places, during our training. But he was about to explain why we do not just use young people from our own time. D'Alembert?"

"Thank you, Ahna. It is precisely *because* they are from this time and culture that so many of our young people are unsuitable for the sort of mission in question."

"That doesn't tell us anything," Adam said sourly.

"No, it doesn't," D'Alembert agreed placidly. "But consider. When the teenagers of today, of 2345, were born, Earth had been at peace, all her people happy, healthy, safe, and free, for generations. All the worlds of the Solar System that could be settled, had been settled. Hard times, bad times, didn't exist anymore, and the character traits needed to get through them—courage, stubbornness, self-reliance, a whole collection of things that we have come to refer to collectively as 'grit'—were no longer as important as they once were. They even fell into disfavor. People who were overly stubborn, determined, or daring, were called uncouth, uncultured. Then came the Gift Givers, and suddenly, humanity had need of the traits it had turned its back on."

"So people aren't brave anymore?" asked Aaron. "All your people just give up if things don't go your way?"

"Not at all. Those traits still exist—but they are rarer, because there is less need for people to develop them. And those who have them—such as Ahna, here—are in short supply. We need more than we have. There are only so many young people of just the right age—young enough to survive a sally port jump, but old enough, and wise enough, to deal maturely with what they find on the other end. How many young people of your own times would be able to take on the tasks that Ahna has accepted?"

There was silence for a moment, which Ahna took as something of a compliment. But at last Roberto spoke.

"Excuse me, Dom D'Alembert, *Senhor Spirito*, but are you saying that we three from the past have this special something, this grit? How can you know? How can you tell?"

"I think I figured that one out," said Adam. He grinned at Ahna. "We three—we only know what we have done in our own lives so far. But this is the future. You know what we will do later in our lives."

D'Alembert hesitated a moment. "An interesting notion," he said. "But, even if we knew the particulars, even if your biographies were in the historical record, we could not discuss such matters with you. You cannot know your own futures. If you did, that knowledge could not help but influence you, distract you, perhaps make you overconfident.''

"If you already know you're going to win the game, maybe you won't try so hard to win," Ahna put in. "If you know you'll lose, maybe you won't try as hard, and lose even worse. Maybe you relax a little bit—just enough to make you lose. And that could make for complications, the future affecting the past, that we don't need to talk about just now." The situation was complex enough, Ahna told herself, without getting into world lines and time-travel paradoxes.

"But we do know our futures," Adam protested. "Or at least something about them. We know we were brought here. We'll see things about your time. Suppose we run across something in a book or something that mentions something about things that happened in our lifetimes—wars, or inventions, or something?"

"I won't need to look far to find out about my near future," Aaron said, and nodded at Adam. "You're from only sixty years in my future, and, well, Germany was sort of at the center of things in 1938. You probably know a lot about what happened next in my time."

Ahna and Adam exchanged glances with each other. She could tell he knew at least something about what happened next to German Jews, and to Germany. "Well, uh, yeah, I suppose so." Adam said slowly. He looked to Ahna. "Are there any rules about that?"

"The safest thing is for you not to say anything," Ahna said firmly. "That goes for both you and Aaron when it comes to Brazilian history as well."

Aaron nodded. "I can see that. For what it's worth, we never studied about nineteenth-century Brazil in our schools. So there's not much I could say."

"We didn't study Brazil much either," said Adam. "But that doesn't get around the main problem. We know about the future now. How do you keep us from knowing about it after this, when we go back?"

A sudden look of alarm appeared on Aaron's face. "You are going to send us back, aren't you? You're not going to keep us here forever to keep us from talking, or something, are you?"

Ahna's eyes widened in shock. "Goodness no!" she cried out. "We could never do such a thing. No. Unless something goes terribly, terribly wrong, you will all be returned home to your own times, to just a moment or two after you were Yanked."

"Ah, if you could make it an hour or two later in my case, I think it might be healthier for me," said Aaron, a grim little smile on his lips.

Ahna smiled back. "I think we can arrange that," she said.

"But we'll know about the future," Adam objected. "You just said that can't be permitted."

Ahna paused for a moment. The mission rules made it clear that it was her choice in regard to what to tell them, and when. Some other groups had been rushed through training so quickly that, lucky for them, there had never been time to discuss such matters.

"One moment, please," D'Alembert said, his voice coming from out of nowhere with a bit more firmness and urgency than usual. "If you three young gentlemen will excuse us, I think I must ask Ahna to step out into the hallway for a moment."

"D'Alembert!" Ahna protested.

"I'm afraid I must insist."

"All right!" she said. She stood up, and stalked toward the door. It slid open ahead of her, and shut behind her as she stepped out into the hall. To her not very great surprise, Giotto was just coming around the corner, sliding silently up to her on his hover system.

"All right," she said. "The two of you want to gang up on me where the three of them can't hear us. What is it?"

"I was of course monitoring the conversation," Giotto began.

"I know, I know!" Ahna said. "So what's the problem?"

"I think you know," said D'Alembert.

Ahna didn't answer at first, but neither D'Alembert nor Giotto was the sort to play along with such games. "Don't be childish," said D'Alembert. "Do you think that if you don't say the words, the problem won't exist?"

Ahna glared at the point in midair where D'Alembert's voice seemed to be coming from at the moment. "No, of course not," she snapped. "But I can't ask these three boys to work and maybe fight alongside me at the same time I'm lying to them."

"We cannot possibly tell them everything about the situation in the amount of time we have left before mission-start. Not telling someone everything is not always the same as lying," said Giotto.

"But sometimes it is," Ahna said. "*This* time it is. Besides, it's too late. Just by not answering certain questions we've told them all they need to figure it out for themselves."

Giotto spoke. "This group of Yank subjects *was* selected in part because of their ability to think in nonconventional ways and work from incomplete information, as well as for their tenacity. Ahna has a point. We cannot expect such a group to ignore a puzzle such as the one we have given them—especially when it concerns them directly, and does so in such unusual circumstances."

"You both think they will figure it out for themselves?" D'Alembert asked.

"If they haven't done so already," Ahna replied.

"They give no sign of having done so," said D'Alembert. "I am still monitoring the conference room, and they are not talking among themselves about any substantive matter.''

''Yet,'' said Ahna. None of the three of them spoke for a moment. Ahna waited as long as she dared, then launched into the silence. ''This is supposed to be my mission, with me making the decisions. So either accept my decisions, or take me off the job and put someone else in.''

''You've made up your mind, then?'' asked D'Alembert.

''I *have* to tell them. I don't see any choice.''

''Very well,'' D'Alembert said, plainly reluctant.

Giotto and Ahna went back into the conference room where the boys were waiting. The three of them looked at her expectantly.

''Well?'' asked Aaron.

''D'Alembert and Giotto and I had to discuss something,'' she said. ''Let's go back to your question, Adam. The answer is pretty simple. Before we send you back, we'll induce a very specific amnesia that will only cover your time here.''

''I don't understand,'' said Roberto.

''They'll make us forget,'' said Aaron. ''They'll make sure we can never remember that we were ever here.''

DECISIONS

Adam should have felt surprised by Ahna's news, but somehow he wasn't. Some part of his mind had seen enough moves ahead to work it out, and see the logic of it before he was told. "That doesn't sound very fair," he objected.

"No, it isn't," Ahna said. "But we are desperate, and desperate people can rarely worry a great deal about being fair."

"Very little of my life has been fair," Roberto said evenly.

"Mine either," said Aaron. "These people pulled me out of my time about ten seconds before I was going to be beaten to a pulp, or worse. I'm willing to take a few risks for them in exchange, even if I don't remember it all afterward."

"I slept in a bed finer than the bed of Dom Luis last night," said Roberto. "I took my first proper bath, with hot water and soap. I ate my fill at breakfast, and no one struck my hand when I reached for more. To live like this, even for a little time, is a great gift, at least to me."

Adam considered his two fellow Yank subjects for a

moment. A slave and a German Jewish boy who was used to being hated, who couldn't possibly realize how horrible the years to come would be for him and his people.

It dawned on him that he was the only one who got up in the morning expecting life to be fair, assuming he would get a break, get a chance to defend himself or try again. Mr. Benton and Mrs. Meredith had offered to let him undo his mistake. Neither Roberto nor Aaron would ever get a chance like that. Probably both of them had been punished for no reason at all, dozens of times, far more severely than he would ever be for things he had done.

"A question, please," said Aaron. "I think I understand the reasons you must make us forget, when this is over—but if you can make us forget everything, then why can't we find out about our own futures? It would be most exciting to know what will happen next in my own world, even if I can only know it for a little while."

Adam looked sharply at Ahna. He had no doubt that she was thinking the same thing he was—that letting Aaron know his future, and the future of his country and his people, would be no favor at all.

But that was not the answer she gave. "Memory erasure is not always perfect," she said. "I'm no expert on it, but different sorts of memories are mapped to different parts of your brain. We can locate experiential memories of a given time period pretty easily, but reported information memories could be located in any number of synaptic matrices that—"

"I'm sorry, excuse me," said Aaron. He tapped the broca amplifier on the side of his head. "This thing is working all right, and giving me the words you're saying, but I don't know what the words mean."

"I didn't quite follow it either," said Adam.

"If I might assist," said Giotto, "I think I can explain

the problem in an analogy that might make more sense to our visitors.''

''Yes, please,'' said Ahna.

''Imagine a chest of drawers, or a set of cubbyholes, where things can be stored in an orderly manner. We understand how memories of your own personal experience are stored, and how to find them. That set of rules is more or less the same in nearly every person. We can find the ones we need and erase them, if need be.

''But if I told Adam something about his little sister's next birthday party, would his brain store the memory as the words I spoke to him? Or would he visualize the story, and store it with the idea of birthdays, or parties, or sisters—or all three, or with party decorations, or with some other, completely unexpected, association of ideas?

''We can find what 'drawers' to look in for memories of recent direct physical experience, things that happen to you, personally, but it is much more difficult to look in all the 'drawers' for things that aren't linked to direct experience. Thus it is much safer to tell you as little as possible about your own futures to start with.''

Roberto frowned for a moment, and then nodded. ''Your magic is good, but not perfect. I understand. If you don't tell me what I shouldn't know, you won't have to go clean it up later.''

''Yes. Exactly,'' said Ahna. ''But we have yet to tell you anything about the mission itself. Before I do, let me say that any of you can decide to leave, to be sent home, now, or anytime until one hour after this briefing is finished. Ask before then and we will send you at once, with no questions asked. Up until the actual moment the mission itself starts, you can still ask to be returned—but as we get closer to mission-start, it will become harder and harder to make the arrangements, and there could be delays. In any event, after the mission ends, you will be returned to your own home time and place.''

"Unless something goes wrong, of course," said Aaron. "Whatever it is we're supposed to do, it's not going to be one hundred percent safe. Someone could get hurt, or worse."

"Yes," said Ahna, a bit stiffly. "That's true. The odds are against it. Very much against it. And we could all be killed by a meteorite smashing into this building in the next five seconds—but the odds are against that, too."

"Odds in favor, odds against," said Aaron, and shrugged. "I just want to be sure I have the full picture here. I don't want to give up and go home before the game even starts."

"Nor do I," said Roberto.

Adam glanced at the others and nodded, just a heartbeat too late for it to be altogether convincing. "Me neither," he said. He felt as if he were a little behind the others. If they were all there because they had this "grit" the 2345 A.D. people kept talking about, why wasn't he as brave as the others seemed to be?

"Excellent," said Ahna. "Now, there is one other point." She glanced at Giotto, then at the point in space where that D'Alembert guy's voice had been coming from. "Adam and Aaron knew how to read when they got here. Their broca amplifiers have linked to the proper skill centers in their brains, so they read and write our language. But Roberto doesn't know how to read or write. He's going to have to learn how before we leave."

The robot she called Giotto spun its head around and focused both eye cameras on her. "That's far too high a level of interference!" it said.

"That sort of memory, memory of a skill or trained ability, is almost impossible to erase," D'Alembert protested. "It is a significant interference with his brain's underlying pattern. We can't send him back to his own time knowing how to read. How could that ever be explained?"

"If you can't remove the skill memories—*if* you can't—he'll go back to nineteenth-century, Portuguese-speaking, Brazil knowing how to read *our* language—not theirs. The ability won't be of any use back there."

"What good will it do him here and now?" Giotto demanded.

"You forget the role he is to play," said Ahna. "We need to convince the Devlin that these three are truly part of the team they are joining. We might be able to hide some gaps in their knowledge—but suppose someone hands Roberto a paper to read, or asks him to take notes at a meeting? Don't you think it will seem a little odd for Earth to employ illiterate diplomats?"

There was silence for a moment before D'Alembert spoke. "You point is well taken," the bodiless voice replied.

"Wait a moment," said Aaron. "Diplomats? We're going to be *diplomats*? We don't even know what's going on."

"You can teach me to read?" Roberto asked. "You can do that? It is possible? It is permitted?"

"Teach him to read?!" Adam protested. "That'd take *months*. I thought this whole thing was a rush project."

"One at a time, please," said Ahna. "We don't expect you to be diplomats—you'll be in the background while the team members from our time do the negotiating. We just need to make sure you can pretend well enough to satisfy the aliens. And yes, Roberto, we can teach you to read. And don't worry, Adam, the same broca amplifier he's got on can do the job more or less instantly. It's just a question of activating a few extra circuits."

"I will be able to *read*? *Today*?" Roberto asked.

"Yes," said Ahna, "a little later today. Reading is a difficult skill that takes practice and effort to master—but we can implant all of the basic rote knowledge of

76

letters and words that you will need. That is, assuming that D'Alembert approves it.''

There was a long moment of quiet in the room, but at last D'Alembert spoke. ''Very well,'' he said. ''It is a violation of standard procedure, but under the circumstances, I will approve it—reluctantly.''

''Thank you, D'Alembert,'' said Ahna.

''*Muito obrigado, Senhor D'Alembert*,'' said Roberto. ''*Muito, muito obrigado*.''

''*De nada, Robertinho. De nada*.''

''Whatever that means,'' Aaron said evenly. ''But dearest Miss Ahna, you have been promising to explain what all this is about for a good long time now. What's this mission you keep talking about?''

''Quite right,'' said Ahna. ''Very well, then. Humankind has encountered a number of alien races—intelligent beings who aren't Human and who come from other planets. Some of these aliens have been friendly, some have shown little or no interest in us—and some have been very close to hostile.''

''The species we know the least about, and the one that seems to be the most hostile to us, are the Devlin. We have virtually no direct information about them, other than the fact that they received the same 'gift' of the sally ports roughly when we did, and they have been working feverishly to expand their sphere of influence. And we seem to be in their way.

''Beyond all that, there is one other matter concerning the Devlin. You have been told how only young people can transit the sally ports. It is not youth, exactly, that is the factor. It is *growth*. A Human who is still growing is able to pass through sally ports with little or no difficulty. A full-grown Human cannot. That same restriction seems to hold for all the other races we have encountered, with two exceptions. One is the Thogemag, who get around the problem in a way that needn't concern us for the moment. The other species is the Devlin.

77

They simply keep growing, their whole lives through. The older they are, the bigger they are.''

Adam saw the problem. "So they can send their adults through sally ports, but we can't." He turned to Ahna. "And that puts us at a disadvantage. No offense."

"None taken," she said. "I agree."

"But all the news isn't bad," said Giotto. "Thanks to the K'lugu."

"Who are they?" asked Roberto.

"Another alien race—and a far friendlier one," D'Alembert replied. "They served as mediators through a long, complicated, series of painstaking negotiations. Thanks to the K'lugu, it has been agreed that a party of Humans will meet with a party of Devlin on an island on a K'lugu world, a planet with a name that translates from the K'lugu as 'Bogwater.' ''

Ahna took it up from there. "But the K'lugu aren't the problem. The Devlin are. No one knows what they want. Humanity knows far too little about them, about their motives and goals. We want to go and find out."

"Wait a second," said Adam. "Does this sally port gizmo hurt machines? Giotto, would you be hurt if you went through it?"

"No. It has no particular effect on robots or other forms of artificial intellect," Giotto replied.

"Then why doesn't our side just send a bunch of robots?"

"An excellent question," said Giotto. "The Devlin, no doubt seeking to press home their advantage, insisted on a meeting of 'true' beings—actual Humans and actual Devlin, flesh and blood. Our side agreed to the 'true' beings rule, and agreed to a first meeting on a neutral site—on condition that the *second* meeting take place in our Solar System, where we can bring in adult diplomats and other specialists. However, auxiliary members of the delegation can be robots. I will, therefore, be in attendance—but I am not to have any contact at all with the Devlin."

Aaron broke the silence. "So your side—our side, I guess—is going to meet with their side. What are you all going to talk about?"

Ahna smiled. "The Human agenda for Meeting One is, in large part, to get it over with, so everyone can adjourn to the Solar System and the grown-ups can take over. We will make the first face-to-face contact with the Devlin—"

"You mean haven't even *seen* them up until now?" Roberto said.

Ahna frowned. "Didn't I make that clear? We haven't ever met them. We have some data, a few intercepted transmissions, some images and basic bio-data we got from the K'lugu, but no Human has ever met a Devlin in the flesh. At least so far as we know."

From the way Ahna said the last thing, Adam could tell it was important in some way. " 'So far as we know' leaves a lot of possibilities open," he said. "Do you think there are some encounters you don't know about?"

Ahna glanced at Giotto, and at where D'Alembert's voice had last come from. "Maybe they picked the right people for this job after all," she said. "Very sharp. Exactly. You cover this part, D'Alembert."

"The Devlin seem to know more about Humans than they should, given the extremely limited nature of the contacts between the two races," said D'Alembert. "There is strong evidence that the Devlin have some secret source of information on Humans. They asked certain questions of the K'lugu that suggested prior knowledge of us, knowledge they shouldn't have had. And their knowledge has odd gaps in it. We looked at information they have, thought about where it might have come from, and compared it to their areas of apparent ignorance. We think there is a very high probability that the Devlin have stumbled across a lost colony ship somewhere.''

"Lost colony ship?"

"A whole fleet of ships were sent out almost as soon as the sally ports were opened, before we understood them very well," said Ahna. "The whole operation was a disaster. It was only then that we learned adults can't survive the trip through an interstellar sally port. The loss of so many ships was part of what taught us—or retaught us—that the universe is a dangerous place. Some of those ships have been found—some with everyone on board dead, some with survivors. But nine such ships are still utterly unaccounted for.''

"One clue makes us think the Devlin have found a particular derelict ship. We intercepted a Devlin message that was accidentally sent unencoded and unencrypted. Most of it is unintelligible, but there is one word that sounds as if it were recorded Human speech, cut-and-pasted into an audio report because the Devlin had trouble pronouncing it. It is the word 'Roanoke.'"

Adam said bolt upright. "Roanoke!" he repeated.

"Ah, yes," said D'Alembert. "You are from that part of the world, though from several centuries in the future of the incident. You would know about Roanoke."

"But Roberto and I wouldn't," said Aaron.

"I read about in history class," said Adam. "In fact I've been there. Roanoke was a colony established by the English in North Carolina, hundreds of years ago. A ship left the settlement to go back to England for supplies. When it returned, the place was deserted. No one ever found out what happened."

"*Roanoke* was also the name of one of the colony ships that vanished," said Ahna.

"It doesn't sound like such a lucky name to give to anything," said Roberto.

"You might have a point," Ahna said dryly. "Maybe we'd better not use it again. But for the moment, it seems very likely that the Devlin encountered the *Roanoke,* or survivors from her, somehow."

"So what are we supposed to do?" asked Adam.

"Snoop around," said Ahna. "While the main negotiation team is meeting with the Devlin, you three, the Yank team, will pose as support staff, and try to find the source of the Devlin's knowledge regarding Humans. Maybe we've got it all wrong about the *Roanoke,* and they just listened in on our transmissions, the same way we listened in on theirs, and learned about us that way. Or maybe there *is* a lost colony group out there. If so, and it's possible to do so, you Yanks and I will try to contact them and prepare rescue and relief as needed."

"But from what you're saying, these *Roanoke* people could be anywhere in space," Adam protested. "None of us even know how to turn the lights on and off in this room. How are we supposed to contact them? We can't fly a spaceship to go look for them, even if we knew where they were."

"It's most unlikely that you'll have to travel in a spacecraft," said Giotto. "It is far more likely that the Devlin will be doing what we will be doing—using t-ports to keep their base on Bogwater linked to their network of sally ports and t-ports. Our belief is that there will be a sally port link held open between Bogwater and wherever the *Roanoke* people are being held. The *Roanoke,* or her people, serve, in effect, as the Devlin's library of information about us. All it will require is following their sally port network back to the proper nexus."

"Great," said Adam. "That makes it sound *much* easier."

"It is, beyond question, a delicate, dangerous situation," said D'Alembert.

"Just wait," Ahna said. "It gets better." Her tone of voice shifted and took on a slightly singsong tone, as if she were quoting some sort of orders or instructions from memory. "While your team is researching the *Roanoke* lead, you are not to interfere with or upset the Devlin, or to take any actions or steps that might disrupt Meeting One. Peaceful relations with Devlin are to take precedence over hypothetical contact with the theoretical lost colony group. However, *if* the lost colony group has established itself on a habitable world, bear in mind that such a world is a jewel of great value. Establishing and retaining claim to such a world would take precedence over relations with the Devlin."

Aaron let out a low whistle. "A lot of balls they want to juggle, isn't it?"

Ahna smiled sadly. "They don't make it sound easy, do they?" she asked. "But in any event, that's pretty much all I had to say. Giotto?"

"That concludes this initial briefing," the robot said. "As stated earlier, you have one hour to decide whether to proceed with the mission, or whether to return to your own times at once."

"What happens in an hour if we decide to stay and work for you?" asked Roberto.

"Oh, yes," said Ahna. "That was the one thing I forgot to mention. If you decide to stay, we'll leave at once for Edge Station Three."

"Which is where, please?" asked Aaron.

"On the Edge, obviously," said Ahna, with a mischievous grin.

"Of course," said Aaron wryly. "How could I ask such a silly question?"

"Sorry," said Ahna. "That was a stupid joke. On the Edge of the Solar System. Just outside the orbit of Neptune. With the walks between t-port stations, it should take us just about ten minutes to get there."

STARING AT THE SUN

Before Adam had a chance to think things through, the hour was over. The four of them—Adam, Ahna, Roberto, and Aaron—were walking the corridors of the C.O.B. pyramid, toward the first of the t-ports.

Adam was not quite sure how, or when, he had agreed to go along on the mission. It just sort of happened.

The other two boys never seemed to have a moment's hesitation. Maybe it was just that his life was so much more comfortable and secure than theirs. Roberto and Aaron were living, breathing reminders of what life was like for a lot of people, even in 1999. Make that most people. They had nothing to lose.

He didn't get much further in his thinking than that before they entered a room, the door of which was marked TELEPORT CHAMBER. Inside the room, in the center of the floor, was a booth, glassed-in on three sides. Two technicians stood behind a complicated-looking control console that was festooned with video displays, key-control panels, and odd transparent cubes that shifted color from moment to moment. One of the techs looked up at Ahna. "Ready when your people are."

"We're ready," said Ahna.

"What about Giotto?" Adam asked.

"We're just headed off to the Edge Station to get you three a bit more trained and oriented," Ahna said. "Giotto has other work to do in the meantime. He'll join us on Bogwater."

"Oh, okay," said Adam. He looked a bit doubtfully at the booth. "How does that work?"

Ahna grinned wickedly again. "No one really knows. Ever since the Gift Givers gave us t-ports, our scientists and technicians have been tearing their hair out trying to figure it out. We can operate them, and manufacture them, and we even figured out how to make t-ports that reached through time as well as space. Even so, no one is quite sure how they work. But if you're asking what you need to do, it's pretty easy. Just stand in the booth until you notice that you're somewhere else. I'll go first, and then come back, just so you three know it works. All right?"

Roberto shrugged. "Everything else so far has been magic, and it has all worked. Why should we doubt this trick will work as well?"

"Still, it couldn't hurt to see her come back," said Aaron, folding his arms thoughtfully as he stared at the t-port booth. "Go ahead, *Fräulein* Ahna. Go, and come back. I'd feel better."

Ahna stepped into the booth and nodded to the techs. One of them nodded, the second pushed a button—and nothing happened.

The second tech noticed that the three boys looked confused and smiled. "It takes a few seconds for the potentials to build up," he said.

And, then, without any fuss, Ahna simply vanished.

"There you go," the tech said triumphantly. She looked down at the console. "Edge Station Three confirms arrival. Standing by for return leg."

"Just so you know," said the second technician,

"she's really taking a lot out of herself by going an extra round-trip to show you it can be done. One jump to an Edge Station won't slow you down, but two or three, back and forth, one right after another, is no fun."

"Thank you for telling us," said Roberto. "It is important to know that our hostess is making so much effort for us."

"Stand by for incoming," said the first tech.

And just as suddenly as she had gone, Ahna was back in the booth. "You see?" she asked with a smile. "No problem."

"No problem," said Adam. He looked at her closely. Somehow her smile looked a little forced. "I guess it's my turn now," he said, and stepped toward the booth as Ahna moved out of it. He couldn't help but notice that neither of the other boys seemed eager to go next.

He stepped into the booth. His heart was pounding, and his hands had balled up into fists. He uncurled his fingers and put his arms at his side, palms flat against his hips. "Ready," he said. It was the biggest lie he had ever told. How could he possibly be ready for whatever was on the other side? Maybe there was still time to tell them to stop—

But then he saw the technician push the button, and that was enough to freeze him to the spot. Supposing he moved, and had, say, a leg outside the booth when the gizmo activated? Would the leg stay where it was, neatly sliced off by the effects of super-gravitionizalized trans-axial displacement, or whatever the techno-talk would be?

Adam was just about to cry out and call for them to stop—

—when the quiet, careful world of the C.O.B. pyramid vanished—

—and the bustling, busy, bright-lit deck of Edge Station Three popped into view in its place.

* * *

Adam stepped out of a t-port booth identical to the one back on Earth, but the room outside was completely different. The walls and floors were painted in bright, primary colors—blue floor, red walls, yellow ceiling. One wall was clear glass from about waist level on up. On the other side of the wall was a line of people—well, mostly people, anyway—who were apparently waiting for their turn to use the t-port.

But they'd have to wait just a little longer. The other members of his own team were still coming through, one after the other. First Aaron, then Roberto, then Ahna, making her third trip in five minutes between Earth and the Outer Solar System. She looked decidedly peaked as she came out of the booth, but she waved off Roberto's offer of help. She seemed to be herself again after a moment or two.

Adam was feeling woozy himself, and by the look of things, so were Roberto and Aaron. But a single t-port jump wasn't supposed to bother a teenager that much. Maybe it was the mere *fact* of the jump that bothered him, the shocking, absurd idea that he was suddenly billions of miles away from Earth.

"Clear the chamber please," said one of the techs. "Several parties are waiting to depart."

"Come on," said Ahna. "This way."

Aaron and Roberto, both wide-eyed and quiet, fell into step behind her. Adam followed, feeling a little wobbly in the legs. He almost tripped over his own feet once or twice as they walked out of the t-port chamber and into what appeared to be a main station corridor. Had his legs gone to sleep somehow? It took him three or four strides to realize that *he* wasn't wobbly—it was gravity itself that was a bit off, somehow. He tried an experimental hop that should have lifted him six inches at most. Instead it lifted him a good foot off the deckplates. He landed clumsily, cried out, and fell over, landing on his side.

"It's real," he said to himself as the others hurried back and helped him up. It was the first time, the first moment, he truly believed it all. Everything else might have been faked, somehow. Hollywood, 1999, *could* have tricked up nearly everything else he had seen and heard. They might even have been able to do the t-port. Shoot him full of some superfast tranquilizer drug. Knock him out, hustle him to another set somewhere in the movie studio, wake him up and tell him he's out past Neptune.

But *gravity*? How do you go about faking reduced gravity? Even Hollywood couldn't make Adam think he weighed half as much or make him fall half as fast as he did back home.

Ahna smiled as she helped him to his feet. "Yes," she said. "It's real." She turned to the others. "It's about half Earth gravity here," she said. "I should have mentioned it, but with so much going on, I forgot."

"Half Earth what?" Roberto asked.

"Gravity. The force that holds you to the floor or the ground," she said.

"What she means is that the reason we all feel funny is that we weigh half as much as we did on Earth," said Adam.

Roberto's eyes widened further, if such a thing could be. "*Impossível*," he said. "I ate well. I have not been sick. I am no thinner."

Ahna laughed. "Even so," she said, "Adam is right. Yes, you are healthy and strong—but even if your strong body is still all there, it only weighs half of what it did. And you might as well enjoy it while you can. On Bogwater, we will weigh about five percent more than we do on Earth."

Roberto frowned again. "What is percent?"

"One-hundredth part," said Ahna. "Five percent means five-hundredths. One-twentieth."

Roberto just looked more puzzled. Clearly that explanation didn't help either.

"Never mind," said Ahna. "There are other things to worry about. Come this way."

They followed, walking carefully, openly gawking at everything they saw. There were strange machines on all sides. It was impossible to guess what anything was for. A boxy thing about as tall as Adam might have been a robot, judging by the way it hovered down the hall— but it looked remarkably like an old-fashioned filing cabinet with arms. What appeared to be a foot-wide metallic spider was hanging from the ceiling by four of its legs, and busily doing some sort of repair work with the other four. One leg held a perfectly normal-looking screwdriver, but the other three held gizmos Adam couldn't even guess at. They passed a transparent room that seemed to be filled with small, multicolored beach balls that someone was bouncing off the walls and ceilings— unless the balls were bouncing themselves.

The colors on everything from the walls to the doors to the clothes people wore seemed wildly vivid, almost lurid, after the pale, careful pastels everywhere in evidence at the C.O.B. pyramid.

Even the people were brightly colored. Not just their clothes—though they seemed dazzlingly bright as well. Many—well, at least some—of the people had done things—quite a few things—to their skin, and to their hair. A bald, blue-skinned man wearing red pants and a green shirt strolled past them, reading some papers and thoughtfully stroking his gleaming gold beard. A woman dressed in a khaki jacket and dun-colored trousers walked in front of them down a cross corridor. She could be forgiven the dull clothing. Anything fancier would have simply distracted from the leopard-spotted pattern of her short-cut hair.

"Quite a show, isn't it?" asked Ahna. "The theory is to combat isolation and the unchanging environment with extremes of fashion and design and constant change. Fads run through here in about two or three weeks."

Ahna directed them to a door with a placard that read OPERATION HOURGLASS TRAINING CENTER. The door opened on its own, and they went in.

If the low gravity hadn't made Adam believe, once and for all, that they were in the future and off Earth, then the viewport of the main training room would have done so with no effort at all. What he saw through the big, circular window was too real, too sharp, too breathtakingly unexpected, to be anything but real.

The stars! Never had he seen so many of them, never had they been so bright, against a sky so dark. And closer in, the sky was filled with spacecraft of all types. Big, small, every size in between. Some were little more than open frameworks of girders that cargo could be attached to. Others were fat white cylinders with all manner of antennae and detectors and things Adam could not even guess at sprouting out of the hulls at all angles.

"Look at that!" Roberto cried out, pointing to the porthole. "A new star in the sky! And so bright!"

"Where?" asked Aaron.

"There. In Leo, the Lion. Do you call the star patterns by the same name as we do in Brazil? Can't you see it? There! It has never been there before."

There *was* a very bright star, remarkably bright, framed in the center of the window. But Adam wasn't even going to bother pretending he knew the stars and constellations remotely well enough to notice a new one in the sky.

"You've seen that star many times before," Ahna said gently. "It's the Sun."

All three boys stared at the fat dot of light hanging in the darkness. A jump out past the orbit of Neptune didn't even rate as a walk around the block in comparison to the leap they would make through the sally port, but it was far enough to shrink the Sun down to a fat dot. Adam wondered if one of the stars he could see right now was the one that shone down on Bogwater.

"What's that?" Aaron asked, pointing out the view-port to a faint bluish green dot, scarcely more than a point of light itself.

"Neptune," said Ahna. "The Station's orbit is nearly at conjunction—that is, closest approach—to it."

"Is Neptune a world, a planet like Earth?" asked Roberto.

"That's right," said Ahna.

"It's not very big," said Roberto.

"It's five times as big around as Earth, and weighs seventeen times as much," said Ahna. "It's just that we're so far from it that it's hard to see."

"From Earth, you can't see Neptune at all, except with a telescope," said Aaron. "I read that somewhere."

The three boys from the past stared out the viewport at the universe beyond, at the dark and the emptiness that surrounded the station.

"Come on," Ahna said at last. "We have a lot of work to do, and very little time to do it. We have lecturers coming in to brief you, equipment to explain, and I want to arrange private sessions and tutoring for each of you as well. It's time we got busy."

EDUCATION

The suit technician held up what looked like an odd-looking set of coveralls. "This is an s-suit. 'S' for safety, 'S' for security, 'S' for system. The s-suit will take care of you—if you take care of it. This model is one of the more advanced in use. It includes heating and cooling systems to control your body temperature. It has a supply of drinking water, which it replenishes by condensing water vapor out of the air. It has a tracking device, so your team members will be able to locate you at all times. It likewise includes a communications system. Add a helmet, gloves, boots, and an environment pack, and it can serve as a space suit for use in a vacuum in an emergency."

She spread the suit out on the table before the three boys. "So much for a quick overview. Now we'll go over the suit, piece by piece, and teach you how to use it . . ."

". . . Your team will be carrying one special, expensive, and important piece of equipment: a miniature sally port inducer. It is a spherical device about fifty centimeters across. Once activated, it will generate a sally port linked to a matched port orbiting the Sun, near us here at Edge Station Three. If your team actually finds survivors of a lost colony, you are to get as close as you can to their location and activate the inducer. However, the odds against your successfully locating the colony are great— and inducers, as I believe they said in your times, don't grow on bushes. So we'll tell you not only how and when to use the inducer—but also spend a lot of time making sure you know when *not* to use it. . . ."

The technician sat down beside Roberto, close enough to make Roberto feel more than a little nervous. She reached up and put one hand on his forehead, and the other at the back of his neck as she examined his broca amplifier.

Roberto did not like to have others touch him. Dona Flora was never shy about punishing the household servants when she thought they were being lazy, or even if she were merely in a bad mood. Whenever anyone got their hands too close to Roberto, he flinched, bracing himself for the blows that were likely to start falling. Dona Flora had a particular fondness for boxing his ears.

But this woman, this technician, had a most gentle touch. There was something detached, almost impersonal, about the way she examined him. "No problem," she said. "That's a perfectly standard attachment of the amplifier. Now, it's going to sting just a little when I remove it, and once it's off, you won't able to understand most of my speech—except for whatever your brain has picked up in its native speech centers. I'm just going to activate its visual-language and reading module. It will probably tingle just a bit when I put it back on. So don't be scared, all right?"

Roberto could scarcely suppress a smile. "Yes, it will be all right. Please go ahead." Even with the magic language machine teacher, the amulet, the charm—no, those were not the proper words—the *broca amplifier* attached to the side of his head, he couldn't understand half of what everyone was saying. He could hear and comprehend the words, but so many of them were meaningless. There was nothing in his own life to which he could attach the words "robot," "t-port," or "radio."

The technician moved her hands gently, and he could just barely feel them brushing his skin. There was the slightest of tingles, the merest moment of brief discomfort. To someone who had endured Dona Flora's beatings, or worse, that time with the lash, such a little fleabite was not worthy to be called pain. That was all. The—amulet?—language charm?—what *was* it called?—was off.

"Glana fatu adblust the ambbliger," the woman next to him said. "Idbwill tok juzp a second." The words were gibberish. He couldn't understand the worker—no, that wasn't it—the, the—what was it? There was a special word, a special job-name for this woman. He had known it only moments before. Why couldn't he remember!?

He knew why not, and forced himself to remain calm. She needed to adjust the—the charm—and then put it back on him. When she did, all the words would come back, and he would be able to read. To read.

Roberto relaxed, and let the woman with the job-name he could not remember get on with her work.

Adam and Aaron sat at the table in the main training room. Adam had lost track of the names of all the lecturers and briefers and trainers. There were too many of them, and they came and went too fast. He couldn't keep them all straight.

Aaron was doing a bit better at it than Adam. Adam leaned over and whispered to him. "Aaron—who's this guy again?" he asked.

"Dr. Halshaw," Aaron hissed back. "The director of

the whole Meeting One project. He's supposed to show us maps and tell us the lay of the land where we're going.''

"Oh, right," Adam said.

"Are you two boys finished whispering?" Dr. Halshaw asked, glaring at both of them.

"Yes, sir," they answered in unison.

"Very well," said Dr. Halshaw. "None of our map specialists are available here at Edge Three, and I have some experience in that area. Therefore, I will provide you with the basic cartographic information important to Meeting One with the Devlin." Dr. Halshaw's tone of voice, facial expression, and even the way he held himself ramrod straight all shouted louder than words ever could that he did not like this situation. He was older, decades older, than most of the other briefing officers. Many of the other staff experts on this and that subject were barely older than Adam—in their mid or late teens, or their early twenties. Dr. Halshaw was somewhere in his mid-fifties. But age was not the only difference. Most of the other briefers had been patient and good-natured in dealing with the three boys from the past, and all the things they did not know, but Dr. Halshaw was making no secret of his impatience. "Shall we begin?"

"*Herr Doktor* Halshaw?" Aaron asked, cautiously raising his hand.

"Yes, Alvin, what is it?"

"My name's Aaron, sir," he said. "Sir, Roberto isn't here."

"Thank you, but I was aware of that. My powers of observation haven't failed me completely."

"Shouldn't we wait for him?"

"No, we should not. As you might recall, *Aaron*, your little friend from the back of beyond is illiterate. Illiterates can't read words, and if you can't read words, you can't read maps. He could not understand what I'll be saying. Therefore, I don't think we will wait for your friend the noble savage.''

Aaron ignored the insult and focused on the issue at hand. "Roberto is getting his broca amplifier modified right now, Dr. Halshaw," he said. "Supposedly he'll at least be able to read really simple things almost at once."

"How nice that you assume my maps must be 'really simple.' Nevertheless, I'm going to take the risk that your newly literate friend might miss some little thing and go on without him.

Adam thought he understood Dr. Halshaw's impatience. The Gift Givers had shown up fifteen years before. The teens and adults who were training them today would have still been in diapers, and the thirty-year-olds would have been Adam's age. But Dr. Halshaw would already have been in his mid-thirties, just starting to come into his own. And then the stars had been thrown open—but not for him. For children, for upstarts, for babes in arms who had paid no dues, put in no time, made no sacrifices. He didn't have to take out his frustrations on the Yanks, though. Still, they needed to know what this grumpy old man could tell them. *We'll just have to go over it all with Roberto later*, Adam told himself.

"Look, Dr. Halshaw," he said. "I'm sorry. None of this was our idea. No one asked us if we wanted to come here. We're just trying to do our best. Maybe we should just talk about the Meeting One site."

Dr. Halshaw glared at Adam for a solid twenty seconds. At last he spoke. "All right, then." He touched a control that caused a map-image to appear on the table before him. "Pay attention. The K'lugu let us send in a robotic survey team. Our survey 'bots did aerial and satellite imaging, ground-walks, and so on. No Human being has yet set foot on any of the islands—or on the planet of Bogwater for that matter. That means we probably know the important basics, but there are likely to be surprises.

"The site chosen for Meeting One is an island that is part of a chain of about twenty small islands straddling the equator at 115 degrees west longitude. The archipelago is home to all sorts of wildlife, including various species of giant flightless aquatic birds that have evolved into creatures not unlike seals and sea lions. That's why we've nicknamed the island group the Canary Islands." Halshaw paused, and Adam realized that the man had tried to tell a joke. A pretty lame one. Both boys just stared at him. "It's a humorous reference to the megabirds, which look nothing like canaries. The team named most of the other islands in the group after various waterbirds."

He pointed to various smaller outer islands. "There's Sandpiper, Osprey, Cormorant, Pelican, and so on. All the place names I'm giving you are the informal ones dreamed up by our people. Presumably the K'lugu have their own names for them, and probably the Devlin have invented their own as well.

"The largest island is about 112 acres, or forty-five hectares. At first we called it Stork, but it's come to be called Negotiation Island.

"Both the Human and K'lugu embassies are on Negotiation Island, the K'lugu in a half-buried structure near this beach, and the Human embassy five hundred meters—a bit more than five hundred yards—inland, on a low rise that has more or less been officially named Human Hill."

"Don't bother translating to yards and feet and pounds," said Adam. "I'm pretty good with the metric system, and no one else around here knows American weights and measures."

"I am relieved to hear it," said Dr. Halshaw. "Your measurement system was incredibly unwieldy. In any event, our embassy, assembled by our robots from prefabricated sections, is already complete, ahead of schedule and before the Devlin finished.''

Dr. Halshaw sounded pleased by that. Adam wondered what the big deal was in finishing first, but decided it would be smarter not to ask.

"As you will see, there is a wide expanse of open space below Human Hill—Parley Meadow. Negotiations will take place in a pavilion being built there, by the K'lugu, an extremely simple structure, little more than a roof held up by four corner posts. The Devlin insisted on that, we think because it would be harder to booby-trap."

"*They* sound like a very trusting bunch," said Aaron.

"They are not," Dr. Halshaw said, agreeing with the sarcastic tone of Aaron's voice, rather than the words he spoke. "Getting them to agree to anything at all, even what time of day to meet for the first session, took heroic effort. Things are very delicate. Do something wrong, offend someone, and you might ruin a meeting that took years to set up."

Dr. Halshaw glared at both of them again. *Great*, thought Adam. *Just what we need. More pressure on us.*

"The Devlin were invited to build their embassy complex on Negotiation Island as well, but refused," Dr. Halshaw went on. "Instead, they built it on nearby, slightly smaller Blackback island. Their embassy is currently undergoing final assembly. Their robots are building it."

Aaron and Adam studied the maps for a moment. "Do you have a map that shows Blackback Island bigger, maybe?" asked Aaron.

Dr. Halshaw adjusted a few controls, and the image in the map table recentered itself on Blackback, with more detail appearing as it grew larger. The map erupted up out of the tabletop, so they were staring at a three-dimensional image of the island.

The map going three-dee startled Adam, but Aaron

didn't seem bothered. Maybe one miracle more or less didn't matter to him.

Aaron studied the model, frowning intently. It was a rounded lump of land, about half the size of Negotiation. The shoreline facing the open sea was all low, gentle beaches, but the shore nearest Negotiation Island was rocky and rough. The interior of the island was a series of low hummocky hills and gently sloping valleys covered by patchy scrub forest, intermingled with grass and meadows. Aaron pointed at a slightly fuzzy image of a clump of buildings visible in one of the meadows. "That's their embassy?" he asked.

"That's right."

Aaron frowned again. "If I've got the sight lines straight in my head, you can't see that compound at all from Negotiation Island—but *they* could watch practically *all* of Negotiation from *that* hill on their island." Aaron stabbed a finger at the model.

Dr. Halshaw raised one eyebrow just a trifle. "Quite right," he said with some surprise.

"So they can watch us, but we can't watch them," said Adam. "What about spy satellites, or something like that? Can we snoop on them that way? Or is that where all this came from?"

Dr. Halshaw looked surprised once again. "Ah, yes," he said. "You're the one from 1999. There were space-based sensors of a sort in use by then, weren't there? Yes. The imagery data used to produce this model and the maps were in part derived from space-based detectors, though not from anything orbiting the planet.

"In the agreement for Meeting One, the K'lugu allow the Humans and the Devlin one embassy ship each, but the ships must remain in deep space. Our ship is the *Benjamin Franklin*. She's on station, about as far from Bogwater as Edge Three is from Earth. It took a lot of time and patience, and a good dose of luck, for her to get these images from that far off."

"So it wasn't easy taking the pictures," said Aaron.

"No, it wasn't. And I wouldn't count on getting more anytime soon. There has been constant cloud cover over Blackback Island since four days ago, though the skies over the rest of the Canaries have been mostly clear. We think the Devlin have been using cloud generators to hide from our cameras—and from K'lugu cameras as well. Presumably the K'lugu have satellites in close orbit, watching everything."

Adam frowned. It seemed it would be more or less impossible to spy on the Devlin embassy compound, either from space or from Negotiation Island. But knowing what the Devlin were up to was going to be a very big part of their job.

He was starting to get an idea. Adam leaned in close to the three-dimensional model. "Can you show us Negotiation Island like this?" he asked. "I want to see something."

The woman with a job-name Roberto could not recall moved in closer and reattached the charm to the side of his head. There was a sharp tingling sensation over his ear.

Roberto looked toward her and blinked. He felt a little strange, much more so than he had the first time they had put on the broca amplifier—*amplifier*, that was the word!

"How do you feel?" the technician—*technician*!—asked him, speaking slowly and carefully. "Can you understand me?"

"Yes!" Roberto said excitedly. "Yes, I can."

"That's half the battle, then," said the technician. "Let's see if the rest of it worked."

She opened a cabinet, revealing a shelf full of data viewers and old-fashioned books—these future people called them flatbooks. "Here," she said, opening one of the flatbooks and offering it to him. "Try this one. It's

99

a very basic book for little kids. You're much too old for it, of course, but it will at least tell us if the amp modification worked.''

He took the slim book, his hands trembling slightly. Roberto opened it up and looked first at the picture, and, hardly daring, looked at the words, the jumble of strange, spidery marks that had always defeated him, there under the drawing.

And then—

—And then it was like a key turning in a lock, like a door swinging wide, like a whole new world opening up to him.

''The—the cat sat on the mat,'' he read, scarcely believing what he was doing. ''The fat cat ate a rat on the mat.'' He looked up at the technician, and her eyes were shining. ''On the mat!'' he said again, almost shouting it.

''Yes, yes,'' said the technician, smiling widely. ''What a naughty, *naughty* cat!''

She reached out, and held his hand tight, and Roberto did not mind her touching him at all.

THE GAME OF WORLDS

Adam had seen Thompson, the xeno-psych specialist, two or three times since they had arrived on the station. Adam wasn't sure if Thompson was his first name, his last name, or the only name he had. He was a young man, pale, tall, and slender, with a thick shock of blond hair that seemed to drift into his eyes at the slightest provocation. He was constantly sweeping it up out of his eyes with his left hand—a left hand, Adam could not help but notice, with the pinky and the ring finger each missing a fingertip. And there was a long, faint, puckery scar, barely visible but still there, running along his left jaw line.

He was just a bit late, arriving after all four of them were there. Instead of standing at one end of the table and lecturing them like a schoolteacher, he sat down with Ahna and the three boys, opened his briefcase, and spread his data viewers and notes on the table.

"Ready for me?" he asked, and flashed a big, lopsided grin that made the faint scar on his jaw vanish, at least for a moment.

"I don't think any of us feel the least bit ready for

anything," Aaron said. "Everything is so new."

"That's a nice, realistic attitude," Thompson said. "A lot better than being overconfident." His grin faded just a bit. "A lot better," he said. Then he brightened again and looked around the table. "So, whom do we tackle first—the K'lugu or the Devlin?"

Roberto shrugged. "How about the K'lugu? All anyone has talked about is the Devlin. I'd like to hear something about our hosts."

Thompson dug around in his data viewers and paper notes. "K'lugu. K'lugu," he muttered to himself as he shuffled through all the material. "Right. We like to think we have a fairly good basic grasp of K'lugu psychology," Thompson began, "but it is important for you to understand that a lot of it is guesswork. If it will make you feel any better, the K'lugu and the Devlin don't know much about us, either.

"Now that all *that's* cleared up, let's get started. The K'lugu resemble terrestrial amphibians. We believe their average life span is about fifty to sixty standard Earth years. They have two sexes, as we do, but the males are vastly outnumbered by the females. That right there is probably the fact that makes them most different from Humans . . ."

". . . As for the Devlin, the short-form answer to just about everything is 'We don't know.' How long do they live? What is their basic family and social structure? Are they truly as hostile as they seem to be, or are we just missing some vital insight that would explain them to us? They always *seem* aggressive to us, but we have yet actually to prove they have committed any deliberately hostile act."

"I thought that there'd been space battles between them and us," said Adam.

"There have been," Thompson agreed. "But it's

never been absolutely clear who started them. Each side always says the other did something aggressive first, and each side says whatever they did was misunderstood. The whole point of Meeting One is to start finding out the truth about the Devlin, plus all the other jobs they want you to do."

Ahna frowned and shook her head. "It's too much. I'm too young for this," she said.

"I know," said Thompson, and rubbed the scar on his face with his mangled left hand. "I was too young for it. They made me a diplomat when I was your age. I worked on the first contact with the Berylians. And then, all of a sudden, just as I was beginning to think I knew what I was doing, I was too old to make a sally port jump. I still don't know whether I'm glad it's over—or whether I'll never miss anything as much."

Roberto sat up in bed and walked alongside Holmes and Watson as they investigated *The Hound of the Baskervilles*. He didn't want the story to end, but at the same time he was eager to get through it. He had found a data view book on the Gift Givers that seemed like it might be useful. And he had come across, treasure of treasures, a pair of books on Brazilian history: *The Masters and the Slaves* and *The Mansions and the Shanties*. It was shock to realize how little he knew about the history of his own country.

And then there was a twenty-second-century adventure story that looked almost as exciting as Sherlock Holmes, and there were two strange books full of remarkable pictures about a girl called Alice, and then, and then—he blinked and sat up in bed again. He was having trouble staying awake. But sleep was a waste of time in a world where so much was his for the taking. Roberto yawned prodigiously. He'd read just a few more pages, and then maybe rest his eyes for a moment. . . .

In a bed half-buried in books and data viewers, Roberto dozed off just as the great detective and his faithful companion were plotting their next move.

"These briefing books provide a list of prominent Humans that the K'lugu have dealt with, or have heard of, and will likely expect you to know about. Read the book over. If you can memorize it, all the better. . . ."

"In front of you is a standard-issue wilderness survival pack. If things go very, very wrong, it ought to contain everything you need to survive until we arrange for pickup. . . ."

"Most of the plants and animals on K'lugu are inedible to us. Basically, the chemistry is just different enough that your body wouldn't know how to process them if you ate them. However you might have to eat K'lugu food—or even Devlin food—at a banquet. These enzyme packs will ensure that none of their food will actively harm you, and will alter the chemistry enough that you'll get some nutrition out of it. . . ."

On and on the lessons went, until they ran out of time. The four of them met for dinner, the last night before departure, in the station refectory. All the information, all the advice, all the guesses, all the suggestions were like bees buzzing around in their heads. All of them were exhausted. All of them were too tired to eat, their heads too jam-packed with ideas, information, instructions, and advice.

But Edge Station Three served good food, and somehow all of them emptied their plates, and were even able to contemplate dessert—something that Ahna called a "glib tart."

"So tomorrow is the big day," Aaron said. "We go

to Bogwater. Do any of you feel ready for it? *I* sure don't." He turned toward the Brazilian boy. "How about you, Roberto?"

But Roberto had his nose buried in a data viewer, as usual. Aaron had decided that Roberto was trying to make up for a lifetime of not reading, all at once.

"Roberto?" he asked again.

"Hmmm? What?"

"What are you reading this time?" Aaron asked gently.

"*The Art of War*, by Sun-Tzu. A Chinese general."

"Put it away for now," said Adam. "We've got to do some talking." Roberto shut off the viewer and was all attention.

"Last night it was Machiavelli," said Adam, nodding toward Roberto as he spoke to Ahna. "*The Prince*, if you know what that is."

"Sort of," said Ahna. "It's kind of like *The Art of War*. It's all about how to trick people and bully them and make them do what you want. Very nasty stuff. The diplomatic classes are supposed to teach it, but none of the teachers can bring themselves to assign it."

"Maybe they should start," Aaron said. "From everything I've heard, you people are up against some very rough customers, but instead of figuring out how to deal with them, you pride yourself on how kind and gentle and decent you are."

"What's wrong with being decent and gentle?" Ahna asked.

Aaron shrugged and made a vague open-palm gesture with both hands. "Nothing, when you live in a gentle world. You guys lived in one, up until these Gift Giver characters showed up. Roberto and I sure don't. Adam's world sounds a lot nicer than mine or Roberto's, but I bet there were plenty of nasty customers and people who played dirty."

"That's for sure," said Adam. He hesitated, then

shrugged. "I might as well admit it. Sometimes, I was one of them."

"We had to learn how to handle the rough characters," said Aaron to Ahna. "Now you people have to relearn that. Know how to outtrick them, beat them at their own game."

"If it helps to think of it that way, I remember I read somewhere that diplomacy was the game of nations," said Adam.

"Yes," Ahna said eagerly. "But it's not nations anymore. "We're playing the game of worlds. And that's just how high the stakes are. If we play it just right, maybe we win a whole new world for humanity, if we've guessed right about the *Roanoke*. But if we lose, and the Devlin discover they can push us around and get whatever they want, they'll show up for Meeting Two on Earth with all the advantages on their side. Maybe they'd go on to dominate *our* world. We don't know much about them, but what we do know doesn't make me think they play nice—or fair."

"Then maybe we shouldn't either," said Aaron. "If they play rough when the stakes are high, we have to be ready to fight back, and give back as good as we get."

"I know," said Ahna. "I might not like it, but there it is—and it's a big part of why you're all here. We've lived in such a nice world for so long we've forgotten how to face up to bullies. We haven't had to do it."

"So when do we get a chance to start showing you how?" Aaron asked.

"Tomorrow," said Ahna. "When we get to Bogwater."

"No," said Aaron, grinning fiercely. "Tonight. *Before* we go."

"What do you mean?"

Adam leaned in toward Ahna. "Aaron and Roberto and I have been working on a few ideas. Some stuff that might give us some advantages, get the Devlin to underestimate us, and maybe get us some information.''

"Lesson one in being sneaky," said Aaron. "Plan ahead. Know your ground, know the situation, figure out how to use it. The night you people picked me up, I wouldn't have stayed alive as long as I had if I didn't know those alleys backwards and forwards.''

"The Devlin at Meeting One are going to be adults," said Adam. "They're going to sneer at us for being kids. We can use that.''

"Lesson two," said Aaron. "Encourage the other guy when he's not taking you seriously. These Devlin sound awful sure of themselves because they're adults. So we let them think we're really *dumb* kids.''

"And I bet they think the way the islands are laid out make them safe," said Roberto. "Why not encourage that notion as well? Maybe even distract them.''

"Lesson three," said Aaron. "Get them to look left when you run to the right.''

"All right," Ahna said, leaning her head in close. "You've got ideas? Let's hear them. Maybe I can add a few.''

"You?" Aaron said in mock surprise. "You, Ahna the angel from the peaceful-perfect future? *You're* going to help *us* be sneaky?''

Ahna grinned in that slightly scary way she had. "I might be a little out of practice, but I learn fast. If I didn't have *some* talent for it, they wouldn't have picked me for the diplomatic corps. Come on," she said, in her best conspiratorial voice. "Talk to me.''

LEAST HARM

"Least will be here again soon," Markus said, leaning in the doorway of their cabin. "We've got to decide what we're going to do." He craned his neck to look around the doorway, up along the path leading to the Devlin t-port bunker.

They were finished with the chores around the compound, at least for the day. Not much point in starting anything new, with daylight about to give way to dusk.

Maurha, sitting in the sunlight on the doorstep, glanced up at her brother, then looked back down at her daughter. Little Ginny was playing in the dirt in front of the house, digging holes and carefully filling them with pebbles. Maurha smiled. Ginny's expression was so serious, and her concentration so intense, as if the fate of worlds depended on her filling each little hole with exactly the right number of pebbles.

Maybe they were all too serious about a lot of things.

"We have to give him something," Maurha said.

"But what?" Markus asked. He let his eyes take in all of the debris field. The smashed bits and pieces of the *Roanoke* lay all about them, like the bleached bones of some long-dead beast. Even the cabin they lived in was nothing more than a cargo container scavenged from the ruined ship. It was as if they had lived for fifteen years in a graveyard. "Do we tell what he wants to know? What he *ought* to know? What we *want* to tell him?"

"I'm not even sure what any of those would be, exactly," said Maurha. "Do you trust him?"

"No," Markus said flatly. "There's something that doesn't ring true about his story. And somehow—I don't know—he acts like *he* doesn't quite like it, either—as if someone else had told him to lie to us."

Maurha nodded. "Right. As if he had been ordered to tell us a certain story, but he wasn't happy about it."

"Here comes Ethan, in from the fields," Markus said, waving to his sister's husband as he came down the path.

Ethan spotted them, grinned, and waved. Behind him, a knot of younger farmhands came into view. Even after a hard day in the fields, the young ones were full of energy. Two boys started a race, and suddenly all the rest joined in. They tumbled into camp in a cloud of dust and a chorus of joyful shouts. Only Ethan, calmly walking along at his own pace, was left behind. Ginny spotted her father and clapped her hands together in glee. "Daddy's home! Daddy's home!" she cried out, and ran up the hill to meet him. Ethan knelt and opened up his arms, and Ginny flung herself at him. He caught her in a bear hug, then hoisted her up and balanced her on his hip to carry her one-handed.

Maurha ducked inside the cabin to get her husband something to drink. She took a mug down from the shelf and filled it from the inside water barrel. The word *Roanoke* was emblazoned proudly on the side of the stoneware mug. Like nearly everything else they had, the mug had been dug out of the ship's wreckage. She carried the mug out with her just as her husband was walking up to the cabin.

Ethan set Ginny down, took the mug gratefully, and

drank the water down in one gulp. "Thanks," he said. "I needed that."

"How's the cornfield look?" Markus asked.

Ethan shrugged, and looked back along the path to the crop fields. Fourteen years' worth of weary footsteps had worn that path, fourteen years of struggle to learn the art of farming. "We'll have a better crop this year than last, for whatever that's worth," he said, sitting down on the doorstep. "The younger ones are getting old enough to be a real help. We'll eat this winter."

One of the Ford kids had brought out a much-used ball, and organized a game of catch. As usual, Ginny tried to join in, but she was too young, just three. All of the others were fifteen or older, survivors of the crash of the *Roanoke*, orphaned by the disaster. Ginny was the first—and so far the only—Human child born on this world.

"We were discussing our friend Least," Maurha said, sitting down next to her husband. "And how he wanted to know all our history, all about Humans, just in case our legends matched up with some bit of gossip out there." She waved a work-hardened hand up at the sky. "Just in case someone out there had heard the story."

"You don't buy that any more than I do," said Ethan.

"No," said Maurha. None of them were as trusting or as innocent as they had been, back before the crash. They had learned the hard way that the universe was not a safe place, that life was often full of nasty surprises.

"So we agree he's lying," said Markus, still leaning in the doorway. "And if he's lying about why he wants the information, we can't trust him. We can't give him anything that might hurt Earth. But we have to keep him happy. He's our only link to the outside universe."

"And we have no idea what could hurt Earth," said Maurha, watching the young ones running around the camp. "All of you!" she cried out. "Don't get too riled up. Dinner will be ready soon. Ginny! Take it easy."

Her warnings didn't seem to slow any of them up for more than half a minute.

"Maybe we know more than we think," Markus said. "If Least is lying about wanting information to help us, then it seems pretty obvious to me he wants the information to help the Devlin. And the Devlin wouldn't need information about Earth, and Humans, unless they were already in *some* sort of contact with Humans. But Least didn't come here wanting to know about our technology. Why not?"

"You can learn a lot about technology by spying from long range with special instruments," Ethan replied. "You can get some idea about what someone's hardware can do and how powerful it is. What you can't tell with that sort of spying is what the people running the hardware will want to use it for. Suppose the Devlin know something about how our machines work. Least is here to find out how *we* work—how Humans think, what we're likely to do in a given situation."

"So he asks for our history," Markus said. "He asks for our legends and works of fiction."

"Right," said Ethan. "So they'll know how we act."

"It makes sense," Maurha conceded. Trickery. Deceit. If Least was practicing such things on them, he could be no friend. Therefore he was—he was—an *enemy*. The mere thought of the word made her shudder. It was one thing to accept that the blind forces of nature could hurt them. But the idea that an intelligent being could intend them deliberate, willful harm was far worse, far more terrifying. "I wish we knew how *they* acted."

"We all wish that." Markus agreed. "But I doubt we'll find out anytime soon. On the other hand, if Ethan is right, then all of a sudden we're facing a very interesting question. We've got a bunch of aliens trying to trick us into telling them what Humans are like. Okay. Let's pretend they've tricked us into telling. What are *we* going to trick *them* into believing?"

ONE SMALL STEP

The next morning, the three Yanks dressed in their s-suits, then met Ahna in the main training room for one last briefing—this one from her.

"We'll make the transit to Bogwater in two stages," she said, "going first through the interstellar sally port that links Edge Station Three with the embassy ship *Benjamin Franklin*. This is a different sort of teleport system than the one you went through to get here. That was an intermittent booth. This one is a constant portal."

"Do all the short-range t-ports use booths, and all the long-range sally ports use these constant things?" Adam asked.

"No," said Ahna. "You can use either kind of booth in any situation, and either can be just about any size. We happen to be going through a sally port conveniently large enough for people to walk through, but there are sally ports large enough for a whole ship to transit through. Same thing with the intermittent booths. They can be any size.

"Edge Station One has some sally ports built by the Gift Givers. With one of *those* ports, you can transit from the Station direct to a planetary surface—and you don't get a blinding headache, either. Edge Station Two has older, sort of clunkier, Human-built sally ports. Here on Edge Three, we've got the latest Human-built designs—better than Edge Two's, but nowhere near as good as the ones the Gift Givers made. The Human-built sally ports can only transport you to a point in deep space. They can't get you to a planetary surface. You have to use a shorter-range t-port to get back and forth from a planet, the way we did to get here from Earth. And we're a long way from building sally ports that won't give you a pounder of a headache. Our people are working on it—but they haven't managed it yet.

"We choose what kind to use when depending on power constraints, how flat space-time is near both ends of the port, how much interference there is from other t-ports, how much use the port is going to use, and so on."

"Fine, so that's how they're alike," said Aaron. "What's the difference between them?"

"We used an intermittent booth to get from Earth to here. You start with the t-port link off, get in, and then activate the link. Constant portals are kept on more or less all the time. They work across a flat plane, rather than on a volume of space like a booth, if you see what I mean. Most of the t-ports on Earth are what they call 'gray plane' constant portals. You can't see the other side before you go through. Just a sort of gray mist. The links from Edge Three are the new and more advanced 'clear plane' constant portals—you can see the other side. You just walk through it from one side to the other. As best we know, the K'lugu tend to prefer intermittent booths, but the Devlin seem to use nothing but constant portals."

Adam's eyebrows went up. "That is very interesting," he said. "Very, very interesting."

"Interesting or not," said Roberto, "I think we had

best go, before we have time to think about it and decide against the trip.''

"All right then," Ahna said. "Right this way."

Ahna led them out of the training room and through the maze of corridors—all done up in stark blacks and whites at the moment—to a door marked SALLY PORT TRANSIT CENTER—SECURED AREA. Adam was expecting someone to check their IDs, or fingerprints, and run them through metal detectors or futuristic X-ray machines. But Ahna just stood in front of the doors for a moment until they opened on their own. Adam decided that a real security system would be smart enough to do its scans and checks without bothering anybody. Or maybe D'Alembert was monitoring, and he had cleared them through personally.

The three boys followed Ahna in through the doors, and they found themselves in a round-walled room. Massive heavy-duty doors, a dozen of them, were set into the walls. There were display screens over the top of each door. Three of the screens made some sense to Adam: EDGE STATION ONE, EDGE STATION TWO, EMBASSY SHIP FRANKLIN (BOGWATER). But SLEEPSHIP DORMOUSE, PENTACLE NODE, PLANET ICEBALL, and DONTASK were mysteries to him—and likely to remain so.

Adam's suspicion that D'Alembert had cleared them through security was confirmed when his mellifluous voice spoke out of the center of the chamber. "Welcome," he said. "It would appear you are all ready for the trip. Please stand by while I adjust air pressure here in the antechamber to match pressure with the *Franklin.*"

"What about our um—special equipment?" Aaron asked.

What sounded almost like a chuckle rumbled out of the middle of the air. "The kites and your other toys have already been transported," D'Alembert replied. "Commencing air pressure adjustment."

There was a hum of air pumps working, and Adam could feel the pressure drop in his eardrums. He worked his jaw muscles and yawned until he felt his ears pop, and Ahna did the same. He saw Aaron and Roberto reaching up to their ears and looking a bit confused. Neither of them had ever had to deal with a rapid change in air pressure before. When would a nineteenth-century child of slaves or a 1930s ghetto kid fly in a plane or go up a mountain? "It's the air-pressure change," he said to them, raising his voice a bit so they could hear him with their ears clogged up. "You feel it in your ears. It's okay. It feels weird, but it can't hurt you. It'll clear up if you yawn and work your jaw muscles."

The two boys did as he said, and it was clear by the expressions of relief on their faces that it had worked.

"Pressure matched," D'Alembert said. "Inside hatch opening." The door marked EMBASSY SHIP FRANKLIN (BOGWATER) swung open—and the path to the stars was clear.

But, somehow, it didn't *look* like the way to the stars. It looked like a corridor. There was a complicated-looking doorframe, festooned with all sorts of controls and displays, about halfway along the length of the corridor.

Adam stared across the threshold of the sally port. "Just how far away is the other side?" he asked.

Ahna shrugged. "About fifty-two light-years," she said. "Or maybe about a meter and a half. You can measure it either way."

Adam shook his head. "You've got yourself a pretty strange future going here," he said. "Come on. Let's get this over with."

"You don't want me to go first?" Ahna asked.

"No," said Adam. "Not this time. I want to go first."

"Be my guest," said Aaron.

"And mine," said Roberto.

Adam hesitated for just a moment. *Fifty-two light-years*. It was utterly impossible for him even to conceive of such a distance. And yet he was about to cross it, by moving through a doorway between two halves of a corridor. He was about to cross through a sally port between the stars, a crossing that would kill an adult.

There were big sally ports, large enough for ships to pass through. Going that way would seem more like star travel than this. Never mind. What was that old saying? "A journey of a thousand miles begins with a single step."

Adam O'Connor took a deep breath, walked down the corridor, and stepped through the doorway————

TWO GIANT LEAPS

—**A**nd nearly fell flat on his face. His feet flew out from under him, and he went sprawling onto the floor of the compartment, just barely getting his hands in front of him in time to cushion the blow.

At the same moment, a stinging pain shot through the base of his skull, as if someone had hit him hard on the back of his head. It didn't hurt as bad as the jump through centuries of time, but the t-port jump across hundreds of light-years didn't exactly feel good, either.

Light-years! Was that part true? Had he really crossed the heavens, to a whole new star system? He had to find out. Just the mere possibility was exciting enough to make him forget the pain at the base of his skull.

Unfortunately, it also made him forget his sudden clumsiness. He scrambled to his feet—and found himself sprawled out on the deck again.

"Adam! Are you all right?"

It was Ahna, calling from the other end of the corridor, the other side of the sally port, a few feet, and an impossible distance, away. He had almost forgotten the others were there.

117

"Yeah, yeah, I'm fine," said Adam. "My legs are a little wobbly, that's all."

"It's the stronger gravity," Ahna said. "The gravity aboard the *Franklin* is adjusted to match Bogwater's surface."

"Oh," said Adam. "Right." He couldn't help but think of how he had explained changes in air pressure to Roberto and Aaron just a few minutes before, and how he had felt a bit smug about being more sophisticated than they were. It was probably no bad thing at all for him to be reminded that he was as much of a low-tech bumpkin as either of them in this world.

He noticed there were handrails on both walls, running the length of the corridor at about waist level, and he grabbed on to the left hand one and stood again, more slowly and carefully.

This time he got to his feet without any trouble. He stood there for a moment, his hand still on the railing, and bounced up and down on his heels. Ahna was right. He was a bit heavier, just enough to throw off his balance.

"Okay," he said. "I think I've got the hang of it."

"Me next," said Aaron. "But," he said with a grin, "I think I'll use the handrail, if you don't mind."

Adam grinned back at him. Sometimes the joke was on you, and there was nothing to do but laugh at it yourself.

Aaron moved cautiously through the sally port, grabbing at the rail before he stepped across. Adam could see nothing out of the ordinary as his friend crossed the sally port barrier. No flicker of blue light, no surging of strange energies, no shimmering around Aaron's body, as required in all the science-fiction TV shows. The only things the slightest bit strange about it were Aaron's worried look before he stepped through—and the plainly obvious look of sharp pain after he did.

"That hurts," Aaron said ruefully. "A *good* sharp kick in the head."

Roberto came across taking hold of the rail, and Ahna brought up the rear, both wincing in pain as they traveled through light-years. All four of them walked to the end of the corridor. Ahna pushed a button, and the airlock swung open—into a room that looked out on wonders.

A massive circular viewport, almost as tall as Adam, stood directly across from the airlock door. Through it they could see a sky full of glory, a nebula of blue and gold and red, a cloud of gas that looked for all the world like a looming thunderhead shot through with stars that glowed from behind.

All around the nebula, the sky seemed far more crowded with stars than the skies of Earth had ever been, stars of every conceivable color, stars that seemed so bright and clear that Adam felt as if he could reach through the viewport and touch them.

"The K'lugu call that the Brightmorning Nebula," said Ahna. "Not all of the names they come up with are funny to us."

Adam tore his eyes away from the spectacle out the viewport. He moved a step or two farther toward the center of the vestibule, then paused to look around. The airlock door they had just come through had a sign reading EDGE STATION THREE over it. There were two other airlocks. The sign over one was blank, but over the other were the words NEGOTIATION ISLAND, BOGWATER.

"Welcome to the Earth Embassy Ship *Benjamin Franklin*," said a tall, dark-featured boy standing by the viewport. "We've been waiting for you. Good to see you again, Ahna."

"Good to see you, Johan." She turned to the three boys from the past. "This is Johan Tavennos," she said. "My coleader on the diplomatic team."

"Or at least what's left of it," Johan said bitterly. "Not your fault, but bringing in the three of you meant

119

we had to bump three of the eight of the original team. The meeting rules only allowed eight Humans, eight Devlin, and eight K'lugu to attend Meeting One. And the powers that be decided that the three of you would be of more use than three of our original team members.''

Johan was taller than Adam, but somewhat more slender. There was a lean, wiry look to him, emphasized by his s-suit. He appeared to be of Northern European stock, with pale skin, brownish black hair, and dark brown eyes.

''You're right, Johan,'' said Ahna. ''It's not their fault. And they *have* thought of things we missed. I think it will turn out to be worth having them along.''

''Good,'' said Johan. ''We could use a few pleasant surprises. Come along. The others are waiting, and we don't have much time.'' He turned around, opened the hatch behind him, and walked away, without waiting to see if the others were following. Ahna, standing apart from the others, looked toward them, then hurried after Johan, with the three boys from the past following.

''Can I start in on not liking this Johan now? Or should I wait a little while?'' Roberto muttered to Aaron and Adam as they walked along together, watching Johan lead the way.

''Give him a chance,'' Ahna said, dropping back a step or two to walk with the three boys. ''Things haven't been easy for him. For any of them. You must be patient.''

''Your hearing is quite good, *Dona* Ahna,'' Roberto said, a note of amusement in his voice. ''But very well. I will not start to dislike him—just yet.''

Johan Tavennos ushered the newcomers into a large, high-ceilinged compartment filled with cargo and equipment. Robots of all sorts and sizes were swarming over the machinery and supplies, checking things over. Three girls, all wearing s-suits, were overseeing the operation.

"This is the prep room for the job," said Johan. "As you can see, there's a lot of last-minute things we have to do. We're scheduled to be on planet for the arrival ceremonies, in precisely one hour and five minutes—and we've got to be *exactly* on time. So there isn't much time to brief you. Maybe we can get to it once we're there, but right now I need you three Yank boys to just sit quietly, out of the way, while Ahna helps the rest of us check this gear out, and make sure we have everything."

"No," said Ahna.

"What do you mean, 'no'?" Johan demanded.

"I mean you're not in sole charge here, and I mean meeting your new teammates is more important—much more important—than watching the robots double-check our inventory. We're all supposed to have been working together for months to get ready for this meeting. How convincing are we going to be if we don't even know each other's names?"

"She's right," said one of the girls who had been checking cargo. She was fair-haired, with a serious look on her face. "We need to get to know each other, and be sure they know what's going on."

Johan frowned, then shrugged. "All right, you have a point." He looked over the three boys from the past. "Which one of you is which?"

"I am Aaron Schwartz."

"My name is Roberto Galvão."

"I'm Adam O'Connor."

The blonde girl set down her data reader, came forward and smiled at the boys. "I'm V'toria Montkirc," she said. "Most people call me Torry."

She gestured toward one of the other two girls. "This is Marget Felis," she said.

"Hello," said Marget, and gave them a distant little smile. She was small, slight, and strikingly elegant, with

121

bronze-colored skin and big, expressive eyes. Her gleaming hair hung in a braid that reached the small of her back, and was a remarkable rich black-gray, a shade that Adam had never seen before. No one on Earth in 1999 had hair like it. Adam wondered if it was hair dye, or if Marget herself had come out of some sort of test tube. Gene-splicing, or cloning, or something. There was something just a bit *too* perfect about her.

"Nice to meet you," said Adam, and Aaron and Roberto murmured their own shy hellos.

"And this," said Torry, "is Suza Godduff."

"Hi!" said Suza, a big grin on her face. If Marget seemed elegant and sophisticated, thought Adam, then Suza was plainly quite the opposite. She was tall, skinny and gawky, all knees and elbows. She was pale-skinned and freckle-faced, and her thick brown hair was cut in a short bob. "Glad you finally got here!" she said, and obviously meant it.

"So are we," Adam said, with a laugh.

None of the others had offered their hands to shake, but Suza did—stiffly and awkwardly, as if she didn't have much practice at it. "That's what you do when you say hello, isn't it?" she asked. "We don't do it much anymore."

"That's right," Adam, taking her hand. "That's what we do."

Suza grabbed his hand and pumped it vigorously. "Great!" she said. She shook Roberto's hand, then Aaron's.

"Fine," said Johan. "Now that we're all friends, do you feel better, Ahna?"

"Some. But the four of us who just got here need to know more about the current situation."

"Yeah, like, for starters, where are we, and what happens next?" Adam asked. "We kept getting briefings from people who said someone else would explain the details later. We're sort of running out of later."

Suza sat down on a packing crate and shoved a few loose strands of hair away from her face. "Well, you know we're aboard the *Benjamin Franklin*," she said. "We're currently in a distant orbit of Bogwater's sun, a star locally known as Swampwarmer."

"The K'lugu seem to have a talent for interesting names," said Aaron.

Suza smiled again. "It seems like it's a very poetic and elegant name to *them*. I guess warm swamps are a good thing, so far as they are concerned. Anyway, the welcoming ceremonies for us are supposed to start in just over an hour. We—all of us here—are to t-port to Negotiation Island just as they start. The Devlin are aboard their own ship—which we're watching as best we can, but it's on the other side of the planetary system—and they are to t-port in at the same time we are. The K'lugu are already on-planet, of course."

"Our embassy on Negotiation Island is complete and ready to go," said Marget, "and as best we can tell, the K'lugu and the Devlin are ready as well. Most of our stuff has already been t-ported down. All this"—she gestured to indicate all the equipment in the compartment—"is mostly backups and gear we don't think we'll need but want to have handy just in case."

"What about our cargo?" Aaron asked.

Johan gave Aaron a funny look. "Don't worry," he said. "All your toys have already been t-ported down."

"Excuse me, please," said Roberto, "but there is one thing, a very important thing, that no one has spoken of. I think as Adam said, each of our teachers has assumed the others would speak of it. What do these K'lugu and Devlin *look like*?"

"Big frogs," said Suza. "The K'lugu look like big frogs, but they walk upright, like us. They like the water, and are great swimmers, but they can live quite happily on dry land, too."

"Which reminds me," said Ahna. "*We* stay away

123

from the water. We don't go swimming, we don't go down to the beach, we avoid getting near the shore if we can help it. We don't even use boats, but insist on using aircars instead. In fact, we use the most complicated machines and hardware we can to avoid contact with the water."

"Why?" asked Johan.

"I was looking forward to a swim," Torry objected.

Ahna nodded toward the three boys from the past. "They've come up with a plan," she said. "And it will help if we make the Devlin think they don't have to watch the water very carefully."

"But what *about* the Devlin?" Roberto asked again. "What do they look like?"

Johan laughed. "That's easy," he said. "I can give a complete answer based on all the information we've swapped with the K'lugu. Nobody knows. No human, or K'lugu, has ever actually seen a Devlin."

"Or," said Torry unhappily, "if they have, they didn't live to tell about it."

Roberto stared out the massive viewport at the wondrous sky beyond. The others would be along in a minute, but he had slipped away from the conversation just a bit early. He wanted a moment or two alone with the viewport, and the magnificent sky it revealed.

The countless stars and the glowing nebula seemed magical things, beyond all possibility. He could see farther than he had ever dreamed of. His world, his universe, had expanded beyond all reckoning. A few days before, he had been an illiterate slave, living in a hovel on the grounds of a minor *fazenda* in a remote corner of Brazil, with only the vaguest notion that the larger world beyond the city of Fortaleza even existed.

And now—now he could read, now he could write. Now he had traveled to the stars. Now he had seen the planet Neptune floating like a ball in the sky's inky seas.

Now he was representing all of humanity in a meeting with a great and dangerous potential foe. His heart swelled with pride. He had been chosen to receive great gifts in hopes that he could do great things. He was determined to show himself worthy of all the honors he had received.

He heard a bustle and a murmur of conversation growing louder behind him as the others made their way back to the airlock vestibule. He turned and welcomed his three good friends and their four new acquaintances. He saw that the five children of the future—Ahna, Marget, Johan, Torry, and Suza—were now wearing broca amplifiers identical to his own. He wondered why, when his own amplifier allowed him to speak their language? But then the answer—the very obvious answer—came to him. The aliens. They would need the amplifiers to comprehend the aliens' speech.

"Ready to go?" Ahna asked.

"As ready as any of you," Roberto said with a sly smile.

"That might not be saying too much," Ahna said, laughing. "But we're not going to get any more ready. Let's do it. Do we have to cycle the airlock?"

Suza worked the airlock controls. "Nope," she said. "We're already matched with Bogwater's sea-level air pressure. All we have to do is open the door. She stabbed her finger down on a button, and the door marked NEGOTIATION ISLAND, BOGWATER swung open. A shaft of light, the clear golden light of the seashore in morning, stabbed out from the airlock chamber. The clean, salt-sweet smell of ocean air wafted out over them, and a warm breeze gusted into the vestibule.

There, at the end of the airlock's shipboard corridor, was the sea, the shore, the sandy soil of an island, thick grasses rustling in the breeze, a blue sky half-covered with thick, puffy clouds. Roberto could hear the distant thunder of waves crashing on a beach somewhere nearby.

He had almost forgotten the sounds, the sights, the smells of the ocean shore, but now he remembered, and longed for them all. Roberto had to hold himself back to keep from racing down that corridor and to the island beyond. They would have to make a dignified entrance.

"Wow," said Adam.

"Amazing," Aaron agreed.

"It's really pretty," Ahna agreed, "but we don't have time to think about it. Come on, let's get lined up. We want to put on a good show on arrival, just in case there's an audience."

Supposedly, they were arriving in private at the Human embassy before making their official appearance at the Parley Pavilion, the site of the conference. But there was at least a fair chance the K'lugu or the Devlin would try to watch the arrival of the Human contingent. Just in case, it seemed sensible to try and make it dignified.

As much because no one could think of any better way to do it, they had decided for the eight of them to walk through the t-port in two lines of four, the girls on one side, boys on the other, each line ordered from shortest to tallest. Maybe doing it that way would be a deadly insult to the Devlin, or maybe it would be meaningless, or a grand compliment. But they knew so little that the same could be said of any possible arrangement.

As it happened, the arrangement put Roberto and Suza in front, leading the way, representing all of humanity. Roberto could barely contain his pride. He, the illiterate slave, was the *bandeirante*, the pathfinder.

The eight of them, in two columns of four, strode down the corridor, through the t-port—and onto a new world.

16

GREETINGS

The stabbing headache came again—but for Roberto, at least, the clean, fresh, new world they stepped into seemed to sweep it away instantly.

The sun—or rather the star that the K'lugu called Swampwarmer—shone down out of a perfect summer sky, a sky painted a slightly darker, richer, shade of blue than Roberto had ever seen over Fortaleza. A playful breeze ruffled his hair and tugged at the fabric of his s-suit. Roberto smiled. He had returned to his home, to the seashore.

Yet it was not entirely like home. Waves of fanlike fronds, rather than grass, sprouted out of the sandy soil. The birds that circled overhead were like none he had ever seen—and he could not even be sure they were birds at all. He breathed in a deep lungful of the fresh air. It was sea air, and vastly better than the canned, sterile air of Edge Station Three. Yet it was different from the air of home in a dozen subtle ways—taste, smell, the feel of the wind itself.

He looked around and compared what he saw to his memories of the maps Adam and Aaron had shown him.

Plainly, they were right where they were supposed to be, on top of Human Hill. The Human Embassy, a small, white, two-story building, was just off to one side of the t-port machine. Down below was Parley Meadow, and past that, what had to be the K'lugu Embassy, just by a white sandy beach. And there, in the near distance, just across a narrow stretch of water, was Blackback Island. The Devlin Embassy was there. Roberto knew he wouldn't be able to see it from where he stood, but he stared all the same. Out there were the mysterious aliens they had come so far to see. *Aliens. Not-Humans.* What a strange, impossible notion. A week ago in his life, he would not even have been able to conceive of such a thing.

He turned around to watch the rest of the team come through. Ahna and Johan, the tallest boy and girl, brought up the rear.

Behind them stood the t-port generator, a complex mass of machinery with a wide corridor standing in its center—the airlock corridor of the *Benjamin Franklin.*

"Hey!" said Suza, pointing behind Roberto. "Look who's here!"

"Welcome to all of you," said an oddly familiar voice behind Roberto. He turned and saw Giotto, the robot who had worked with them back on Earth, quietly floating his usual half meter off the ground.

"I almost forgot you would be on Bogwater," said Roberto.

"Of course I am here," Giotto replied, and it was hard not to imagine a hint of smugness in his voice. "I was especially programmed for this mission."

"Good to see you again, Giotto," said Suza. "We missed you."

"I am delighted to see you as well, Suza," said the robot. "But we do not have much time for pleasantries at the moment. Our schedule is extremely tight. The

K'lugu and Devlin delegations are expecting you at the arrival ceremony in exactly ten minutes, thirty seconds, and the conference site is a good five minute walk from here. I suggest you all get going at once.''

"Aren't you coming with us?" asked Roberto.

"You are forgetting that the Devlin insisted that all those who attend the conference itself must be 'true beings,' " Giotto said, making no effort to hide his distaste for the phrase. "I will be waiting here for your return. Now go!''

Ahna looked around at all the others. "You heard him," she said. "Come on. Let's do our job." The eight of them formed two columns of four again and started down.

Roberto and Suza led the way, with Marget and Aaron next, then Adam and Torry, and Ahna and Johan bringing up the rear. Adam's heart was pounding so hard he half wondered if Torry could hear it. He glanced over at her, expecting her to be looking straight ahead, cool, collected, the ice princess he had met aboard the embassy ship.

But instead Torry seemed anxious, even scared. She looked about fretfully, first in the direction they were going, then behind them, then to either side.

"What are you so nervous about?" Adam whispered. "You know what you're doing. You've done this before."

"We might have the training," Torry whispered back, "but none of us have ever done any real fieldwork. This is the first mission for all of us."

"But I thought that—" Adam began, but then he stopped. He hadn't thought. He had *assumed*. Torry and Ahna and all the others acted so confident, so experienced and grown-up, he had assumed they'd all done it before. He'd have to be careful about jumping to conclusions like that. They were all headed straight into the unknown, where one good long jump could be all it took to get everybody killed.

They walked on toward the Parley Pavilion in silence.

"Looks as if we're the first ones here," Aaron said as they arrived at the Parley Pavilion. They stopped outside the structure without actually going in.

"Looks like," Adam agreed.

"So now what?" asked Aaron as he looked the place over. The structure was just as the briefers had described it—a square slab floor about thirty feet on a side, with a white peaked roof over it. The roof was supported by slim pillars in the four corners of the Pavilion.

There were three identical tables under the Pavilion roof. The tables were about three meters long and one meter wide. They stood along three of the Pavilion's four sides, each about two meters in from the edge. The table had eight chairs apiece, all of them facing the center of the Pavilion.

There were tables along the southern, western, and northern sides of the Pavilion. The eastern side, the one facing the shore, stood empty.

"We're on that side," said Ahna, pointing to the table on the south side of the Pavilion.

"Good," said Adam. The "chairs" behind the other two tables looked wildly uncomfortable, if you could even call them chairs. He stepped toward the pavilion, eager to take a seat, but Ahna grabbed his wrist and pulled him back.

"No," she said. "We don't set foot in Parley Pavilion until the others are here."

"And they should be here by now," said Johan, "or at least on their way." He glanced at his wristcomp. "The greeting ceremony is supposed to start in exactly four minutes. The Devlin pushed very hard to get exactly the starting time they wanted. You'd think they could at least show up."

"What about the K'lugu?" asked Roberto. "Should not our hosts be here to greet us?"

"Different etiquette, apparently," said Torry. "At a K'lugu gathering, the host leaves the meeting place and does not appear until all the guests are there. We're not quite sure why."

"What if they gave an interstellar conference," muttered Adam, "and nobody came?"

"Quiet!" Ahna said sharply. "They could be monitoring us somehow. We have to behave ourselves and be dignified. Line up, one of us behind each chair. Johan and me in the middle with me to the left. Torry, to my left, and Suza, and then Marget."

Johan pointed at Roberto. "You, at the far right end, Adam next to you, and you, ah, Aaron, between me and Adam. Get to your places, stand there, and be quiet!"

The eight of them lined up and waited. Adam checked his own wristcomp again and again, watching the seconds slip away.

"Two minutes left," Johan announced. "Where *are* they?"

Just then there was a loud, thundering boom, from off in the distance—and then another, and another, then a whole flurry of booms that echoed back against the hill.

"Over there!" cried out Roberto, pointing toward the horizon. "Over Blackback Island!"

There were eight black dots over the island, moving in formation, straight up into the sky.

"Did something blow up?" Aaron asked. "What were those explosions?"

"I think they were sonic booms," said Adam. "That's the noise something makes when it passes through the sound barrier. And if they drop below the speed of sound, we'll get sonic booms again. My guess is those are eight fancy aircraft, one for each Devlin delegate."

"But they're only a few hundred meters up," protested Aaron. "How could they take off so fast?"

"I think we're supposed to be impressed by the fact that they did," Johan said.

The eight black dots streaked up into the sky, fading away almost into invisibility before they arced over, still in perfect formation, and started to dive back down—straight toward the Parley Pavilion.

"All of you, stand where you are!" Johan called out. "Don't run, or duck, or flinch. They're trying to scare us and impress us with a lot of noise and power. Don't let them. Stay where you are, and watch them land. Pretend you see this every day."

"Suppose they *don't* land?" asked Aaron. "Suppose those aren't aircraft? Maybe they're bombs."

"If they are," said Johan grimly, "then running isn't going to do us any good anyway. If they want to kill us, they can."

"That would be crazy," Ahna protested. "Why go to all this trouble to kill eight Human kids on a K'lugu world? And the K'lugu have to be monitoring the island with cameras from somewhere. There'll be witnesses."

"You're right," said Johan. "Let's hope the Devlin know that."

Adam turned to Roberto. "Roberto, you okay?"

"I am," Roberto said. "I will not run, just because I am frightened. This is a time when running would do no good."

"Hang on," Adam said, trying to sound more confident than he felt. "They're just trying to scare us."

"They're doing a good job," said Aaron.

"Join hands!" Ahna shouted. "Hold on to one another."

Adam took Roberto's right hand in his left, and Aaron's left in his right, and held on tight to both of them.

The eight black dots were directly overhead, formed up into a hollow circle formation, diving straight for them, moving almost faster than the eye could see. A bare two hundred meters above the ground, the eight dots braked to a seemingly instantaneous halt. The sky roared with the sound of eight simultaneous sonic booms, deafeningly loud.

And suddenly, there were eight jet-black spheres hanging motionless in the sky over their heads, forming a perfect circle in the sky over the Parley Pavilion.

Adam checked his wristcomp again, and watched as the last few moments until the designated start time for the meeting melted away. Thirty seconds before zero hour, the eight spheres fell, dropping like stones, but holding their perfect formation.

A scant ten meters off the ground, sun-bright tongues of red fire lashed out from the bases of all eight spheres, retro-rockets that roared with ten times the noise the sonic booms had. Adam felt himself grabbing harder and harder, holding on to Roberto's and Aaron's hands for dear life. He knew that if he had not been holding their hands, he would have turned and run, all the way back up Human Hill. The Devlin ships were all around them, landing ahead of them, to either side, behind them.

The retro-rockets stabbed down into the ground and kicked up a torrent of dirt and debris. Suddenly the air was filled with blinding, billowing clouds of dust. Adam closed his eyes and ducked his head, trying to keep the dust out of his face. He wanted to put his hands up to his face to shield it, but he did not dare let go of Roberto or Aaron.

And suddenly it was over. The retro-rockets stopped their thunderous roar, and the world was silent once again.

A gust of wind blew in off the beach and swept away the smoke and the dust.

The eight black, featureless spheres had landed in perfect formation on all sides of the Parley Pavilion.

They were surrounded.

THREATS

From somewhere deep inside, Adam pulled together enough self-control to stand up straight. It took a determined effort of will to let go of his friends' hands. When he finally did, he blinked, wiped the dust off his face, and looked around.

None of the others looked any calmer than he felt. The deafening roar of the retro-rockets had left a ringing in Adam's ears, and he was sure the others couldn't hear any better than he could.

The eight featureless spheres sat on the ground, motionless and silent. The sounds of the island—the wind, the surf, the call of seabirds—gradually reasserted themselves in the quiet after the storm of the Devlin's arrival.

But why had they done it? Adam turned to Johan. "Could Humans build things like those sphere-ships that could fly like that?" he asked.

Johan shrugged. "Sure, I guess. Something pretty close, anyway. But I don't know why we'd want to."

"The question is, why did the *Devlin* want to?" asked Adam.

"Ships like that sure aren't—aren't *practical* for

much of anything," said Marget, still a little frazzled. "That's a pretty inefficient way to get from one island to another."

"Stuka," said Aaron. "They are Stukas, like the Nazis used in Spain."

"What?" Johan asked.

"The Stuka dive-bomber," said Aaron. "Half of what it does is drop bombs. But the other half is to drop the bombs in such a way to scare everyone to death so they won't have the nerve to fight back."

"They're trying to psych us out," Adam agreed. "Throw us off our game so we'll make mistakes."

"Well, now what?" asked Aaron. "Do they just sit in those black-ball things forever? Are we supposed to go up and knock, and ask them to come out?"

"Maybe those spheres *are* the Devlin," Marget suggested. "We don't know anything reliable about what they look like. Or maybe those are Devlin eggs."

"Complete with built-in rocket packs?" Johan asked skeptically.

Marget shrugged. "I don't know. Why not?"

The spheres sat there, giving them no clues.

"The K'lugu!" said Adam. "The rules are that the hosts arrive after the last of the guests have arrived safely. The Devlin are waiting on the K'lugu."

"But why wait?" Torry objected. "If that arrival was supposed to scare us or impress us, waiting for the K'lugu just gives us time to calm down."

No one had an answer for that at first—but then it came to Adam. "Witnesses," he said. "They need someone, a third party besides them or us, to see what they're going to do."

"Gee," said Suza. "*That's* sure a comforting idea."

"Over there!" Roberto cried out. "Coming out of the water!"

Adam looked where Roberto was pointing. A line of— of *heads* had appeared just outside the surf, a hundred meters or so off the shore. They came in, closer and closer, their bodies coming up out of the water and the crashing waves far more gracefully than any Human could have managed.

Eight spindly figures walked out of the surf, up onto shore, and moved steadily toward the Pavilion. The eight Human teenagers watched as the K'lugu came forward.

Aliens, Adam thought. *Actual, authentic aliens. People from another world.* All the other wonders, all the technological magic and miracles, were as nothing compared to the sight of eight K'lugu rising up out of the water and walking toward Adam.

They walked side by side. Something in the way they formed up told him that was the way that came naturally to them: no leaders, no followers, but the whole group moving together. They kept in line, but as individuals, with no effort to match their strides or march in rhythm.

They were upright bipeds, but not in the least like Humans in appearance. Ostriches, after all, were upright bipeds. Walking on two legs didn't automatically make for all that much family resemblance.

They had two legs, two arms, and a head in the same arrangement as Humans. That much was familiar. They had compact, slender bodies, and their long, flexible arms accentuated the smallness of their frames. They were a dark greenish gray over most of their bodies, with their bellies slightly lighter and more yellowish in color. No doubt that marking pattern made for excellent camouflage in ocean water. Their skin was smooth, with neither scales nor fur. They had no clothing, but several wore what appeared to be wide tool belts slung around their waists.

At first, as Adam watched them approach, he thought they had an extra set of joints in their arms and legs, but then he realized that one more pair of knees and elbows, or even two or three, wouldn't be enough to account for so great a range of motion. Their limbs seemed to be completely flexible, capable of bending and moving in any direction. What sort of bones and skeleton, if any, did the K'lugu have? How could their legs be that flexible, and yet be strong enough to walk upon?

They had no fingers or toes. Instead, their hands and feet ended in four flat, flexible ridges of muscle, rather like the webbing on a frog's foot, made thick and strong enough that there was no need for the supporting digits in between.

One of the eight turned its head to look along the shore, and demonstrated that K'lugu had the rather disconcerting ability to rotate their necks a full three-quarters of the way around.

Adam found himself staring at the K'lugus' heads, their faces, as they drew closer.

Their heads were streamlined, almost bullet-shaped. One of them happened to look straight up. With its head thus lined up with its body, neck and shoulders merged perfectly into one streamlined form, the way a fish's head streamlined into its body. Above water, the K'lugu held their heads as Humans did, but beneath the waves, Adam was willing to bet they pointed their eyes and mouth straight ahead into the water, like a dolphin.

The K'lugu that had checked the sky looked down, and its eyes, which had been recessed back into its head, popped up and about halfway out of their sockets. It was a normal, smooth-looking motion. Probably another adaptation to amphibious life. The eyes retracted for underwater vision, and popped out a bit for better vision in the world of solid land and clear air.

Suza had said they looked like giant frogs, but Adam didn't think so. To him, they looked more like turtles stripped of their shells. There was definitely more of the turtle than the frog in their gentle faces.

They were graceful, handsome beings, and Adam took a liking to them at first sight.

They walked straight from the beach to Parley

Meadow. One of the eight Devlin spheres was directly in their path. They paid it no mind, but simply walked around it, three to the left, five to the right, before forming again.

The K'lugu did not acknowledge the Humans in any way as they came around to the western side of the Pavilion and stood behind the chairs there. Then they stared straight ahead at the beach, and the water beyond, silent and motionless.

"Now what?" Adam whispered to Aaron and Roberto.

"I have no idea," said Aaron.

"Manners," Roberto whispered. "Look to the rules we know. They are the hosts, and must not show themselves until all the guests arrive. But they must show equal courtesy to all. They have waited until we have all arrived—but they cannot greet us until they can also greet the Devlin in the same moment."

"So they have to pretend we're not here until the Devlin figure that out for themselves, climb out of their ships, and come to the Pavilion?" Adam asked.

"I believe so."

"Well, if you're right, let's hope the Devlin can figure it out nice and fast," muttered Aaron. "I'm getting tired of standing here."

Aaron's wish came true almost at once. Less than a minute after the K'lugu had lined up behind their table, the eight Devlin spheres opened up simultaneously. The side of each sphere that faced in toward the Pavilion split open vertically down the center, and the two halves swung out of the way to either side.

And inside each sphere-ship was what had to be a Devlin. A *big* Devlin. They seemed to come in a variety of sizes, but the smallest was Johan's height, and the largest was well over two meters tall, maybe bigger.

All of the Devlin wore what seemed to be form-fitting armored suits made of a dark, gleaming material. The suits had a self-camouflaging feature that made it hard to see them clearly.

They resembled earless and bigger-brained grizzly bears with oddly wide-set eyes. Their heads were covered with short, light brown fur, the same color as a golden retriever's coat.

They walked on two legs—very muscular legs. But the Devlin had not one, but *two* pairs of arms. There was an outer, larger arm-pair. Even on the smallest of the Devlin, those arms were massive. The bigger arm-pair hung from shoulders that were more or less where human shoulders would be. The smaller arms were closer to the chest and below the larger arms, sprouting out from where the rib cage would be on a Human. Their outer-arm hands were big, beefy, four-fingered affairs. The hands of the inner arms were likewise four-fingered, but more delicate, better suited to fine work.

Each Devlin was carrying a weapon in each of its four hands, and more in sheaths and quivers strapped to their armor suits. Adam saw swords, knives, handguns, long guns, and other things he couldn't identify that were probably just as nasty.

"Bringing weapons to the meeting? That's allowed?" Aaron asked nervously.

Ahna shook her head. "I . . . we . . . it never occurred to us that diplomats might come armed!" she said. "We never thought to put anything about it in the premeeting rules."

Adam looked at her in amazement. No wonder these innocent future Humans needed help from the past. What else had they "never thought" about?

"Nice-looking toys they brought," Aaron whispered to Adam. "How scared are you?"

"Very," Adam whispered back. "How about you?"

"The same. But if we're smart, we won't let *them* know that."

With eight heavily armed and belligerent-looking aliens surrounding them, it might be hard to keep it secret, Adam told himself. But Aaron was right. They couldn't afford to be the ones to blink first.

The Devlin came on, moving in toward the Pavilion, contracting the perimeter. When they were about five meters or so from the Pavilion, they stopped, weapons raised. It was very hard to miss the message that the Devlin had them surrounded.

The moment held, no one—Devlin, K'lugu, or Human—speaking or moving.

Adam saw a flicker of movement out of the corner of his eye. He glanced over quickly. Marget, her eyes wide with terror, was staring at the biggest Devlin herself—and backing away. A lot of good that would do her, with the other Devlin closing in from behind her. He had to at least try and calm her down, and do so without the Devlin noticing.

"Marget, stand where you are!" Adam whispered, trying to speak without moving his lips. "Stay calm. They're not going to hurt you, or any of us. It's just a show to scare us."

Marget blinked suddenly, momentarily surprised to hear the voice from out of nowhere. "How—how can you know that?" Marget whispered back, the fear plain in her voice.

"Because if they wanted to kill us, they could have done it by now," Roberto whispered grimly through motionless lips. "They want to show us the whip, not use it."

"Killing us wouldn't do them any good," Aaron whispered in agreement. "They need to negotiate, and they can't do that if we're dead. Besides, the K'lugu would see it. Why would they want witnesses?"

"But—" Marget protested.

"But nothing," Adam whispered back. "Don't be afraid. They don't dare hurt us." He tried to sound sure about that. But the Devlin were aliens. Who knew what their logic, their manner of thinking, was like? Maybe killing a bunch of teenagers was their way to score debating points.

After what might have been a half a minute or half a lifetime, the largest of the Devlin, the one closest to the Human's table, stepped forward, all its weapons still at the ready.

It? Something in Adam's subconscious told him that this one, the biggest one, was female.

All eyes were on her. She spoke, and the sound was closer to a lion's roar than Human speech. Adam's broca amplifier translated, speaking in a low, gravelly voice that was some sort of approximation of what the Devlin sounded like.

"I am Eldest," she said. "I am local Prime. I speak for Devlin." She put her weapons away in several of the complicated sheaths and holsters strapped around her body. She moved around to stand in front of one of the massive, thronelike chairs behind the Devlin table. She gestured to the other Devlin. Three stayed on guard, guns and knives at the ready, but the other four holstered their weapons, then stepped forward and started to work removing the Devlin table and the other seven chairs. "None other of my clan need stay," Prime announced. "Prime alone will deal with the others here."

"Greetings to you, to Devlin, to Prime," said one of the K'lugu, the one closest to the Human table. To Adam's ear, the K'lugu's words were little more than clicks, buzzes, gurgles, and hums, but the broca amplifier translated the words into a smooth, elegant, cultured sound, a slightly high-pitched voice that reminded Adam of the high-school librarian back home.

"Greetings likewise to the Humans," said another K'lugu.

"All and each K'lugu speak for each and all," said a third. "May we remind our Devlin guests that it was agreed that each species would have eight delegates?"

The other Devlin were done moving furniture. Prime sat in the sole remaining chair on the Devlin side. She snorted derisively. "I, Prime, grew weary of the argument over numbers, and so agreed to eight. Prime is more than able to deal with eight Humans and eight K'lugu by herself in such a matter as this. Prime agreed to bring seven lesser Devlin to smooth the matter, but now Prime dismisses the lesser Devlin to other duties."

Adam glanced down the line of his fellow Humans. All of them seemed rooted to the spot, too confused, too disoriented—and too afraid—to act. And that, Adam saw, was what the Devlin, what Prime, had wanted. To throw them off, to start the meeting by establishing that Devlin could break the rules, that Humans were a lesser breed, of no great concern, the junior delegation that need not be taken seriously. Prime couldn't be allowed to get away with it—but it was working so far. Aside from one short word of welcome from the third K'lugu, neither the K'lugu nor the Devlin had so much as acknowledged the Humans' presence.

It didn't help matters much that Prime was an adult, and a big, scary-looking, heavily armed authority figure, facing a bunch of Human kids who all came from times and places where deference and respect for authority were as natural as breathing. They'd stand there until someone invited them to sit down.

Well, Adam told himself, it was a good thing *he* knew all about flouting authority. His heart pounding in his chest, he stepped forward and onto the platform of the Pavilion. The moment he started moving, all the lesser Devlin aimed their weapons at his head. *They could have killed us by now, if they had wanted*, he told himself. *They're schoolyard bullies hoping they can scare us into giving them our lunch money without a fight*. The Devlin had the firepower to kill all the Humans and K'lugu here in a heartbeat—but they'd be fools to think that would be the end of it. Kill the Humans and K'lugu here, and they might well be looking at an interstellar war. *It's all bluff and bluster*, Adam told himself. *If this crowd was sure they could win a fight, they'd have started it by now*. Hoping his logic was as strong as it sounded, Adam moved forward, pulled his chair out, and sat down, forcing himself to move calmly, casually. "I'm Adam O'Connor," he said, leaning back in his chair, and trying to sound polite, but snide, the way he did when he was messing with a teacher. "I speak for myself, and whoever agrees with me. And from where I come from, it's rude to point weapons at people. You want to tell your lessers to knock it off?"

Prime glared at Adam. "Your request is denied. Your request interrupts my speech with the K'lugu. You will speak when spoken to, and not before."

"No," said Adam. "I will speak, and my friends will speak, whenever they choose, and they'll speak with whomever they want. But we don't negotiate with guns pointed at us."

"The honor of Prime required that she be armed and protected!" Prime roared, standing up from her throne. "It is our right. And no one will tell Prime to sit with lesser ones!"

"While it is true weapons were not explicitly excluded, that was a regrettable oversight, not an expression of protocol or precedent," said Clearwater.

"Weapons were not forbidden!" Prime snapped.

"The meeting protocols do not prohibit the delegates eating each other," said one of the K'lugu. "But that does not mean such behavior would be acceptable."

"But the protocols do call for us K'lugu, as hosts, to rule on such matters," said another K'lugu. "The Human Adam O'Connor is quite right. Weapons are not acceptable at the negotiation table."

"You threaten the honor of Devlin and Prime!" Prime bellowed. At a signal from Prime, three of the Devlin trained their weapons at the K'lugu.

"We do no such thing," said another of the K'lugu calmly. "We remind the Devlin of the rules for this meeting, including the right of the host to adjudicate issues not covered in the initial protocols. We remind the Devlin Prime that her people agreed to comply with those rules."

"We do not choose to honor that agreement or your adjudication," said Prime. "This meeting will continue with all Devlin bearing weapons."

"That's it," said Aaron, his voice firm and forceful. "I already know how this comes out," he said. "I live in that world back home." He stepped forward, to stand next to Adam's chair.

No one else was close enough to see it, but Adam saw how pale Aaron was, how his hands were trembling. Adam had never known violence firsthand, but a Jew in the Germany of 1938 knew from deep inside, from his own scars and nightmares and memories. Aaron might well have seen friends and family killed on the street. Aaron knew what real fear was. But there he stood.

"I am Aaron Schwartz, and I speak for Humans who won't be bullied," he said. "If the weapons stay, we leave."

"The Humans will remain!" Prime bellowed. "All shall stay where they are until we conclude the Human surrender."

There was a gasp of amazement from behind Adam. He was out of his seat without even realizing it. The rest of the Human delegation moved forward as one onto the platform.

"Surrender?" Johan asked. "We are here to establish friendly relations with your people. Why would we come here to surrender ourselves to you?"

Prime gestured toward the Devlin on her right, one only slightly smaller than herself. The second Devlin spoke, even as he kept his weapons trained on the Humans.

"I am local Secondary," the Devlin announced. His real voice sounded exactly like Prime's. But the broca amplifier put out a male voice, a low, condescending purr. "Prime will not address you directly. We are not here to accept your personal surrenders," said Secondary. "The situation has changed. Some days ago, a Human ship encountered a Devlin ship in Devlin space, and the two ships entered into battle. The Human ship was defeated and destroyed. Devlin Law supersedes all other laws in all times and all places. By the Devlin law of Single Ship Combat, defeat of that Human ship by a Devlin ship represents defeat of all Humans by all Devlin.

"We are here," Secondary went on, "to claim victory and accept the surrender of the entire Human race."

BLUFFS

Shocked silence hung over the Pavilion, no one knowing what to say or do. At last Aaron spoke.

"No," he said. "No to it all, no for a dozen reasons. We will leave." He turned around and stepped out of the Pavilion. "All of us," he said. "We must leave."

Adam stood up and followed him. He wanted to protest, to shout at the Devlin, to argue with them, but he knew Aaron was right. They had to leave.

"We can't just go!" Johan protested, grabbing Adam by the arm. "We have to stay and talk this out with them."

"Quiet!" Adam hissed. "Don't let them hear." He gestured for everyone to gather in close. All eight of the group huddled in together, and spoke in low whispers.

"Maybe we can stay and work something out," said Torry.

"No!" said Aaron. "We have to go. Now."

"If we go, they'll shoot us," said Marget.

"Then they shoot us," said Aaron. He looked at Johan, and then at Marget, Suza, Ahna, and Torry. "This is why you brought us here," he said to them. "For when you need what you call *grit*. Don't you see? There is nothing, nothing at all to work out here. How do we compromise? Maybe we surrender half of Earth to them, and in return they agree to shoot only half of us? We can't start off talking to them by letting them break all the rules and play tricks and threaten us."

"But everything we've worked for—"

"Is lost and gone already if we stay," said Roberto. "It is lost *if* the first thing this Devlin Prime learns about you is that you will allow her to scare you, to beat you. Teach her you will not give in to threats, and—perhaps—the threats will stop."

"He's right," said Adam. "And we can't let the Devlin see us arguing about it. We have to go. And we have to go *now*."

The Devlin were bluffing. Adam knew it, knew it in his bones. It was time for the Humans to bluff right back. But the threat to leave and not come back had to be convincing. A half second's hesitation was all it took for your opponent to know your bluff wasn't real. When you bluffed, you had to bluff all the way. They had to leave at once, and act like they were never coming back.

But he couldn't tell Ahna and Johan that, not with the Devlin watching and listening. Whispering was not much of a defense against whatever high-tech spy gear the Devlin might have.

Finally, Ahna nodded. "I agree. We have to go."

Johan shook his head, confused and frustrated. "All right. I don't understand, but let's do it."

"Form up the same way we walked in," Aaron whispered urgently. "Walk past the Devlin like they're not there. And *walk*. Slowly, calmly, the way we came in. No matter what happens, just keep walking."

"But—" Marget protested.

"Later!" said Aaron. "When they're not watching and listening. Come on."

They lined up into two rows of four, turned their

backs on the Parley Pavilion, and started the walk back to Human Hill.

"Halt!" Secondary called out. "Stop!"

"Just keep walking," said Adam. "Don't look back. Hold hands with the person next to you. It helps to have someone to hold on to."

"What if they shoot?" Suza asked, her voice half-choked with fear.

Adam saw that she was crying. Well, who could blame her?

"Either they shoot to kill, and we die, or they shoot to scare us, and we don't get hurt," said Aaron, his voice hard, his face grim. "But if they meant to kill us, they would have done it by now."

"Be strong," said Roberto. "It will not take us long to get away."

Adam wasn't so sure about that. He looked ahead, toward the Human Embassy, on the brow of Human Hill. It had been a short walk from it, but with guns at their back, the walk back looked miles long.

"Halt!" another Devlin voice called from behind them. "Halt, or we shoot!"

Adam suddenly realized that both Roberto and Aaron were praying, quietly, to themselves, one in Portuguese, the other in Hebrew. He wanted to start praying himself, but fear had scared all the fine, formal prayers and words of praise right out of his head. *Please don't let me get killed*, he thought. It would have to do.

"This is your final warning!" the Devlin voice called. "Come back at once!"

"Hang on," Adam said. "Hold on to each other. Ahna, if this is it, thanks for letting me—"

BLAM!

A red spear of light touched the hillside behind them, and a cloud of dust and dirt blasted up into the air.

All of them flinched back from the explosion, and raised their free hands to shield their faces from the blast debris. Marget screamed, and Torry stumbled and almost hit the ground before Adam could pull her upright.

"Warning shot!" Adam called out. "Just a warning shot!"

Please let us have it figured out right. Please let that warning shot mean they're just bluffing. How much of the future of Humanity had three boys from the past just bet on how a bunch of alien bullies thought?

WHAM!

Another blast, off to the right and just ahead of them. Another flash of light, and Adam felt a sudden sharp sting on the right side of his face. Some bit of gravel had caught him just under the eye.

"Keep going!" he shouted, but the last shot had been too close and deafeningly loud. He couldn't hear himself—or anything else.

Somehow, they held together, walking two by two, hand in hand, moving up the hill toward whatever safety the Human Embassy might afford them. Another blast to the left, and another to the right.

Adam felt something warm on his lips and wiped it away with his free hand. He looked down to see blood smeared across the back of his head. Somehow his nose had started bleeding. *They could have hit us by now*, he thought. *They're just trying to scare us. And they're managing to do it.* But being scared didn't matter. Not giving into the fear. That was what would hold them together, keep the Devlin from winning.

KA-BLAM!

Another blast, right in front of them, not ten meters from where they stood. Bigger, brighter, louder than any of the others, loud enough to be heard through Adam's deafened ears. It knocked all of them down, and the flash of light was blindingly bright, like the world's biggest camera flash going off in their faces.

They sat where they had fallen—dazed, deafened, and momentarily blinded by the bright flash. It was long seconds before any of them began to recover, staggering to their feet.

"Keep going!" Adam shouted at the top of his lungs. His own ears were ringing so badly that he could barely hear himself. He gestured frantically, urging them to get up, urging them to keep going toward the Embassy. "Keep going!"

They were going to live through this. Now he knew it. That last blast had told him as much. It had been something like the stun grenades riot police used, meant to scare and confuse, not kill. If a real bomb or rocket had hit that close, they'd have all been dead in less than a heartbeat. The Devlin had overplayed their hand.

"Come on," he said again. "Come on! If they wanted to kill us, we'd be dead by now. Keep going."

The eight of them, moaning, caked with dirt, tears and blood and sweat streaming down their faces, got up. Somehow, they kept going. And somehow, they got to the Embassy.

They entered the Human Embassy stunned, bloody, terrified. But there were no further attacks. Either the Devlin felt that firing on an embassy was worse than firing on ambassadors, or else they had given up after the flash-bomb failed to scare the eight human delegates into running.

Giotto and the other, less advanced robots were immediately everywhere at once, busily tending to their injuries—all of which turned out to be fairly minor. Adam had only a few cuts and bruises. His nose had stopped bleeding by the time he had gotten to the embassy.

Giotto spent less than a minute on him. "You're a mess," the robot told Adam. "But none of it's worth worrying about. Go clean yourself up." And with that, the robot turned his attention to Marget's far nastier cuts and scrapes.

150

Adam longed to take a shower and get all the mud and blood off himself and change into a fresh s-suit, but there wasn't time. They had to talk things out now, immediately, before anything else could happen, before the Devlin could make some other move.

He contented himself with washing his hands and running his head under the tap in the washroom and toweling off as hard as he could. And his s-suit seemed to know a few tricks about shedding dirt. By the time he had freshened himself, it seemed almost as fresh as it had at the start of the day.

He returned to the main room of the embassy just as Giotto was finished patching everyone up. The other seven Human members of the team were sitting around the conference table while Giotto hovered in midair to the right of the one open seat at the table.

Adam sat down between Giotto and Aaron and looked around the table—and saw every other set of eyes looking at him, and at Aaron. Well, fair enough. They had gotten into this mess by listening to Aaron and him. Who else were they going to look to as they tried to figure how to get back out?

"All right," said Johan. "Adam's back, and we're all here. Giotto, how much were you able to observe from back here?"

"I was able to monitor just about all of it through the sight and sound senders concealed in Ahna's s-suit," said Giotto. "I saw what happened. But I do not understand what I saw and heard."

"I do," said Adam. "They're bullies, that's all. The kind of bullies who break the rules, just to see if anyone has the nerve to try and stop them. If no one does, they take what they want." He shook his head. "But they sure pushed it hard."

"But why—why didn't they kill us?"

"Because they can't," said Adam. "They don't dare. Killing diplomats? That probably *would* start a war—

with us, with the K'lugu, maybe both. But if they had managed to bluff us into *thinking* they'd kill us, and got us to do whatever they said, they could get everything they want without actually having to take the risk of fighting.''

"But even if they had gotten us to agree to all that stuff—to their having weapons at the negotiating table, and Devlin law taking precedence over any other law—and having Earth surrender to them—it wouldn't do them any good,'' Ahna objected. "None of the people back home, the adults running things, would agree to any of it. They wouldn't—they *couldn't*—honor agreements like that.''

"Of course not,'' said Aaron. "But that's the trick. The man who leads my country—a very bad man—has played it many times. He agrees to a meeting with other leaders to discuss thus and such. But when the other leaders get there, our leader suddenly starts demanding a hundred times more than he could possibly get. And so the other leaders 'compromise' with him. They give him less than he demands—and ten, twenty times more than they expected to give him before the meeting.''

"But that's not right!'' Johan protested.

"No, but it works,'' said Adam. He paused for a minute, choosing his words carefully. He wasn't supposed to talk about the future of Aaron's world in front of him, but he had to say a little bit about it. "I don't know as much about that part of history as I should, but Hitler, the man Aaron is talking about, won a lot of fights just because he demanded so much, and made such terrible threats, that giving away nearly everything to him seemed like a good deal by comparison. The other thing he did was pretend he was a lot stronger than he really was, with a bigger army and so on. He built his army up as fast as he could, but he *acted* like he had a strong military for years before he *really* had one—and everyone believed him. So no one was willing to start a fight with him. He won without *having* to fight, over and over again. He bluffed out all the other countries.''

"It's the sort of trick Machiavelli talks about in *The Prince*," said Roberto.

Ahna looked at the three boys from the past thoughtfully. "So what you're all saying is that the Devlin were hoping to get us to agree to impossible things, not because they thought they'd *get* them, but so they'd have a much better bargaining position when they met with our diplomats on Earth. We here would promise them everything, so they'll take *half* of everything from the real diplomats, and act like they were being generous because they didn't take more.''

"But they overdid it," Giotto objected. "They pushed far too hard, right at the beginning, as if they thought we'd give in instantly.''

"Maybe we would have, without our friends from the past here," said Suza. "I was plenty scared. I'm *still* plenty scared.''

"Even so," said Giotto. "If what Aaron and Adam and Roberto say is true, then the Devlin are merely bluffers and bullies.''

"It might not all be bluff," Roberto cautioned. "They could still have a sky full of weapons ready to use. We are here, talking, instead of being dead. That proves they were bluffing about *using* their weapons *here*, *today*. It does not mean they do not *have* them.''

"Yes, yes," said Giotto. "And bullies can fight hard, when they need to, or want to. We must not think the Devlin are less dangerous just because they tried to play a trick on us. But I am trying to make a different point.'' He turned to Adam. "Forgive me, if I am somewhat—indelicate—for a moment. From what I know of your life, back in your own time, you were a bit of a bully yourself at times. Is that not the case?''

Adam squirmed a bit in his chair and resisted the temptation to deny it. They must have studied him like crazy before they went to all the time and trouble of yanking him into the future. They already *knew* he had been—heck, still was—a bit of a troublemaker, a bit of a bully. Giotto was just being polite. "Well, yes," he said. "I guess so. What about it?"

"All right then. Look at the situation the way a bully would. If you knew nothing at all about another teen-ager—not how strong he was, how smart he was, how tough or weak, how brave or cowardly he was, or how many friends he had, and if you couldn't tell by looking at him—would you try and push him around, the very first time you met him, before you had a chance to find out anything?"

"No way," said Adam. "I wouldn't try—a bully wouldn't try—to pick on someone who could turn out to be stronger than I—than he—was. Instead the bully would wait around until he knew more, until he heard some gossip or got a chance to watch him a little."

"That is about what I expected," said Giotto.

"Wait just a moment!" said Roberto. "What about the reason we three from the past are here in the first place? We're not here to be at the conference. We're here to find out if the Devlin found one of the lost colony ships."

"Quite right," said Giotto, sounding pleased. "Quite right indeed."

Adam suddenly understood. "That explains it. The Devlin thought they could bully Humans because they thought they knew Humans, because—"

"Because they *do* know Humans!" Ahna finished.

"Exactly," said Giotto. "Their behavior today suggests, very subtly, that they know something about Humans. That they have met Humans, and learned something that made them think, rightly or wrongly, that Humans could be pushed around. It's a slender thread, and certainly not enough to base all our plans on, but the logic is there."

"Then we can't go," said Johan. "We can't leave Bogwater. We have to stay and give you three from the past a chance to do your job."

"You're right," said Adam. "We can't leave. But we have to *pretend* we're going to leave. We have to call the Devlin's bluff by bluffing right back. And we can't bluff halfway. We have to make it *seem* real by making it *be* real. We have to start packing everything up, and we have to do it out where they can see it."

"What will that accomplish?" Suza demanded.

"One of two things," said Adam. He held up his right hand and raised his index finger. "One. The Devlin might see us getting ready to go, and see that we mean it, and then not do anything to stop us, and leave themselves. It will mean they were just here to try and throw a scare into us, put guns to our heads to make us do what they say, and they weren't really interested in talking."

Adam held up a second finger. "Two. They blink first. The Devlin stay, and come to us with their excuse to explain what they did. If they do that, they'll be *admitting* that threatening us and demanding the surrender of humanity were just tricks. That'll be hard for them to do, so they'll only do it if they really *need* to talk with us. They won't like coming to us, because they'll be admitting to us that they know Humans can't be pushed around, and that talking to Humans is important enough that they have to come up with excuses. And they'll know that we know that they know it." Adam grinned mischievously. "It'll drive them crazy."

"What could possibly excuse their shooting at you?" Giotto asked. "What could they say that we would believe?"

"It doesn't matter," said Adam. "It might be anything. The dog ate their homework. The alarm clock didn't work. The sun was in their eyes."

"We do not have to *believe* it," said Roberto. "In

fact, I would guess they will not *expect* us to believe it." He paused, and considered for a moment. "But I think Adam's guesses are right. If he is correct, we must *pretend* to believe whatever explanation they give. Let them save face. We must not attack their pride."

Ahna frowned and stared down at the table for a moment. "If—if you are right, and if they do come to us," she said, "then in a sense we'll have accomplished our mission. They'll have admitted they need to deal with us."

"And if we had rice, we could have rice and beans, if we had beans, and water and a pot and a fire," said Roberto.

Ahna looked up at him in confusion. "What? What do you mean?"

Roberto smiled. "I mean that we have many 'ifs' and 'maybes' and guesses about beings we met for the first time today. We could have it all wrong."

Marget shrugged. "There's not much we can do about it if we do have it wrong."

"So we wait?" said Torry.

"We wait, and we start packing, and we do it out where they can see us."

"Speaking of seeing," said Adam, "I'd like to see what *they're* doing, the K'lugu and the Devlin."

"I have been monitoring Parley Pavilion and the surrounding area with long-range cameras and other detectors," said Giotto.

"So what's been happening?"

"I will present the imagery to you," the robot replied.

One wall of the room shimmered, then transformed itself into a video screen with a view of the Pavilion.

The image was reasonably sharp and clear, with just a bit of the shakiness and fuzziness produced by long-range lenses pushed a little past their optimum settings. "We are not getting good enough sound to do any sort of on-the-fly translation," said Giotto. "We're recording whatever sound we get for later processing, if need be. But even without hearing the words, I think we can safely guess there is an argument in progress."

The Devlin Prime was standing outside the Pavilion, gesticulating wildly. She pointed two arms at other Devlin, one at herself, and the fourth to Human Hill. Secondary and the rest of the Devlin were standing lined up in two ranks, one of three, the other of four, in what appeared to be the Devlin equivalent of attention. The subordinate Devlin were clearly ill at ease. They seemed to be looking nervously at each other whenever Prime had her back turned to them, and they shifted back and forth on their feet.

The K'lugu, however, watched Prime's performance calmly. One, then another, then another, would answer Prime, with no apparent pattern to who spoke in what order.

"What about them?" Adam asked Giotto. "The Devlin I can sort of understand, but I don't know much about the K'lugu."

"They're patient, honorable, and determined," said Giotto. "Once they come to do a job, they don't give up on it. At times such as these, they are likely to try and make things work out by sheer stubbornness, in the hopes this will impress the rest of us, and encourage us to keep trying. If we do walk out, and the Devlin follow, they won't give up trying to make the conference work. They might just remain at the Pavilion and wait. Even if everyone else were to abandon the talks, my guess is that the K'lugu would stay at the Pavilion until tomorrow, or perhaps the day after, in the hopes that we'd return," said Giotto. "And if we didn't, they'd go out after the Devlin, and after us, again and again, urging us to try one more time."

"They're likable, and they're good people," said Ahna. "They want things to be fair and honest—but they might have a different idea about what those concepts mean than we do. So don't assume they're on our side."

"But we may want them to be in the future," said Giotto. "Part of our mission here is to further improve and strengthen our relationship with the K'lugu. We may need allies someday."

Especially, thought Adam, *in a universe that has the Devlin in it.*

"Our side or their side, the K'lugu don't seem too worried about calming Devlin Prime down," said Aaron. "She looks even madder than before, if that's possible."

"Perhaps," said Giotto. "However, it would appear they have reached some sort of agreement."

As they watched, the subordinate Devlin broke ranks and moved back a little way from the Pavilion. Prime moved to join them.

The seven other Devlin clustered themselves around Prime and faced themselves outward, putting her in the center of a defensive circle. Adam remembered seeing pictures of musk oxen doing the same sort of thing. The way the Devlin did it made it look like a reflex, as automatic as a dog going around in a circle once or twice before lying down and curling up, or a Human unconsciously tapping her feet in time to music.

"They're settling in," said Ahna. "It looks like they're going to wait right there."

"Wait for what?" asked Marget.

"An answer from us," said Aaron, pointing at the K'lugu. One of them was turning away from the group, and starting to walk straight toward the camera—toward the Human Embassy. "An answer to whatever question that K'lugu is about to ask us."

"All right then," said Adam. "It's showtime. Let's get our packing started. And remember, we need to look like we really mean to go."

Ahna looked toward Johan. "I think he's right," she said. "What about it?"

Johan folded his arms and watched the K'lugu head toward them. He shook his head and shrugged. "Okay," he said. "I guess it makes sense. Let's do it."

Five minutes later, the first of the cargo was heading through the t-port to the *Franklin*. Service robots were moving equipment out of the embassy, and the Meeting One team members were hard at work as well, checking cargo off and giving orders to the robots. Ahna hoped the aliens would see a Human delegation so insulted that it could not possibly remain. But suppose they saw it as a panicky retreat—or as a bunch of teenagers milling around and trying to look busy?

She turned to look down the hill at the K'lugu making its—her? his?—leisurely way up the slope of Human Hill. She walked toward the K'lugu, meeting the alien before he/she/it reached the Human Embassy.

"Greetings," Ahna said, spreading her arms outward and bowing slightly. "You are welcome in our place," she said, and the translator spoke in her voice to the K'lugu.

The K'lugu replied, and Ahna's broca amp relayed their meaning. "Greetings likewise to you," the K'lugu said, and bowed, imitating Ahna's gesture exactly. "I am most pleased to be welcome."

"I am Ahna Varkan of the Human delegation," said Ahna.

"And I am Clearwater, daughter of the K'lugu." Clearwater straightened up and regarded the hustle and bustle behind Ahna for a moment. "I perceive that your people are departing."

"Regretfully, yes," said Ahna. "We could not remain. To do so would be to say we accepted the right of the Devlin to break whatever rules they chose, as well as their right to threaten and attack us."

"Yes," said Clearwater. "I perceive the logic of your thoughts. However, I am here to ask you to remain."

"Have the Devlin ordered you to ask this?" Ahna asked.

Clearwater stiffened, and stared hard at Ahna. "No," she said. "K'lugu are not commanded by the Devlin. The Devlin *requested* that a K'lugu go to you, and we K'lugu agreed to this request."

"Good," said Ahna. "I am glad to hear it." And glad to see that Clearwater was offended by the idea that a Devlin could order her around. "But the Devlin have given us very good reasons for leaving. Can they give us better reasons for staying?"

"They wish to speak with you."

"So they can demand our surrender again?"

"The Devlin Prime says that was all a misunderstanding. The word 'surrender' was a mistake. A fault in the translation machines, perhaps." Clearwater rolled her head up to the vertical for a moment, and then back down, in what seemed the equivalent of a shrug. "So says the Devlin Prime."

"What says the K'lugu Clearwater?"

"I am here to bring a message, not to offer an opinion."

"I see." Ahna tried to think. *The word 'surrender' was a mistake.* Was it a mistake because they thought the word meant something else—or because the gambit of trying for a surrender was a mistake? Ambiguity had its uses. If both sides accepted the words, and moved on, it scarcely mattered if each side thought the words meant a different thing. "I agree that the word 'surrender' was a mistake," said Ahna. "What of the weapons fired at us? All of us suffered small injuries. It was mere chance that none of us were badly hurt, or killed."

"Another misunderstanding. Prime wished you would desire to remain of your own free will. Her subordinates thought she wished to detain you." Again the shrug. "So says the Devlin Prime."

Ahna nodded, but said nothing for a moment. The

boys from the past had been right again. The Devlin had come up with excuses, not explanations. Now she could either accept the feeble excuses, and get back to the conference—or denounce them for the lies they were. She couldn't do both.

But perhaps she could stall, and get a better feel for the situation. "I will return to the Pavilion with you, and bring one companion," she said. "I am curious to hear more about these—misunderstandings."

"I am glad to hear it," said Clearwater.

Ahna gestured toward Giotto, who was waiting nearby. The robot knew to play the part of servant, rather than advisor, in front of aliens. "Tell Master Johan to join me," she said. She wished she could bring one of the boys from the past, but Johan was the team's co-leader, after all, and she didn't want to bring along too large a group—in case something went wrong. She would just have to do the job herself. She resolved to be as suspicious and sneaky as anyone from the past. "Johan and I will return to the Pavilion. While we are gone, keep packing," she said. "I want our people and equipment ready for departure in one hour. We will return before then."

Giotto dipped his body down on its levitator for a moment—the robotic equivalent of a bow. "It will be done, Mistress," he said.

Ahna nodded, turned her back on Giotto, and waited for Johan to join her. This was going to be tricky.

Ahna, Johan, and Clearwater walked past the blast craters made by Devlin weapons and toward the Parley Pavilion, the scars on the land serving as quite unnecessary reminders of the danger they were in. The Devlin were still clustered together by their side of the Pavilion, and the K'lugu stood near their side of the structure. Clearwater went to stand with her own people.

"Come on," said Ahna to Johan. She led him straight

to the Human side of the Pavilion and took one of the center seats at the table. Johan hesitated for the barest moment, then followed her lead.

"We are preparing to leave this planet," Ahna said, not waiting for the Devlin or the K'lugu to have a chance to take their places, let alone speak first. "We have no reason to stay. It is only out of respect for our good friends the K'lugu that we agreed to delay our departure, however briefly."

"The Devlin ask that you remain and reconsider," said Clearwater.

"We have not heard the Devlin ask for anything at all," said Johan.

The eight Devlin still stood crowded together, just outside the Pavilion, Prime in the middle. Both humans and all eight K'lugu turned to look at them expectantly.

None of the Devlin moved at first, but at last the smallest of them, one hardly larger than Ahna, popped out of the side of the group of Devlin—almost as if he had received a good swift kick from the inside.

He moved forward, slowly, reluctantly, and stepped up into the middle of the Pavilion floor. He faced Ahna and Johan, spread his four arms wide, and rocked backward slightly. It was plainly a formal gesture, meant to show his hands were empty and that he was leaving himself open to attack. *I surrender, I apologize*, the pose said. He held that position for a moment, then dropped his hands to his sides and stood upright before the two Humans.

"I am Least," he said, "smallest and youngest of our Prime's followers here present. I offer most sincere apologies for the recent misunderstandings between our two delegations."

"For whom do you speak?" Ahna asked.

Least slumped all four of his shoulders in misery. "I— I speak for myself," he said. "The Least of our group speaks for no one else. It is the task of the Least of any group to take on all blame, all failure, all punishment.''

"So whatever errors Prime or Secondary, or any other Devlin of your group might commit, all blame must fall on you?'' asked Ahna.

"I know it is different for your people,'' said Least, "but that is our way. Yes. Whatever punishments there are will be mine to suffer.''

"Your people threatened us,'' said Ahna.

"Yes,'' said Least.

"They tried to trick us, and frighten us.''

"Yes,'' said Least.

"They fired weapons at us, and almost caused us serious harm.''

"All this is true, and I must take the blame for it all,'' Least said. "Our Prime, in all her wisdom, did not realize that our translation equipment was converting some words and concepts incorrectly. For example, our word for 'clothing' was translated as 'weapon.' This caused much confusion.''

"So you thought we objected to your having clothing at the conference.'' said Ahna. *I don't believe that for a minute*, she thought, *but it's just barely plausible*. That was all the Devlin needed. Something that *might* be true, something that would let them save face.

"And what of the weapons fired at us?'' Johan asked. "Was there some failure in translating Devlin into Devlin?''

Least looked even more miserable, if such a thing were possible. "Unlikely as it sounds, sir, you have guessed right. Our group is gathered from many different Devlin domains. There was indeed confusion of dialect. There is a group where the phrase 'urge them' or 'persuade them' is used as a slang term for firing near-miss shots in certain cases. Our great Prime urged persuasion— and her lessers did their best to obey with eager zeal.''

"And the demand for the surrender of the entire Human race?'' Johan asked. ''Another slight misunderstanding?''

''Secondary spoke those words,'' said Least. ''Only the words of the Prime have authority, unless that authority is properly delegated. I am at present so delegated. Secondary had no such delegation of authority when he spoke of your surrender. I offer my profound apologies for all these mistakes and misunderstandings.''

''We take note of your apologies,'' said Johan. ''We will record them, as we recorded the incidents themselves.'' It was hard to miss that he said nothing about *accepting* the apologies.

''But we have yet to hear any reason why we should stay,'' said Ahna. ''Your misunderstandings and mistakes were very serious. Will they happen again?''

''They will not,'' Least replied, almost too firmly, too eagerly. ''We have taken—precautions—to see that there will be no further problems.''

''No weapons?'' asked Johan. ''No threats? No surrender demands? And we will be treated and addressed as your equals, as indeed we are?''

It didn't seem as if it could be possible for Least to look any more miserable, but he managed it. ''We agree to all these items,'' he said.

''Then we shall remain,'' said Johan. ''At least for now.''

Ahna got an idea, and decided to go for it without even checking with Johan. The moment was right for them to press the Devlin. Later they might not be quite as willing to swallow a Human suggestion.

''There is one more thing,'' she said. ''All our plans for these negotiations were based on all eight of our delegates being here. We note that Prime wished to perform all the negotiations on her own. For reasons of protocol, we think it is important that both sides have the same number of delegates. It would seem a large number is best for us, and a small number best for our

164

friends the Devlin. Perhaps a compromise on this point is in order. Shall we split the difference, and agree on four delegates each?'' She turned and bowed to the K'lugu. ''But this would not apply to our esteemed hosts, of course. So far as we Humans are concerned, this is a K'lugu world. They may bring whatever number they like.''

Least spoke. ''I cannot enter into any such agreement,'' he said. ''Prime alone can decide.'' He turned to look toward the other Devlin. Prime looked decidedly annoyed, even more so than she had before. But she snorted, and waved her inner right-side hand dismissively.

Least turned back toward Johan and Ahna. ''She consents.''

''What did you want that for?'' Johan asked in a low whisper.

''I'll explain later,'' Ahna whispered back. ''Excellent,'' she said in a louder voice.

Clearwater spoke. ''So the parties agree,'' she said. ''But such changes in plan will no doubt require time to arrange. Might we K'lugu suggest that we adjourn until tomorrow at the same time?''

Least glanced back toward Prime, and Prime made the same gesture. ''Agreed,'' said Least.

''Agreed,'' said Johan, as he and Ahna stood up. ''Until tomorrow then.''

Least watched the Humans depart, and felt his spirits fall even lower. He had warned them, warned Prime as strongly as he had dared, that something was wrong. But he had been placed in the extremely awkward position of being the one who brought in the data, as well as the one warning that the data was wrong. Everything he had learned from the *Roanoke* survivors had said Humans were easily intimidated, peaceful, even timid. But the more Prime had wanted to believe it, the more Prime *did* believe it, the more Least had been sure something was wrong.

But the fact that he had warned Prime did Least no good. It was all his fault. Prime's plans to cow the Humans into submission had been based on the information Least had collected. But, as he had quite honestly explained to the Human, Primes did not make mistakes. That was what Leasts were for.

And, of course, those who make mistakes had to be punished. Severely. Least was not looking forward to the evening ahead.

The door of the Human Embassy slid shut behind Ahna and Johan. The two of them made their way into the embassy's main conference room, and dropped into the two chairs closest to the doors, exhausted. The second walk down to the Pavilion and back was nothing at all. But just keeping up appearances, acting calm and in control in front of the aliens that had been trying to kill them an hour before—that had taken its toll on both of them. Giotto and the rest of the team followed them into the room, and took seats around the table.

"So we're back on the job?" Marget asked eagerly as she sat down.

Everyone had watched and listened through the long-range cameras and mikes, but they all wanted to hear it direct from the two who had been there. "Yes," she said. "We start tomorrow. Or at least four of us do."

"What was that about?" Johan asked, a bit irritably. "You shouldn't spring surprises like that. We've already had enough surprises for one day."

"Sorry," said Ahna, "but I didn't think of it until just that second. It just struck me that everything else the Devlin told us was fake—why not their reasons for wanting Prime to negotiate by herself? What if the real story was they needed more people to run things than they had expected? What if, I don't know, their robots weren't performing well or something? I thought that if we made them keep more people at the table, that would leave them short-handed on everything else. And *we've* got reasons for *not* wanting all of us there.'' She gestured at the boys from the past. ''I'm glad the three of you are along—you've saved the day already. But no offense, I couldn't throw away a chance to keep you in the background. The more we keep you away from the conference table, the less you'll have to act like diplomats and the more sneaking and spying you can do.''

''Believe me,'' said Aaron, ''no offense taken. None of us were too crazy about the idea of being at the table.'' Roberto and Adam murmured their agreement.

Johan grinned. ''So you got us what we wanted, and kept them from getting what they wanted, and made it look like a compromise. Very slick indeed.''

''Ahna, I don't think you *need* to read Machiavelli,'' said Roberto. ''You need no more lessons in how to be sneaky.''

Ahna laughed. ''Thanks,'' she said. ''But I have a feeling that we could still learn a few things from you three—but we'll have to leave that for later. We don't have much time. There is a lot we have to do before tomorrow.'' She turned toward Johan. ''Least made a slip when he was talking to us,'' she said. ''Did you catch it?''

Johan nodded. ''Yeah,'' he said. ''I was going to ask you about it. He was talking about whose fault things were. He said 'I know it is different for your people, but that is our way.' The Devlin aren't supposed to know anything about Humans. How does he know anything at all about how we handle blame and responsibility?''

''Right,'' said Ahna. ''He as good as told us they *do* have some sort of information source about Humans.''

''But it could be just an old history book they bought from some trader—or an etiquette book, for that matter,'' Torry objected.

"I don't think so," said Aaron. "He moved differently."

Torry looked at Aaron with a quizzical expression. "What?"

"Least. I was watching on the video display. When he was talking to Ahna and Johan, he didn't move the way the other Devlin moved, or the way he did when he was with the other Devlin." Aaron hooked a thumb over his shoulder to indicate the past. "Back where I come from, you learn to notice how people move. When you need to know,—*is he one of us*? or *is he one of them*?—sometimes what tells you is the hand gestures, or the way a person nods or the way he walks. Least's gestures *changed* when he talked to Johan and Ahna. He shrugged. He nodded. He was imitating Human gestures. You don't learn that out of a book and then do it without thinking when you talk to Humans."

"He's right!" said Giotto. "I do believe he's right. Stand by for a moment, while I review the recorded imagery." Giotto went completely still for the better part of a minute before speaking again. "I apologize for taking so long," he said, "but I wanted to do a full analysis of Least's gestures compared to the other Devlin. Aaron is quite correct. When he was speaking to Ahna and Johan, Least's whole system of body language shifted. He went to what seemed to be an imitation of common Human gestures. I am no judge of Devlin behavior, but it would appear that he did it quite unconsciously."

"That's not the sort of thing you learn from a history book," Adam said excitedly. "Or even from watching movies or videotapes. You pick up gestures by copying what other people do in a conversation."

The room buzzed with excited murmuring. It was a slender thread, but the logic held. Unless they had gotten something very wrong, the Devlin—not just any Devlin, but Least himself—had been in direct contact with Humans, had talked to them face-to-face.

But what Humans, and where? It was tempting, very tempting, to jump to conclusions and assume it had to be survivors of the *Roanoke*—but there was no real proof of that. "Good eye, Aaron," said Ahna. "Everyone else missed that one. But let's move carefully. I think the best thing we can do is stick to the plan our friends from the past worked out. We'll have to change a few things to adjust it to the new situation, but I bet it'll work. Let's get started."

APPEARANCES

Night had fallen, and the stars gleamed down. The Brightmorning Nebula hung low over the water, out beyond Blackback Island, its glory dimmed somewhat by the sea mist.

Their first eventful day on Negotiation Island had come to an end. All the twenty-fourth-century kids, except Ahna, were already in bed, asleep. Despite—or perhaps thanks to—all the excitement, they were just too exhausted to stay awake any longer.

But it was the first time to themselves any of the boys from the past had had since being Yanked into the future. None of them were quite ready to sleep.

Aaron was taking a walk around the island. Roberto had been torn between his love of the seaside and his unquenchable thirst for adventure stories, but the books had won out in the end. He had been curled up with *The Three Musketeers* when Adam had left the Embassy.

Adam had slipped out not long after Aaron had left. He wasn't in much of a mood for a walk. He simply felt the need to be alone for a time.

He sat in the odd not-quite grass atop Human Hill,

and stared out at the sea, the islands, and the sky. But he was looking inward, not up.

Adam found himself thinking about a weird old book he had read, the sort Roberto would like—*The Picture of Dorian Gray*. Adam had read it for English class. He'd picked it because it was one of the shortest books on the extra-credit list, but it hadn't been an easy book to get through. The guy in the story, Dorian, had made a wish always to stay young and handsome, and to let his portrait grow old and corrupt in his place. The wish came true—and the story did not turn out well for Dorian. Adam shuddered just thinking about it.

What the story said was that you couldn't hide who you were—not forever. Dorian Gray had hidden the truth about himself from others. Adam hid the truth about himself *from* himself. He was starting to wonder if maybe fooling yourself was as bad, or worse, than fooling everyone else.

Maybe that was the reason Adam had been so bothered by the book. If he looked at a picture of himself—not of how he looked, but of how he acted, and who he was—what would he see? He did not like the answer he got.

Was he truly any better than the bullying Devlin Prime? *She* didn't worry about what was wrong or right, false or true. All she cared about was what she could get away with, what she could lie her way out of if things went wrong. Was he like her?

He stared, unseeing, at the Brightmorning Nebula for what seemed like hours as the troubling questions swirled around in his head.

"There you are," said a voice out of the darkness.

Adam blinked in surprise and turned around. Ahna was there, faintly silhouetted by the lights of the Human Embassy. "Oh, hi," he said.

"What are you doing out here?" she asked.

"Just thinking," he said.

"Should I leave you alone?"

"No, sit down. I've been staring into space by myself long enough."

Ahna laughed. "Okay, I'll stare into space with you," she said. She sat down next to him, and the two of them admired the glorious Brightmorning Nebula.

"So what have you been 'just thinking' about?" she asked. "The mission? The plan for tomorrow?"

Adam shook his head. "No. Probably I should have been. Mostly I've been thinking about how I got here. Why I got picked."

"Oh," said Ahna in a cautious tone of voice. "You don't have to talk about it with me, if you don't want."

"No, no," said Adam. "I want to. I think I have part of it figured out. You guys chose Roberto because he grew up in an equatorial coastal area not so different from this. That's going to come in handy in the next day or so. Aaron's here because he grew up as a Jew with the Nazis all around him. He knows how to deal with hostile, dangerous people in authority. He knows when to run, and when to fight. And then there's me."

"You're more or less right about the other two," said Ahna, still staring at the sky. "There were other reasons, too, but what you've guessed is correct as far as it goes." She was silent for a moment before she asked the next, obvious, question. "So why do you think *you're* here?"

Adam turned and looked her in the eye. He knew he had to tell the truth, even though it wouldn't be much fun.

"Because I'm sneaky," he said. "Because I know how to trick people, how to get away with things. Though I messed even that up the night before you guys grabbed me."

Ahna looked serious as she replied. She spoke slowly, choosing her words carefully. "All of you come from times and places where it helped to be a bit more—devious—than we are these days. That was part of why you were all selected. But, yes, it was noted that you had special—*ability* in this area.''

''Not exactly the sort of reason for being picked that makes a person feel all proud inside,'' Adam said, staring out at the surf. ''What if that's all I'm ever good at, for the rest of my life? Getting away with things?''

''It won't be,'' said Ahna, staring at him with big, serious eyes. ''I—I can't tell you anything specific about your life to come, but that much I can say, if it's of any help.''

''It is,'' said Adam. ''It is.''

Ahna gave him a friendly pat on the back and stood up. ''Come on,'' she said. ''We need to get some sleep. Tomorrow's a busy day.''

KITES

Least waited on Prime and the others the next morning. It had been a rough night. Prime had punished him most severely for the disasters of the day before. As was fitting to his station, he was to pilot the aircar that transported the negotiation team to the Pavilion. As was fitting to *their* stations, none of the four negotiators acknowledged his existence as they trooped out of the Devlin Embassy and toward the craft. And as was fitting to anyone who wished to survive the day, none of the Lesser Devlin said anything at all about the change in transport. No one seemed even to notice that the entire party was traveling in a single civilian aircar, rather than in a matched formation of eight military assault craft. Everyone pretended very hard that the change had nothing to do with the K'lugu protesting the aerial theatrics that had gone on the day before.

Prime, Secondary, Third, and Fourth came aboard and took their seats, and Least moved forward to the pilot's station. Prime was silent, and seemed moody, even for her. Secondary, Third, and Fourth were all cheerful and upbeat. That was understandable. If Prime had negotiated alone, they would have been on security duty, patrolling the embassy perimeter. Instead, they would spend this day, and the rest of their days on Bogwater, doing very little other than sitting and listening to Prime do all the talking.

Least had no such reason to be cheerful. With three fewer bodies at the Embassy, there would be a great deal more work to do—and he knew perfectly well who would get stuck with most of it. Fifth, Sixth, and Seventh would likely spend most of the day trying to get at least some of the robots up and running, if they could find a way around the corrosion problems.

Least activated the flight systems, and the aircar rose up into the air for the brief flight across the water to Negotiation Island.

Water. Least shuddered. Devlin did not like open water, for a number of very good reasons. For one thing, Devlin did not float. They sank. For another, the waters of the Devlin home world were filled with all manner of extremely hungry creatures, many of them quite a bit more ferocious than the average Devlin. The waters of Bogwater were no more inviting. Huge, loathsome creatures, monstrous, devolved aquatic birds, some of them bigger than Prime, swam in the sea and lounged on the shores of all the islands. Least could not imagine how the K'lugu could endure being so close to them.

No matter. The aircar flew safely over the water, and they had no need to make any sort of physical contact with it.

"I say, Least—what are those?" Third asked as the aircar took to the sky. He spoke quietly to avoid disturbing Prime, who sat in the rear of the craft.

"What—what are what, sir?" Least replied, being sure to keep his own voice down.

"Those," said Third, leaning forward in his seat and pointing with his upper left arm. "Those brightly colored things in the air over the Human Embassy."

"I noticed them when we were still on the ground," said Fourth. "Strange-looking things. They seem to be hovering. Some sort of power system, perhaps?"

"Maybe they're religious symbols," said Fourth.

"Could they be weapons?" asked Third.

"Weapons?" Fourth laughed. "Our pacifist Human friends setting up weapons? That hardly seems likely—especially after the protests they and the K'lugu kicked up yesterday about *our* weapons."

"I don't have quite your touching faith in Humans being harmless," said Third, dropping his voice even lower. "Nor does Least, I believe, though he can't possibly say so where Prime might hear him."

Least doubted very much that the Humans were as harmless as they were supposed to be. But Third was right. It was quite impossible that he could ever contradict his superiors by saying so. Prime had examined Least's work, reached her own conclusions on the matter, dismissed all of Least's respectful disagreements, and ordered an end to debate. That was the end of the matter.

Under the circumstances, however, Least's silence was quite eloquent enough.

"No comment, eh?" Third chuckled. "I can't blame you for that. Well, Least, you'd better find out what they are," he said, leaning back in his chair. "Prime doesn't like mysteries."

"Very good, sir," said Least, trying to keep the note of weary resignation out of his voice. It was one more in the list of endless chores they all threw at him. Least couldn't see how he would ever get them all done. How in the bright wide universe was he supposed to find out what those strange objects in the sky were?

Someday, somehow, he would stop being Least, and he would no longer be stuck with all the awkward jobs. It was too much to hope he would ever be Prime of his own group. But he could at least dream of being traded, and rising to Fifth or Fourth in a new group, with a sensible Prime, or maybe serving in a large group, a Combine of several hundred, maybe big enough that the Lesser weren't rigidly ranked, one number after another, but simply assigned in subgroups of eight or sixty-four. What joy and safety there would be in such anonymity! But the main thing Least dreamed of was having superiors who did not make all problems worse and dump all the work on their inferiors.

He brought the aircar in for a nice quiet landing, a respectful distance from the Parley Pavilion, still wondering how to do the job Third had assigned.

He watched as the delegates trooped out of the aircar and made their way to the Pavilion. At least they weren't trying to scare anyone to death today. That much was progress, at any rate.

As it turned out, finding out what the floating things were could not have been easier. The K'lugu were curious, too, and as Least came out of the aircar, he overheard two or three K'lugu clustered around the tallest male Human, gesturing toward the strange objects. From the vantage point of the Pavilion, Least could plainly see that the objects were hovering in the air off to leeward of the Human Embassy, and seemed to be tethered in some way. He could just make out lines holding several of them to the ground. Two Humans seemed to be holding lines, while other line had apparently been tied off.

"They're called 'kites,'" Johan was saying to the K'lugu. "You could call them tethered gliders, I suppose. They are made of cloth and paper and other materials, and shaped so that an airfoil effect pulls them up into the air, while a line holds them stable in one place. They are traditional outdoor toys, back on Earth. We brought them along, and some other things, to amuse our people during off-duty hours."

"Quite charming," said the K'lugu called Waveripple. "I count at least eight of them up at the moment, and of all quite different design. Is there any significance to the various shapes?"

Johan smiled. "Not really," he said. "Sometimes we make them look like birds or aircraft or whatever for the fun of it, but there is no deep meaning attached to the shapes. The kites are merely for amusement."

Least looked and listened thoughtfully to the conversation. *Toy. Just there to be pretty. Charming. For the fun of it.* Of course. What else could they expect from the simple, gentle, nonthreatening Humans?

He headed toward the Pavilion, to where Prime, Secondary, Third, and Fourth were preparing to take their places with another weary sigh. He could see Third and Fourth, and even Secondary and Prime, glancing up at the odd things hovering in the sky. Prime was plainly bothered by the sight. And Least knew the way Third thought. If Prime was slightly concerned, then Third would feel the need to be downright paranoid.

They couldn't take the Human explanation of the kites at face value, Third would say. Maybe the kites were something else altogether—a signaling device, perhaps. Maybe the story about them being mere toys was a fraud, a fraud as complete as the Devlin pretending that the attack the day before had just been a misunderstanding. But no matter. They had a way of checking up on the Humans, intended for precisely this sort of situation.

In short, Third would send Least to ask the *Roanoke* survivors about it all. It was exactly the sort of thing Third liked to have confirmed—especially when it wasn't Third who had to make the jump from one star system to another to do the confirming.

Ethan was working in the cornfield when he heard the noise behind him. He looked up toward the main wreckage field of the *Roanoke* crash and was surprised to see the heavyset figure of the alien coming over the brow of the hill. Least had visited many times before, but always at the end of the day, when their work was done and dusk was coming on.

"Greetings, Ethan," the alien called out, still some distance away.

"Hello!" Ethan called back, and walked toward his visitor.

"Please forgive me for coming at this time of day, and for rushing so much," Least said. "Our encounter with the alien race that might know something of Humans has begun," he said. "And they have indeed told us something about Humans that seems quite improbable. It's a small, trifling detail, but something we can check, to test if the aliens are honest. I need to return with the answer at once."

"All right," said Ethan, as calmly as he could. This could be tricky—but years of surviving as castaways had made Ethan and the others pretty tricky as well.

The *Roanoke* survivors had given the Devlin a lot of very carefully selected information about Humans. All of it had been true, just in case the Devlin had some way of checking up on what the *Roanoke* people told them—but a lot of it had been misleading. And he would have to follow the same course now. Whatever Least asked him about—military science, space technology, some nasty and brutal incident in Earth history—Ethan would have to tell the truth about it, while maintaining the illusion they crafted so carefully.

The material that he and Markus and Maurha had put together had been designed to make the Devlin underestimate Humans, make Humans look weak, unresourceful, uncourageous. They had *tried* to be clever, tried to outsmart the aliens as best they could. But Humans hadn't had much practice at being sneaky in a long time. Had they been as smart as they thought they had been? Ethan was suddenly scared, scared of Least, scared of the mistakes he might make.

If Least asked the wrong sort of question, or if Ethan gave the wrong sort of answer, the game would be over here and now. But he had no choice but to do his best and answer whatever the question was. "What is it you want to know about?" he asked.

"Tell me," said Least, "everything you know about—kites."

TICK-TOCK

"If we could come to order," said Giotto. "The negotiation team has only forty-eight minutes left on their break before the next session starts, and we have a lot of ground to cover before then." The eight Human members of the team took their seats around the conference table.

"Thank you," said Giotto. "A good morning's work," he said. "A very good morning's work. The kites are working far better than I had dared hope."

Roberto smiled. Kites. Bits of string and cloth and paper. Mere toys. Why take the Humans seriously if they wasted their time playing foolish games with such toys?

But kites were toys that went up into the air, toys that looked down from above—and could, for example, see the Devlin Embassy. They were toys that could carry small devices—such as cameras, motion detectors, infrared sensors. And fiber-optic cable made an admirable kite line, while providing a virtually undetectable means of sending signals up and down between the kite and the ground. Roberto had gotten the idea from reading about man-carrying kites used to carry observers on nineteenth-century battlefields. Once that was in his head, attaching modern, magical eyes and ears and detectors to the old-fashioned toys was an obvious next step.

"All right, then," said Giotto, once the group had come to order. "What I propose to do is run the whole sequence, in chronological order, showing whatever view or imagery that will illustrate the point under discussion. If I may begin?"

The main lights faded, and the wallscreen came to life, showing the brow of Human Hill, with the Embassy in the background. "I have arbitrarily assigned local dawn as elapsed time zero," said Giotto. "Here we are at elapsed time eight minutes, and the launching of the kites—four of them ordinary toys, there as camouflage, and the other four equipped with all manner of sensors and cameras." One after the other, a blue box kite, a red diamond kite, a bright yellow manta-kite, and all the rest soared up into the air.

The image changed to a view from a kite camera, looking down on the ground. The view swiveled and bobbled for a few moments before locking in on Blackback Island and zooming in on a cluster of buildings.

"Elapsed time, fifteen minutes—all eight kites properly launched, and the four spy kites all sending back information. As you can see, we get a good view of the Devlin compound. We start collecting useful data, which we will discuss later."

The image faded out, then faded in again, showing roughly the same view, but with the light somewhat changed with the rising of the local sun, Swampwarmer. Tiny figures came out of one of the buildings. "Elapsed time, two hours, twelve minutes. The Devlin emerge from their Embassy. Five of them board an aircar and land here on Negotiation Island." The view shifted to a long-range camera atop the Human Embassy, looking down and zooming in on the area around Parley Pavilon. "Elapsed time, two hours and sixteen minutes. Our negotiation team—Johan, Marget, Suza, and Torry—walk down to the Pavilion. The K'lugu arrive shortly thereafter. The Devlin disembark, and it is clear they have noticed the kites. They point at them, and seem to discuss them. The Devlin called Least overhears Johan explaining them to the K'lugu, as we had hoped he would." Another cut, to the same view a few minutes later. "Two hours, twenty minutes. Least seems to be talking with Third and Fourth. All the Devlin seem concerned about the kites. Third tells Least something and Least departs at once in the aircar. Two hours, thirty minutes. The negotiation session is called to order."

"And wasn't *that* fun," said Marget. "Prime spent the whole morning still trying to bully us. She demanded all sorts of things. Free passage for Devlin through our sally port network. No tariffs on Devlin goods, but high ones for Human goods. Supremacy of Devlin law on neutral territory."

"In your opinion, how did the Devlin behave?" asked Giotto.

"Nervous," said Marget. "The kites bothered them."

"Let's move on," said Johan.

The view cut away again, to a shot from an embassy camera. "Two hours, forty minutes. The last of the kites is tied off and allowed to fly unattended, while the remaining four 'off-duty' team members—Ahna, Roberto, Adam, and Aaron, start 'playing' on Human Hill, in plain view of the negotiators. They play catch, and then tag, and then a number of games even I couldn't identify. You'll have to tell me about them sometime. In any event, as planned, the more playful and childish they act, the better, so as to make the kites, and what will come later tonight, seem more believable. I might add they do a good job."

"We sure got our exercise," Aaron said with a laugh.

"Moving on," said Giotto, "here we come to the

most crucial sequence." The view jumped back to one of the kite-cams. "Two hours, twenty-five minutes. Least arrives back at the Devlin compound, and immediately enters, not the main Embassy building, but this smaller structure off to one side. It is the right size and shape to house a t-port terminal. He does not emerge until three hours, fifteen minutes, elapsed time. He immediately reboards the aircar, flies back to Negotiation Island, lands, gets out, and has an animated discussion with Third. Third talks with the other Devlin. And, commencing at that moment, the Devlin plainly become more relaxed. They stop glancing over their heads at the kites."

"And they stopped taking us even a little bit seriously," said Torry. "All of a sudden, we weren't negotiators—we were little kids again. Just what we wanted them to think."

"The more they underestimate us, the better," said Giotto. "But that is not the main point. When Least leaves, they are bothered by the kites, and dealing with you more or less as equals. After he returns and tells Third something, they stop doing both things. It's hard not to conclude that he went somewhere to check on our story about kites and toys and whether it was believable that playful, carefree Human children would frolic on a hillside."

"Don't you think we ought to go wherever he did?" asked Adam with a grin.

"It's a nice idea," said Johan. "Let's see if we can make it work. Giotto, what about the Devlin security system? Have you gotten anything useful off the kites' sensors?"

"Quite a bit," said Giotto. "We now have an up-to-date map of their compound. Furthermore, we seem to have spotted some holes in their security arrangements. Judging from the readings off our sensors, they rely on sending low-ranking Devlin on patrol, and on various sorts of technology sensors that detect radio signals, electric output, refined metal, and so on."

"Aren't they using body heat or motion detectors?" asked Marget.

"No," said Giotto, "and for a good reason." The wallscreen shifted to another view off a kite-cam. "Let me just zoom in a bit," said Giotto, and the image of Blackback Island swelled up until it more than filled the screen. Giotto shifted the view again, until a rocky stretch of shoreline became visible.

The shore was alive with what appeared to be two or three species of seal or sea lion. Except seals and sea lions did not have beaks, or crests of vestigial feathers. The huge creatures were moving around on the rocks, galumphing along the shore, diving into the waves, and leaping from the sea back onto land. Two bulls started butting each other's chests and wrestling around. A half dozen young ones were chasing each other about the rocks. "With all that going on, a motion-detection system isn't going to be much use."

"What about their robots?"

A grainy, overenlarged still shot popped up on the screen. It was a frame from a kite-cam, plainly showing two Devlin carrying a robot on an improvised stretcher, heading toward one of the buildings in the compound. "They aren't working too well," Giotto said dryly. "I suspect their robots and other electronics are suffering from corrosion caused by the salt sea air. I have noticed a slight corrosion problem in my own systems, and in the other robots, but we have been able to compensate with no trouble. It would appear, however, that the Devlin robots weren't designed with the seaside in mind."

"The Devlin don't like the water, that's for sure," said Ahna. "You should have seen the looks on their faces when the K'lugu left the morning session and went for a swim. It was like they were too horrified to be

185

disgusted. They won't think of us coming through the water at them.''

"All of this is useful," said Giotto. "We will be able to use it to refine our plans. But now, time grows short. The afternoon session is about to begin."

"We'll go talk some more," said Johan as he stood up. "You 'off-duty' types have fun."

"We'll find something to keep us busy," Ahna said. "See you this evening."

The afternoon negotiating session began at the appointed hour, but it was little more than a shouting match, with Prime doing most of the shouting. By the time the meeting drew toward its end, Johan had a splitting headache, and it was all he could do to keep his temper.

And it would seem that Prime's mood was no better than Johan's. "I grow tired of this!" Prime shouted. "Transit rights, tariff regulations, security arrangements, border demarcation—no matter what I speak of, your answer is the same. Is there no issue between us that you can agree to by yourselves, without saying we must discuss it with your mommies and daddies back on Earth?"

Johan resisted the temptation to make a rude comment about Prime's parents, and spoke in a low, calm voice. "There are many such issues, noble Prime. They are things we must agree to before our seniors, *our* Primes, will be willing to settle any of these other matters. These include diplomatic immunity, the exchange of ambassadors, basic issues of jurisdiction, and an agreed agenda of issues for Meeting Two on Earth." *In other words, all the things both sides agreed to talk about when we set up this meeting*, Johan thought sourly.

"Trivial matters, all of them," Prime said. "We can dispose of them all at once."

"These matters are not trivial, noble Prime," said Clearwater. "As our youthful Human friends might put it, until both sides agree to the same set of rules, how can they possibly play the game together?''

''Life is more than games, K'lugu!'' Prime snapped.

''True enough,'' said Clearwater. ''And some games are played, not for sport, but in deadly earnest. Diplomacy is such a game. But the day is done. Let us rest, and return in the morning, refreshed and ready to start again. Do Humans and Devlin agree to adjourn for the day?''

''Gladly!'' Prime snarled. ''I am weary of all this.''

''Agreed,'' said Johan.

''Yes,'' said Marget. ''We should leave as soon as possible. We are eager to begin our night-flight sports.''

Prime looked at the Humans in annoyed surprise. ''*More* games?'' she asked.

''Oh, yes,'' said Torry. ''We greatly enjoy aircar races. Flying by night over these islands will be most exciting.''

''You are a most frivolous people,'' said Prime as she stood up. ''Why do you expect anyone else in the universe to take you seriously?'' And with that she turned and walked away, without waiting for an answer.

Just wait, Johan said to himself. *Just wait until tonight, and you might find out why.*

FOUR BY SEA

"**G**ood luck out there," Adam said, offering his hand to Johan.

Johan took Adam's hand and shook it vigorously. "Thanks," he said. "But we're the ones with the easy part. You're the ones taking all the risks."

But you'll be the ones inviting the Devlin to shoot at you, Adam thought. On the other hand, his ground team would be facing dangers of its own. "Well, good luck to us, too, then," he said, and left it at that. Johan turned toward his aircar. It had taken a little doing to get eight aircars down from the *Franklin* but they were vital to the plan.

Anyone monitoring the aircars in flight would likely assume all eight were being piloted by Humans. That assumption would only be half-right. Giotto was to fly one car directly, and operate three more by remote control.

If eight cars, and presumably eight Humans, were in the sky, then no one would be looking for *four* of those Humans to be going for a midnight swim. At least, that was what they were all hoping.

The aircars were Honeybees, small, wingless, egg-shaped fliers. Each Bee was a bit under two meters long and one meter wide, painted in black-and-yellow stripes, with a mirrored one-way bubble cockpit. Adam had not the faintest idea how the things flew without wings or visible engines, but they did.

Giotto was in the cockpit of his car, with the three others slaved to his ship and ready to go. The sally port inducer, the whole reason for the trip, was tucked away in the aft cargo compartment of Giotto's car, along with a few other handy gadgets he was supposed to deliver at the other end. Marget, Torry, and Suza were already strapped into their vehicles, waiting for Johan.

"Off we go then," said Johan cheerfully. "Have a nice swim!" He waved once more, climbed into his Honeybee, and swung the bubble top closed.

Ahna, Adam, Aaron, and Roberto watched as the eight Bees shot straight up into the air, one after the other, arranging themselves into a "V" formation. Then, suddenly, all eight ships blazed with light, the yellow stripes glowing, as if lit from the inside, bright enough that it hurt to look at them. Holding formation, they moved faster and faster, until they were nothing more than streaks of yellow light blazing across the sky.

"*That* ought to attract the Devlin's attention," said Ahna.

"It had better," said Aaron. "Come on. Let's get this over with."

"Roberto," said Ahna, "this is where you take over."

Roberto smiled broadly. "With pleasure. Follow me."

They made their way down to the shore, moving carefully in the near darkness. Fortunately, the Brightmorning Nebula cast enough light to see by. Johan and the others might be flying the latest thing in high-tech UFOs, but no one on Adam's team had so much as a flashlight. If the Devlin were using tech-detectors, then it was vital that the ground team made sure not to have any sort of technology on them. They had even gotten rid of their gadget-loaded s-suits. The four of them wore loose-fitting gray cotton shorts, gray tee shirts, and natural-rubber sandals. Each of them had a length of cotton cord and one cloth bag. They carried nothing else at all.

They moved downhill past the Parley Pavilion to the fine, sandy beach at the water's edge. Roberto walked out into the water until it was about ankle-deep and smiled broadly. "It's warm," he said. "Beautiful. Beautiful."

He lifted one foot, and then the other, taking off his sandals. "All right," he said, "let's make a float-belt for Aaron." Roberto, Ahna, and Adam were all strong swimmers, but Aaron had never been in more water than would fit in a bathtub. The others took off their sandals and handed them to Roberto. He used a length of rope to thread the sandals together into a sort of a life preserver. Ahna helped him strap the contraption around a worried-looking Aaron.

"Does anyone really think this is going to work?" Aaron asked.

"Sure thing," said Roberto, supremely confident. "That rubber floats very well. Buoyant, that's the fancy word. You'll float like a cork. Besides, the rest of us will keep an eye on you. Just keep paddling, and we'll get there. No problems."

"Speaking of words," said Ahna. "It's time for us to stop using them. Time to take off our broca amplifiers."

Roberto's smile vanished. "I do not like this," he said.

"None of us do," said Ahna. "But our broca-amps would set off every tech-detector the Devlin have. Giotto will dump fresh ones for us when he drops off the inducer."

Roberto frowned. "I know," he said. "I know." He turned, and looked out across the water, toward Blackback Island, where the Devlin were, then looked toward his friends again. "The current is moving slowly, left to right, here by the shore," he said. "But I think it will be stronger in the open water, and we must be careful of it. I will lead. Watch the direction I swim, and follow after. Aaron, you are after me, then Ahna and Adam. Good luck to us all." He walked back out of the water, onto the shore. "Take it off, if you please, Ahna."

Ahna reached up and gently took Roberto's broca-amp, then removed Adam's and Aaron's.

Adam felt a bit dizzy as the amp came off, and a disturbing sense of loss swept over him. Without the amps, would they be able to communicate well enough?

Adam took Ahna's amp off and handed it to her. She wrapped all four of the amps in her carry-bag, then walked back away from the shore, until she was well above the high-water mark, and stashed the bag in a cleft in the rocks. She pointed very emphatically to where the bag was. The three boys nodded vigorously. They understood.

One after another, they waded out into the warm water and set out for the opposite shore.

Aaron was terrified. It didn't make *sense* that there was so much water. How could there be so much? He had thought the ocean looked big from up on top of Human Hill, but it looked a thousand times larger when you were *in* it. How in the world—even a world like Bog-water—were they supposed to cross all that distance in *water* just by paddling along? People weren't supposed to *float*. Still, the silly life-vest rig was holding him up pretty well. He wasn't going to sink. But no matter what Roberto said, the water was *cold*, much colder than any bath he had ever taken.

Weren't there *things* in the water? Fish, and sharks, swimming in the dark? Things that would eat four Human kids as not more than a nice little snack, maybe?

He wasn't moving very fast, and he knew he was holding up the others. He could see Roberto ahead of him, moving through the water very easily. Aaron didn't like the idea of slowing things down. He kicked his legs and paddled his arms harder, and struggled to keep his head above water. But how, out in the middle of so much water, could they tell if they were moving at all? He was so low in the water he could barely *see* Blackback Island.

He turned to look behind them, and was surprised to see how far away Negotiation Island already was. Half of him was pleased to have made so much progress already, while the other half couldn't help but think how far out in the water they were. But they couldn't turn back. Not now.

Aaron paddled grimly onward.

Roberto felt wonderfully alive, as if he was part of the sea himself, one with the waters that flowed around him. Warm and clean, the gentle waves rolled past them as the currents tugged them toward Blackback Island. The splashing of the water as the four swimmers kicked and paddled seemed the only sound in all the world.

Roberto checked behind him. Adam and Ahna seemed to be doing all right. Aaron was struggling along, doing better than Roberto had expected, but he was going to wear himself out pretty fast. Roberto was not unduly worried. The life vest would keep Aaron's head above water, and, if need be, he would be able to get Aaron to shore.

He felt a slight change in the movement of the water around him. They had left one current and entered another. Now, instead of pushing them toward Blackback, the water was pulling them along, almost parallel to its shore. Roberto shifted course slightly, tacking into the current and swimming harder. He shifted to a backstroke for a moment to check behind again to make sure his three friends were still with him.

The water was colder now, and the waves choppier. The wind was kicking up a little at their backs. Roberto began to hear the crash of surf on shore up ahead. Blackback was close, and getting closer.

They were coming in just north of where he had intended, but that wasn't a problem. However, two things still worried Roberto.

The side of Blackback Island that faced Negotiation Island had no smooth, sandy beaches for the convenience of troublemakers trying to sneak ashore. It was all slippery rock shelves. Worse, powerful waves were crashing into that unforgiving shoreline. Someone could get seriously hurt trying to scramble up out of the water.

The second thing he worried about was the residents of that shore, the enormous seal-like creatures. How would the huge animals react to four humans climbing out of the sea right in the middle of their rookery?

The wind shifted again, and blew from Blackback out toward the swimmers, carrying sounds—and smells—from the shore. One whiff of that pungent reek told Roberto the seal-birds were a lot like other seabirds in at least one way.

The shore was coming closer, closer. A shore current pulled at them, drawing them in toward the black, near-invisible rocks. Roberto wanted to shout a warning, to tell his friends to be careful, but without the magic word machines on their heads, they would not understand him. Surely all of them could see it all as well as he could. And he would have to go ashore first, to be able to help the others.

A wave caught him and threw him forward, in toward the rocks. He swam as hard as he could against the surging water, dragging himself back out of the cresting wave. He trod water for a minute, judging the surf and the timing of the waves.

Roberto saw his moment and lunged forward, catching the tail end of a wave, riding it in just behind the crest.

The hard black shore leapt closer, looming up before him. He scrambled to get his feet under him, and slammed the side of his ankle into a hidden outcropping of rock.

But the surging, eddying, rushing water did not give him time to feel the pain. Another, smaller, wave caught him in the back, and it was all he could do to avoid being knocked head over heels. His reflexes took over, and somehow he got his feet under him—

—and landed, standing upright, in the waist-deep water by the shore, not at all sure how he had gotten there. A jagged rock cliff, two or three meters tall, rose before him. A bigger wave would surely have thrown him straight into that cruel wall.

The cooling wind caught at his bare skin and his thin shirt as he turned around and looked out over the water, straining to see his friends in the dark surf. There! There was Aaron, struggling, making no effort to time the waves or ride one in, but simply paddling straight in toward shore.

A wave, a big one, was coming up behind Aaron, cresting high. It lifted him up, and crashed over his head. Aaron vanished from sight for a moment before reappearing again, bobbing to the surface, still grimly struggling forward.

The next wave was going to catch him, and catch him hard. Aaron had not the least idea there was a big wave behind him, and there was no way to warn him.

Roberto waded through the rushing surf as fast as he could, trying to get to where Aaron was going to land, racing against the incoming wave that was about to catch his friend from behind.

The wave crashed down, catching Aaron in the back of the head. The roaring water buried him and threw him toward the unyielding shore. Roberto lunged to the right, making one last desperate attempt to put himself between Aaron and the cliff face.

A whirling body pinwheeled toward him in the surf as the wave nearly lifted Aaron up over him. Roberto planted his feet and grabbed on to an ankle as his friend flashed past him. He managed to stand up against the crash of the wave, still holding on to Aaron, but the backwash knocked him over and made him lose his grip.

The two boys spluttered and gasped as they got to their feet and stood in the waist-high water.

"*Danke*," said Aaron, but the word meant nothing to Roberto.

"*Vai, agora!*" he shouted to his friend. *Go, now!* Aaron would not understand, but Roberto pointed urgently toward the top of the rock face. Aaron nodded and started to climb, quickly finding plenty of handholds.

Roberto turned his attention back toward the sea, to watch for Ahna and Adam—and was bowled over for a second time as both of them came tumbling in on the same wave. They all crashed into one another. Roberto was thrown against the rocks. His body slammed into the cliff, and the back of his skull bounced off the rocks. He fell forward, half-stunned, into the raging surf.

"Roberto!" a voice cried out. Four strong hands seized his arms. Ahna and Adam pulled his head above water and dragged him toward the shore cliff. Adam put Roberto's hands on the first handholds, and gave him a boost up.

Still dizzy and disoriented, Roberto forced himself to move before another wave hit and chewed them all to pieces against the rocks. *Vai, agora!* he told himself.

Adam and Ahna were right behind him, and followed him up the cliff. At its top was a shelf of rock a good fifty meters wide and perhaps twice as long. They had managed to come in at the highest, steepest part of the shore. The cliff slumped down on both sides of them, allowing far easier access to the water.

Aaron was there, waiting for them—but he was not

alone. The shore was covered with huge, fat, blubbery, sleeping seal-birds.

The smallest of them, obviously the babies, were a bit smaller than Roberto. The largest ones were at least four meters long, and easily weighed more than all four Human teenagers put together.

At first, they looked for all the world like the pictures of seals Roberto had seen in a picture book about the Arctic, but it didn't take long to spot the differences. The seal-birds were covered in thin, hairlike brown-and-black feathers, with bright orange feathers just back of their eyes. The largest ones, which Roberto guessed were bulls, also sported bright red plumes atop their heads. Their wings were mere front flippers, barely large enough to support their weight on the ground, let alone in the air. But their hind legs were powerful-looking, ending in bright yellow webbed feet that were well adapted to swimming.

And the seal-birds had beaks—sharp, hooked, bright orange beaks, like an eagle's or a hawk's, but far larger. Probably any of the bulls could slice through a Human arm or leg with one bite. Fortunately, the seal-birds were remarkably sound sleepers, and had not taken the slightest notice of the Humans.

They were also the most remarkably *loud* sleepers, which might help explain it. The rookery seemed to shake with snorts, snores, bellows, squawks, caws, and odd wheedle-tweet noises from the babies. Now and then a bull would turn over in his sleep, rolling half onto a cow or a pup, who would let out a hoot of protest, then wriggle free, only to land on someone else, setting off another squawk—all without any of them waking up.

The racket was enough to drown out the roar of the surf, and almost enough to make Roberto forget the complicated stink of the place. The rookery stank as badly as any colony of gulls back home in Fortaleza. The smell of rotting fish and the stench of a filthy chicken coop did battle with a rich yeasty odor that reminded Roberto of when the chief slave's private still had blown up.

Aaron stood there, waiting, in wide-eyed alarm, the sandal life vest still around his chest. As soon as Roberto, Ahna, and Adam were all up the low cliff, he pressed a finger to his lips, signaling for silence. The other three nodded vigorous agreement. Roberto, still woozy from being bounced off the rocks, had hoped to be able rest a bit before moving on, but this was plainly no place to stay any longer than they had to.

Adam took the lead, and started threading his way through the snoring giants. It was possible—just—to walk between the creatures here and there, but twice Adam found their way blocked, and they had to backtrack. At last they came to the foot of a grassy slope and clambered up it, leaving the seal-birds to their rookery.

Climbing the slope, they found themselves at the edge of a broad meadow. There, up ahead, by the light of the Brightmorning Nebula, they could plainly see the circle of hills that hid the Devlin Embassy.

Adam pointed toward a line of trees on the other side of the meadow. Roberto nodded his agreement. The trees looked like a much better place to hide than an open meadow. They started moving toward them at a quick walk. Once they were there, they could rest and recover before they moved on uphill.

The good news was that, so far, everything was going according to plan.

The bad news was that, so far, they had only done the easy parts.

EIGHT BY AIR

The ocean was coming up fast beneath him. Johan could hear the roar of the air past the hull of his Honeybee as he dived straight for the cold, hard waters below. A scant two hundred meters above the waves, he pulled up hard on the control stick. His Honeybee pulled level a bare ten meters above the ocean. Johan yanked back on the stick again and opened up the throttle. The little aircar went into a power climb, rushing up into the dark sky, toward the glory of the Brightmorning Nebula.

He checked his heads-up displays, and saw that the rest of the aircars were all over the sky, zigging and zagging wildly all over the place. Good. Good. He rolled left out of his climb and leveled out. He checked the time. Just over an hour since they had taken off from Human Hill and started their performance. Better give Roberto's team just a little longer to get ashore and get themselves organized.

In the hour since takeoff, Johan had, quite deliberately, done some of the stupidest flying of his life. He smiled to think how his parents would react if they saw it.

Races, chases, acrobatic stunts, flying at wavetop level, buzzing Human Hill so low they were actually looking *up* at the top floor of the Embassy—any of it would have been enough to get his flier's permit revoked in a heartbeat back home. And the rest of his team had been no more sensible about any of it. If anything, Giotto and his three slaved-in aircars were more reckless than the Humans.

But it's all in a good cause, he told himself. The Devlin *had* to be tracking them, watching every barrel roll and power dive. And the more they looked at the eight aircars in the northern sky, the less likely it was they'd have time to look for four weary swimmers struggling ashore at the south end of their island. And the longer they watched the eight ships being flown idiotically, the more likey they would come to think Humans were too silly, too giddy, too childish to take seriously. A species that filled its days with kites and games of tag, and its nights with aircar racing, was not much of a threat.

Especially when they were stupid enough to land on the wrong island. *Even stupider when you do it on purpose*, Johan thought, and tried not to think about what sort of defensive system the Devlin had.

Johan flipped the intercom to the all-formation circuit and spoke, mostly for the benefit of any Devlin who might be listening. "Okay, people, time to bring it on home and get to bed."

"Oh, gosh, do we *have* to?" Marget asked, managing to get a remarkably convincing whine into her voice. "It's still *ear*ly."

Johan had to force himself not to laugh. "Come on, now," he said in the sternest voice he could muster. "We've got a big day tomorrow. Move into a V formation, and we'll start heading back." The other seven Honeybees broke off from their aerobatics and homed in on him. He waited until the last of them—Marget's ship—got into formation, then he came about to the south, and started the return to Negotiation Island, leading the rest of the Honeybees back.

He watched his navigation displays as he made the turn. The map overlay showed they were headed out over the water. He adjusted his heading, banking left, until they were lined up on Negotiation Island—and kept right on banking, until they were on a direct heading for Blackback Island. "Negotiation Island, dead ahead," he said. "Let's do one last low pass over the Embassy, and see if we can scare Giotto a little."

If the Devlin were tracking them and listening in—and Johan would be astounded if they weren't—they were about to realize that the Human aircars were headed for a landing on the wrong island. And if they were tracking them, they'd be sure to—

The comm system crackled and spluttered for a moment before the growling voice of the Devlin's translating machine came on the line. "Human ships! You are off course. You are about to enter Devlin Embassy airspace. Turn back! Turn back!"

Johan ignored the call, did not reply, and did not change course. He tried not to think of the guns that might be trained on them already. He fervently prayed that Marget, Torry, and Suza would have nerve enough to stay on course. If they all flew on together, it would look like they weren't receiving the Devlin signal. If even one of them broke off, the Devlin would be far more likely to see through the trick.

"Human ships! This is Devlin Embassy calling—"

Johan shut off the comm system. There was Blackback Island, right in front of them and getting closer every second. The sweat was standing out on his forehead, and somehow his stomach was suddenly cold. If the Devlin panicked and decided to shoot at them, there was nothing, nothing in the world the Honeybees could do to defend themselves. He was a flying target, aiming himself straight for the Devlin's crosshairs. It took all of

Johan's force of will to keep from turning and running, right back to Negotiation Island.

But he kept on, and the rest of the formation stayed with him. He starting shedding altitude, dropping lower and lower as they came in toward Blackback. There! The lights of the Devlin Embassy compound, right where the image data from the kite-cams said they should be.

Lower, lower. If they were going to shoot, they'd have shot by now. Maybe. Maybe they were just waking up Prime to get permission—and Prime didn't seem the sort to wake up in a good mood.

Lower. Closer. Ease back on airspeed. Get set for the low pass. If buzzing their Embassy didn't drive them crazy, Johan couldn't think what would.

Lower. Closer. Slower. His heart was pounding in his chest, and his hand held the flight stick in a death grip. Right at them. Right into the crosshairs.

Lower. Slower. They crossed the northern shoreline of Blackback Island doing a bare two hundred kilometers an hour, a mere hundred meters up. The rolling hills of the island rose up to meet them. Fifty meters up. A hundred ninety kilometers an hour. One-eighty. One-seventy. Johan slowed to 150 kph. Slow enough. *Plenty* slow enough.

They came to the brow of the last hill, passed over it—and saw the Devlin Embassy compound, dead ahead. And suddenly 150 kilometers an hour seemed very fast indeed. The ground and the building blurred past them, almost too fast to be seen.

Johan wheeled his Honeybee around to the right, the rest of the aircars following as they came about and headed toward the Embassy again, slowed down and prepared to hover in for a landing. *No weapons fire yet*, Johan thought. *Maybe we'll be all right. They haven't given us a warning shot—*

BLAM!

The sky lit up to either side of his aircar just as he

brought it into stationary hover. BLAM! BLAM! Two more shots, one to either side of him as his Honeybee hung there, motionless, in the middle of the air.

He cut left and brought the ship down fast, falling more than flying as the ground rose up to meet it.

The Honeybee touched down hard, with a bone-jarring crash so powerful it actually bounced up again, clear of the ground.

More explosions lit the sky, and Johan watched in horror as one of the shots scored a hit on a Honeybee. The explosion was blindingly bright. The stricken aircar's lights died as it lost power. It dropped like a stone and slammed into the ground. The rest of the Honeybees landed safely, and Johan gave thanks for that as he struggled with his flight harness. He got free of it, popped open the canopy of his aircar and stood up in the cockpit.

The canopy popped open on the wrecked Honeybee and the pilot—Marget—jumped out and started to run. She hadn't gotten more than a few meters when the aircar burst into flames. She threw herself flat against the ground just as her Honeybee exploded, sending a tongue of flame lancing into the sky, lighting up the Embassy compound as bright as day. Johan was thrown back down into his cockpit by the blast. Something pinged off his flight helmet hard enough to stun him. It took a second for him to come back to himself enough to climb out of his Honeybee and run to where Marget had fallen.

He dropped down on his knees next to her just as she was rolling over and sitting up. "Are you all right?" he asked.

She nodded weakly. Her face was deathly pale, and she had a bad cut on her right cheek, and it looked like there was blood seeping out of the shoulder of her s-suit. "I—I think so," she said. "I can walk, I think. Let's go. I can fly out with you in your aircar."

He looked at her carefully, by the light of her burning aircar. She looked more or less okay, but he was no judge, and he didn't like the idea of moving an injury victim. But what choice did he have? "All right," he said. "Come on."

He helped her to her feet and steadied her as they walked.

"Stand where you are!" an angry voice cried out. The Embassy's compound lights blazed to life. The eight Devlin had them surrounded, weapons at the ready. Prime herself had an extremely lethal-looking gun pointed straight at Johan's head.

"What are you doing in our Embassy?" Johan demanded. "You can't take over and just start shooting at us!"

"You have invaded *our* Embassy," Prime shouted back. "You fools are on the wrong island. Don't you even have eyes and brains enough to see that much?"

"What are you talking about?" Johan asked, working hard to sound angry, and not scared. "And what gave you the right to shoot at us?" But it didn't really matter how he acted, as long as they all looked at him, at Johan making a fool of himself—anything, just so they didn't notice the four members of Roberto's team, out there in the dark somewhere, slipping through the inner security perimeter. Just so long as they didn't notice the special compartment on Giotto's airship opening up, and the camouflaged cargo container, looking very much like a medium-sized boulder, that would come rolling out of it.

He set about making sure the argument went on for quite a while.

INFILTRATION

Roberto's team moved slowly and quietly up the hill toward the Devlin embassy. Roberto's head was pounding, and he could feel a fat bump forming on the back of his skull, where he had smacked it against the rocks. It should have been an easy walk through the woods, but Roberto had never done anything half so nerve-wracking. Every snap of a twig, every rustle of a leaf, was enough to set his heart pounding, enough to make him imagine the biggest of those Devlin monsters spotting them and giving chase.

They came over the brow of a hill, and Roberto caught sight of the faintest glimmer of light from up ahead somewhere. He paused a moment to get his bearings. He had studied all available maps and images of the island carefully, and after only a moment's thought, he was confident he knew where they were. The Devlin Embassy was only a few hundred meters ahead, hidden by the trees. Satisfied, he nodded and turned to the others.

"*Estamos perto agora*," he said. *We're close now.* He knew full well they couldn't understand him, but the frustration of not talking was getting to be too much. He sat down on the ground, and gestured for the others to do the same. "*Agora, nos esperamos*," he told them. *Now, we wait.*

Adam couldn't decide if he was too scared to be tired, or too tired to be scared. The swim over had been a lot rougher than he had figured, and things hadn't gotten that much easier on dry land. At least now they were in under the trees, more or less hidden from view, so they'd have a chance to rest.

The ground seemed to shake as the V formation of Honeybees swept over their heads at treetop level. Adam jumped to his feet and watched as the eight aircars banked around and headed in for the return pass. They thundered back over their heads, even lower than before, and Adam watched them in slack-jawed astonishment, Ahna and Adam by his side.

"*Vamos! Vamos!*" Roberto was shouting, gesturing for them to get up, get moving. Adam was embarrassed. He was the one who lived in a world full of flying machines. But it was Roberto, the one who had never seen such a thing before a week ago, who kept his head. The whole point of the flyover was to provide a diversion, get the Devlin looking the other way long enough for the four of them to sneak in close.

They got moving, doing their best to move quickly and quietly through the underbrush. Adam tripped once over a root, and another time over a rock, adding to his growing collection of cuts and bruises, but both times he was on his feet and moving again almost at once.

BLAM! An explosion lit up the forest. Adam's heart froze. The Devlin were shooting. Silence for a moment, then two smaller blasts, and more silence.

Just as he had decided it was over, the last, the biggest, the worst of the blasts tore through the forest, and night turned into day. The ground trembled beneath his feet. He could hear the seal-birds at the shore bellowing in fear, and the loud splashes of heavy bodies belly-flopping into the water.

They dared not waste this moment, this chance to move forward. Whatever risk, whatever loss that blast represented, it would be wasted if they didn't take advantage of it to *move*.

The others knew it as well as he did, and all four of them scrambled forward, getting as close as they dared. The forest blocked their view, but the glare of a fire flared and flickered through the trees. Adam could smell burning metal and plastic, and he could hear voices— Prime and Johan, it sounded like. He was straining to hear what they said as he walked when his foot caught on another root. He pitched forward into the dirt, trying to land quietly.

Adam lay there, stock-still for at least half a minute, before he even dared lift his head and look up.

And when he did, he saw the grandest possible stroke of luck staring right at him. A landed Honeybee sat not fifty yards from where he was—and its running lights, those garish yellow stripes that gave the craft its name, were out. The whole point of using Bees was that they drew attention to themselves. Only one Bee was supposed to have its lights out at landing, for the very good reason it was the one they wanted the Devlin to overlook. Giotto's Bee. The one with the cargo carrier aboard. The whole point of landing all eight ships was to provide a big, loud, diversion so that one Bee could deliver the equipment for Roberto's team.

As Adam watched, the rear cargo hatch of the Bee slid silently open, and what looked like a lump of rock rolled out onto the ground. If it had been delivered much closer to Adam, it would have rolled on top of him. He was vastly relieved to have spotted it. Everything they needed, from the sally port inducer to food, fresh clothes, and replacement broca-amps, was waiting inside that phony rock.

Just then, he saw a flicker of movement not more than twenty yards from the other side of the Bee. It was a big, four-armed figure, carrying a rifle-shaped gun and peering into the woods. It stood there, staring out into the darkness, almost straight at Adam, for at least half a minute, before it turned and moved back in toward the center of the clearing, where Johan and Prime were still arguing.

Close as the cargo container was, it might as well have been back on Earth for all the good it could do. There were eight heavily armed and very unhappy Devlin in the woods up ahead.

And until they went away, Adam didn't dare do anything but lie still right where he had fallen.

LOST

Adam woke up, but did not so much as open his eyes for the better part of a minute. Instead, he lay where he was, and *listened.*

Maybe the story told by the noises in the night was finally over. He heard no voices, no shouting, no tramping feet passing too close for comfort. No sounds of Honeybee aircars lifting off in darkness, no crackle of fire or smell of burning machinery from the Bee that would never lift again. No nightmare dream-shouts that might be real or might not, no dreams that merged into reality, or reality that drifted into terror-stricken dreams. Just the normal sounds and smells of an island morning. He could even hear the seal-birds bellowing their good mornings to each other, down at the shore.

Light. Even with his eyes still shut, he could see light through his eyelids. At long last, the real light of day was here. He had never passed a longer night.

He had not moved from where he had fallen the night before. Patrolling Devlin passed too close, a half dozen times, for that. But now, with morning coming on, there would be no darkness for concealment. It was time to get up and search for better cover.

He opened his eyes and lifted his head. All clear. Making sure to note the exact position of the disguised cargo container, he rose up onto his hands and knees and slowly looked around.

A pinecone, or the local equivalent, caught him square between the eyes.

He blinked, and tried to see where it had come from. He saw the barest flick of movement at the base of a big tree a few yards away. He got to his feet and crept toward it as quietly as he could. Aaron, Ahna, and Roberto were all there, crouched down on the other side of it.

Ahna grabbed him and pulled his ear close to her mouth. "Glad you moved finally. Thought you hurt," she said, in her clumsy twentieth-century English. He had almost forgotten she spoke a bit of his language. "Johan team fly out six hour ago. We see Devlin little from here since. We watch, think Devlin be leave soon," she went on. "Five be to go, three stay, we think. But three staying is inside." She looked at him. "You understanding?"

He nodded. "Yes. Good." They could see five of the Devlin were getting ready to leave for the daily meeting, and the other three were inside the Embassy at the moment. But there was something he needed to tell her. "I saw the cargo container. It's very close."

Her eyes widened. She grinned and nodded.

Aaron grabbed at them both and pulled them down. A dark shape moved across the sky, almost directly overhead. "Aircar go," Ahna whispered. "Look for us, or go see Johan?"

Adam shook his head and shrugged. "Your guess is as good as mine."

But the aircar circled once to gain altitude, then set off across the water. Adam let out a sigh of relief. Though there wasn't that much to be relieved about. After all, now they had to sneak into the Devlin Embassy compound.

"Time to go," Ahna whispered. "Cargo can?"

Adam nodded, and gestured for the others to follow him. He led them out from behind the tree, to the one rock in the woods that was no rock at all. He knelt beside it and started looking for the hidden button that would open it, but Ahna found it first. She gave it a twist to the right, another to the left, and then pushed it in. The top of the rock popped open.

There, on top of all the other gear, were the replacement broca-amps. The four lost no time helping each other get them on. Not being able to talk had made everything else almost impossibly difficult.

"Do they work?" Ahna asked in a whisper. "Do you all understand me?"

"Yes!" said the three boys in ragged unison.

"Thank the stars for that much," she said. "Much more of playing pantomime would have driven us all crazy. All right, let's get this gear out and go." There were four backpacks in the container, and each of them pulled one out and put it on. At the bottom of the container was the one thing that mattered most, the reason for everything else—the sally port inducer. It was basically spherical, about twenty inches across, with two carry-handles set into the top, a control panel on the side, and three stubby legs to hold it upright. Adam grabbed one handle, and Aaron the other. They both gave a good hard pull, and managed to lift it clear of the container. It was heavy—probably close to sixty pounds.

"We're not going to be too graceful carrying this around," Aaron muttered.

"As long as we get it where we need to get it," said Ahna.

"Fine," said Aaron. "So let's go, already, before our four-armed friends have a chance to grab us."

"With any luck, they'll all be glued to their detector screens, looking out past their security perimeter while we're already in," said Ahna. "They probably still have no idea we're here."

"Let's hope so," said Roberto. "But we must hurry. There will only be a few minutes before Least flies their aircar back. Come on."

Roberto led the way forward, toward the compound. Adam and Aaron went next, struggling along with the sally port inducer between them, and Ahna keeping watch to the rear.

They came upon the Devlin compound almost immediately. Adam was glad he hadn't known the night before just how close to it they had been.

The Devlin buildings were in a circular clearing surrounded by woods. Roberto gestured for them to halt at the edge of the woods, and circle around to the left. They drifted back into the trees before moving clockwise around the perimeter of the clearing. Adam was the first to spot the burnt-out wreckage of the Honeybee. Ahna gasped when she saw it, and the two other boys stared in silent shock. The aircar was nothing but ashes and wreckage. Adam couldn't see how anyone could have survived the crash and fire, but he saw no sign of a body. What had happened?

But there was no time. Roberto signaled the others to follow him along the perimeter of the compound.

At last they were as close as they were going to get to the low, bunkerlike building that they assumed held the t-port. *It had better be in there*, Adam thought. *If it isn't, the long trip we're planning is going to be awfully short.*

Roberto signaled them to kneel down. He studied the bunker for a long time before gesturing for them to stand up and get ready to go. The door of the bunker was plainly visible from any of the structures in the compound. If any Devlin in the Embassy building took it into his head to look out the window, they were doomed. There was nothing to do but trust to luck. Ahna took her backpack off, pulled what they had in the way of burglary tools out of it, and shoved them in her pockets. She pulled a pair of heavy gloves out of the pack, put them on, flashed a brave smile at the three boys, and ran across the clearing to the door. She knelt in front of it and got to work.

Adam, Aaron, and Roberto watched anxiously as Ahna pulled a laser cutter from her hip pocket and switched it on. The beam sliced into the metal door, sending a thin plume of smoke into the air. Ahna reached into the hole she had cut with her gloved hand and pulled back hard on something.

The door swung open, creaking on its hinges.

Roberto was running across the clearing toward the bunker before the door was open wide enough for him to get through it. Adam and Aaron were close behind him, moving as fast as they could with the sally port inducer slowing them down. They dived inside, hard on Roberto's heels, with Ahna close behind them. She pulled the door shut as gently as she could.

With the door closed, they could risk talking at least in whispers. "I don't think anyone would notice what I did to the door unless they were looking," Ahna said, "but the next time someone tries to open it, they are going to know we've been here."

"So let's keep going," said Aaron, and hooked his thumb at the t-port unit that stood in the center of the bunker. It looked a lot like the Human models—not surprising, considering that both species had received the technology from the mysterious Gift Givers. Maybe that family resemblance in the hardware would be enough to see them through to the end of this crazy scheme. It was the same sort of fancy-looking doorframe they had seen before, but on the other side of that frame, on the other side of the t-port link, they could see some sort of control room, full of consoles and blinking lights.

"All right," said Ahna, pointing at the room they

could see through the t-port. "That's almost certainly the bridge, or whatever they call it, of their support ship, their equivalent of the *Benjamin Franklin*. The Devlin agreed to the same rules we did—no more than eight of their people allowed in-system, and all of them required to live on Bogwater, but with a link to an uncrewed support ship in the outer regions of the system. We don't *think* they cheated, and if they didn't cheat, there isn't going to be anyone aboard to bother us. But if they *did* cheat, and we *do* get caught—we *don't* try to fight our way out. If they kill some of us, or we kill some of them, we could set off a war, and that's the last thing Earth needs. If we get caught, we surrender. Clear?"

"Clear," said Adam, and Roberto nodded.

"I don't like promising I won't fight back," said Aaron.

Adam felt the same way Aaron did, but it wasn't the time to argue the rules. "We're fighting back right now," he said. "But let's not make things worse when we're trying to make them better, okay?"

Aaron shrugged unhappily. "Okay, I guess."

"Then let's go," said Ahna. She stood up and led the way, walking straight into the t-port. Aaron and Adam, still hauling the inducer, went after her, with Roberto bringing up the rear. Adam felt a sharp jolt of pain, right behind his eyes, just as they went through the t-port. Ahna looked surprised, and rubbed her forehead "Ow," she said. "That's a bad one. Much worse than I've had before on an interplanetary t-port." It was plain to see it hit Roberto and Aaron just as badly.

But they didn't have time to worry about such things. "Never mind the headaches," said Aaron. "Where are we, and where do we go?"

"I don't know," said Ahna. "Give me a second." She examined the compartment they were in. It might have looked like a control room from the other side of the t-port, but from the inside it looked a lot like a cargo hold. The control panels they had seen from the other side were certainly complicated enough, but they were the only controls in the cavernous room. The place was big enough to play football in. Boxes, big boxes, of all sizes and shapes, all marked in Devlin script, were neatly stacked up in the center of the deck, with plenty of open space still left over. It was all gleaming white, very clean, very orderly.

The t-port itself, and the control panels, stood off to one side of the oversize chamber. The t-port was still active. From this side they could still see the interior of the Blackback Island t-port bunker through it.

Ahna looked around thoughtfully. "It looks like they just modified some sort of cargo carrier to serve as their support ship, instead of using a purpose-built embassy ship, the way we did with the *Franklin*. In fact, I'm pretty sure this is the only major compartment on this ship. I think the floors and walls and ceilings are the ship's outer hull." She pointed across the chamber. "But look at that," she said. It was a heavy, reinforced door with a little porthole-style window, and a set of wheels and levers just below the window. "That's *got* to be an airlock door. If the ship on the other side of the *Roanoke* sally port is like this one, we won't have any trouble at all deploying our sally port inducer."

"But how do we get where we're going? Where's *their* sally port?" asked Roberto. "On the *Franklin*, there was a whole room full of t-ports and sally ports. How are you supposed to get anywhere else except Bogwater if there is only one door?"

It was a good question, Adam thought as he looked around. But he'd have liked it even better if it had come with an answer.

THE ADVENTURE OF THE MUD-FLECKED
BUTTON

"**Y**our foolish and irresponsible acts have jeopardized this entire series of meetings!" Prime roared, pounding her fist down on the arm of her chair and glaring across the Pavilion at the impassive Human delegation. The day's discussions were off to a rousing start. In fact, they were picking up right where they had left off the night before, when the Human aircars had finally lifted off and flown away.

Least was tired, dead tired. He had been up all night long, shuttling back and forth between the Devlin Embassy and the *Roanoke* colonists. Prime had had a thousand questions for her captive Humans. Do Humans fly aircars at night for pleasure? Why do Humans keep arguing even when it is clear they are wrong? Are young Human males more likely to be belligerent? Are they often assigned as leaders? What sort of navigation systems do Human aircars use? None of it had been useful. The *Roanoke* survivors hadn't been able to provide many useful answers, and Least had no doubt the barrage of strange questions had destroyed all the trust he had struggled so hard to build up.

Least knew he ought to be getting back to the Embassy. There was a great deal of work to be done there. But he was too tired to move right away—and besides, he wanted to hear what the Humans had to say for themselves. Their antics of the night before had not made the least bit of sense.

"I do not, for one moment, believe that your aircars were off course," Prime went on. "You knew, you had to know, where you were landing, and that you were trespassing."

Johan, the eldest of the Human delegates, leaned forward in his chair. "And we do not, for one moment, believe you fired upon us by accident on the first day of our meetings. If we have no rights of safety, no place of privacy and security, then why should you have them?"

"I am weary of your tired old urging about all your tedious rules for diplomacy," Prime snapped.

"We likewise do not understand why the Humans behaved as they did," said one of the K'lugu, "but certainly the incidents demonstrate the usefulness of the concepts the Humans have suggested—diplomatic inviolability and diplomatic immunity, banning the use of threats or force or legal proceeding against diplomats, and this concept of extraterritoriality. A fascinating idea, but one that does not come easily to K'lugu. Would you be so kind as to restate it again, friend Johan Tavennos?"

"Certainly, friend Nightcurrent. It is the idea that any Embassy, and its grounds, must be treated in law as if they were part of the country or planet represented by the Embassy. If there were a Human Embassy on K'lugu, Human law would be in effect inside it. The K'lugu Embassy on Earth would operate under K'lugu law. Also, no one from the host nation or planet can enter an Embassy without permission of the ambassador or his delegate. The host government, or people under its jurisdiction, can't invade an Embassy or take it over."

"Yes, very good!" Prime sneered. "If that rule had been in effect last night, your games with the aircars would have been completely illegal!"

"But they *weren't* in effect last night, friend Prime," said Nightcurrent. She looked toward Johan and nodded. "I suspect that is a great deal of the point."

Prime glared at the K'lugu. "What nonsense is this?" she demanded. "They break the very rules they suggest that we follow—and you listen to them?"

"I would point out the incidents of last night caught *your* attention as well," said Nightcurrent. "I suggest that the Humans were engaged in a bit of theater, demonstrating that an absence of rules harms you as much as them." She turned toward the Humans. "But I would remind you that K'lugu law was very much in effect last night, and still is this morning. Reckless flying and endangering others are serious violations."

"We apologize for any violation of those rules," said Johan. "But how can the Devlin accuse us of trespassing when they refuse to accept the legal concept that would give them rights to the property?"

"But we were there first!" Prime shouted. "We built our Embassy there. It is ours!"

Nightcurrent looked at the Devlin calmly. "Please allow me to remind you, friend Prime, that Blackback Island was merely *loaned* to the Devlin, and that it, and Negotiation Island, are very much on a K'lugu world. *We*, as you put it, were in fact here first. Under the logic your statement suggests, we could lay claim to part of the Devlin home world merely by landing on it and putting up a few structures."

"That is absurd!"

"We quite agree," said Nightcurrent, "but it flows from the logic of your own remarks."

"Perhaps this is a set of principles we can agree to," Clearwater suggested. "Prior and continuous occupation by a species of a place—an embassy, an island, a forest, a moon or a planet or a star system—must be respected, and presumed, absent further issues, to establish possession. Allowing outsiders to construct temporary structures does not, cannot, mean surrendering all rights to the place forever. But when such structures are built to serve as embassies, the rights, safety, and privacy of the representatives must be respected.''

Least was astonished to see that Prime was actually thinking it over, and more astonished when she actually signaled her assent. "Agreed," said Prime. "Anything to keep these Human interlopers away from our places.''

"Friend Johan Tavennos?''

"What? Oh! Yes!'' The Human Johan seemed genuinely surprised. "Agreed. It's most of what we've been asking for since we got here.''

"Excellent," said Brightwater. "This gives us something to start with, something to work on. Let us consider the details of this idea.''

Just then Third happened to glance over to where Least was standing, and frowned at him. "Go home!'' he said in a low voice. "If you hang around here too long, the Humans are going to ask if they can have five delegates, too. Shoo!''

Least sighed and walked back to the aircar, dreading another weary day at the Embassy compound.

Nothing ever happened there.

Adam was getting scared. The longer they were aboard this flying storage locker, the more likely it was that they would get caught. But unless the could find a sally port—not just a sally port, but *the* sally port that would lead them to the *Roanoke* survivors—then everything would be for nothing. Find that sally port, and go through it, find the castaways, deploy and activate the inducer, and that would be it. They'd win. Game over. The inducer would generate a sally port straight back to the Solar System, and help would be on the way to the castaways.

But unless and until they found the sally port that linked to the *Roanoke* survivors, none of it would happen. And there was nothing, nothing else in that enormous cargo hold that looked remotely like a sally port. They had searched every square meter of the place, and confirmed that the only ways out were the t-port they had come through and the airlock leading to outer space. There were no other hatches or doors or portholes. Just the one interplanetary t-port that had gotten them here.

The others were scrambling all over the cargo hold, searching once again for what plainly wasn't there. And besides, it didn't make any sense that the Devlin would have put the sally port in a secret compartment, or stuffed it inside one of those sealed packing cases. No. They couldn't have. They had all watched through the kite-cams when Least had gone into the t-port bunker, and then come out again less than an hour later. That wasn't enough time to dig the sally port out of a hiding place, go forth and back through it, and then hide it again. And besides, why hide it? There were all sorts of interesting things in this cargo bay that a Human spy would be interested in, and none of them were hidden.

All right then, Adam told himself as he stared at the t-port frame. The sally port wasn't concealed. That meant it had to be here, in plain sight, right in front of them—

Right in front of him. The t-port frame. Wait a second. He stared at. There was something about it, something familiar, and yet very out of place. It reminded him of a familiar object back home, tickling the back of his consciousness. Look at it. *Look* at it. A thing like a doorway, with a heavily reinforced frame. It was warm to the touch, and he could at least imagine he heard it humming. Two rows of four slate blue buttons, with a different symbol on each. They looked almost like the buttons in an elevator—

"Elevator buttons!" That was it. That was it! "I've got it!" he shouted. "It's right here in front of us! We were looking for different frames for each port, or else a big complicated way to shift the tuning. But they don't do it like that. They have it automated. They have just one combination t-port and sally port, and they put buttons on it like an elevator." He pointed at the buttons. One of the eight was lighted, and the others were dark. "Just push the button for the floor you want, and it takes you there! Or like a TV remote. Push the button, change the station."

The others gathered around. Ahna examined the t-port, studying the buttons carefully. "You're right," she said. "This frame is way too heavy-duty for just a low-power interplanetary t-port. It's built for interstellar. I should have seen it. Nice work, Adam."

"Yeah, nice work," Aaron agreed. "But now, what button do we push? And if we guess wrong, where do we end up? Devlin High Command, maybe?"

Roberto leaned in close to the buttons and gave them a long, hard look. "That one," he said at last, pointing to the lower left-hand button.

"How can you tell?"

"It's all scratched up, much more than the other ones, and the scratches are fresh. It's been used more. And there's a little fleck of mud on it, as if someone had pushed it in a hurry while there was dirt on his hands."

"So what does that tell us?"

"You couldn't see, last night," Roberto said calmly. "I could. Least went running past at one point and tripped over something. He landed in a half-dried mud puddle. He was a mess when he stood up."

Ahna shrugged. "That almost makes sense, and we don't have much time to fool around. Are you sure, Roberto?"

He nodded solemnly. "I'm sure."

"Either that, or he's been reading too much Sherlock Holmes," said Adam with a grin. "Let's find out."

"All right," said Ahna. "Here goes nothing."

She stabbed her finger down on the button. The button that had been lighted went off, and the button she pushed lit up. Nothing else happened for a moment, but then, in the blink of an eye, the view of the t-port bunker on Bogwater vanished. The t-port went black, and stayed that way.

The four of them exchanged worried glances. "Maybe that was the off switch?" Aaron suggested.

But then there was a strange low humming sound, and suddenly, a new place popped into being on the other side of the t-port frame. It was a ship interior, one that was almost the twin of the one they were in. The only major difference was that everything in it was light blue instead of white.

"Well, that worked, I guess," said Aaron.

"Unless it's the wrong ship," Ahna replied. "And we won't find out if it is from here. Everybody ready?"

"Let's go," said Adam. He gestured to Aaron, and the two of them picked up the inducer again and headed for the sally port.

"Brace yourself for a headache," Adam said.

"Don't remind me," said Aaron.

The two of them walked through the sally port side by side—and got kicked in the head harder than any mule could have done the job. It felt as someone had slammed down Adam's skull with a hammer. Aaron collapsed, passed out cold, and let go of his handle as he fell. The inducer hit the deck with a clang. Adam managed to hang on to his handle and at least steady it as it hit. He tried not to wonder how delicate the hardware inside was.

"Adam! What happened?" Ahna shouted from back on the other side of the sally port.

"The same as going through the other sally port," he said, "but worse. Much, much worse. I'll be all right in a second." He knelt on the deck and rubbed his head. It hurt. It hurt bad.

Aaron came to and sat up, ashen-faced and bleary-eyed.

"Can the two of you stand?" Ahna asked. "Roberto and I have to come through."

"Huh?" Oh, yeah, right." Adam forced himself to stand, then helped Aaron to his feet. They dragged the sally port inducer out of the way. "Come on over," Adam said weakly.

The pain hit Roberto and Ahna just as hard. It was a good five minutes before any of them recovered enough to think clearly. "It must be because t-port jumps don't affect the Devlin," said Ahna, holding her head and gasping with pain. "Our techs are always trying to tune our t-ports and sally ports to make the jumps easier. The Devlin don't bother."

Adam recovered before Ahna and Roberto, if only by a little. Aaron, for whatever reason, had been hit hardest by the passage, and it seemed clear he was going to stay down longest. But the Devlin could discover the break-in at their t-port bunker any second. They couldn't wait for Aaron to recover.

Adam forced himself to think, to work it out. They still didn't know for sure that they were in the right place. This ship didn't have so much as a porthole, and even if it did, it wouldn't do them any good. Long-range interstellar sally ports only worked well away from stars and planets. They must still be billions of kilometers away from whatever ship or planet or prison the *Roanoke* survivors were on. And that, Adam reminded himself, assumed the *Roanoke* survivors were there in the first place. All of it was guesswork. The logic made sense, but there were a million things they could have gotten wrong.

"Airlock," said Ahna, obviously still trying to recover herself. "We—we can put the inducer in the airlock, switch it on, and dump it overboard."

"But we don't know if this is the place," said Adam. "We can't waste the inducer on a guess. We have to know for sure."

And there was one very obvious, very unpleasant way to find out. This t-port frame had only two buttons on the side. One of them was lighted, and the other wasn't.

Adam's head was still pounding from the passage through the interstellar sally port. There was no way at all of knowing what awaited him on the other side of the t-port frame. But what choice did he have? He took all of his remaining courage, all the endurance he had left, and lifted his finger up to push the darkened button. The t-port frame went black, just as it had before—and then a new chamber, a dim-lit, heavy-walled place, popped into being on the other side.

"You get the inducer ready," he said. "I'm going to find out where we are."

And before anyone could say or do anything, he stepped through the t-port frame.

FOUND

Ahna turned back from the airlock and ran toward the t-port frame. They had seen Adam go through it, but he was no longer visible. He must have moved out of view. "Adam!" she cried out. "Adam!"

But there was no answer.

Ahna stared at the t-port frame, unsure what to do. Should she go after Adam and see if he needed any help? But help with what? She looked over at the inducer, then at Aaron, who was still barely able to hold his head up. That made her decide. It took two of them to move the inducer around, and Aaron was in no shape to help. If she left, Roberto wouldn't be able to move it on his own without a lot of struggle that would be hard on him— and the inducer. Besides, she was the only one of them with the slightest experience of airlocks. The best thing she could do to help Adam was to get ready to jettison the inducer.

She looked back at the t-port frame, to see if there was any visible sign of Adam. Instead what she saw made her blood run cold. The sally port frame went dark, black as night and death. And this time it stayed that way.

                    *   *   *

Least climbed out of the aircar and walked sadly back
to the Embassy. It was all going wrong. Prime was digging a hole for them, getting deeper and deeper, further
and further away from any sort of sensible goal. The
Humans were all but fated to be the Devlin's rivals. Anyone who could read a star chart could see that. But there
was no need to turn the Humans into *enemies*. What
hope could there be of building trust and respect between
the two races when all either side could do was bluster
and scheme?

And what of their captives, Ethan and Maurha and the
castaways he had harassed so relentlessly the night before? Least looked toward the t-port bunker, thinking of
all the trips he had made, how much effort had been—

The door! The door to the t-port bunker. Something
was different. No, something was *wrong*.

Least ran over and saw at once that someone had been
here with a hot cutter—a laser, more than likely.

Suddenly it all fell into place. *Diversions*. All the nonsense of the night before had been nothing but a series
of diversions—and they had worked all too well. The
Humans had gotten in. Least had not the slightest doubt
what—or rather whom—the Humans had been after.
The castaways. It all made sense.

Least yanked his sidearm out of its concealed holster
and pulled open the ruined door. Never mind what the
K'lugu said the rules for the meeting were, or who
caught him breaking them. The Humans had broken far
too many rules of their own this time. Least entered the
bunker, gun at the ready. He checked the indicator display, and was greatly surprised to see the Humans had
switched focus off this t-port frame. He punched in the
override, and waited for the link to the support ship to
re-form.

As soon as the link was tuned and stable, Least moved
through the t-port, and onto the deck of the cargo ship.

There was no one there—or at least no one that he could see. There could be eights, even sixty-fours, of Humans hiding in and under and around the packing cases. But Least rejected the possibility. The Humans had not gone to so much trouble just to snoop around the boxes in a cargo bay. They had gone on from here.

But where? Least checked the displays and the indicators, and swore with a proficiency that would have impressed Prime herself. With one chance out of eight, the devils had guessed right. They had linked into the support ship in the star system that held the castaways. And from that ship, there was only one other place they could have gone.

Or maybe they hadn't made the next jump, just yet. Least couldn't power down the castaway-system t-port frame from here, but he could scroll the standby power to barely more than nothing, enough to make the frame go so black it *looked* like it was shut down.

The power would come back up automatically if anyone on the castaway world tried to power up the link from there. And the Humans would be able to ramp the power right back up again from their end—but they would have to know how to do it. Maybe it would slow them down, if only a little. Just long enough to give Least a chance to think of a way out of this mess.

If there *was* a way out.

Adam woke up, and discovered he had fallen flat on his face yet again. The last t-port must have laid him out cold. Judging by the fresh scrapes and cuts on his hands, and the fact that his nose wasn't broken, his reflexes had managed to get him to throw his hands out in front of his face as he went down. That was something, at least.

There didn't seem to be much else to be grateful for. He had t-ported through into some sort of vault or bomb shelter, or something, judging by the thick concrete walls and the very serious-looking steel doors. He looked behind him, to check on the t-port link, and found more bad news there. He could no longer see the light blue interior of the cargo ship. Now there was nothing but inky, featureless black.

No way out, and no way back. He was locked in. Was the place airtight? Just how much breathing air did he have left? He took another look at the steel door and was vastly relieved to see it had a handle on the inside. Well, that made sense, if this bunker had been built to keep the people on the *outside* from getting *in* to where the t-port was.

Adam's hands were sweating as he pulled back on the handle, and the door swung open.

He stepped out onto a lovely hillside, on a world as gentle, as well favored, as Earth or Bogwater. There were strange crystalline hills in the middle distance, and lush plant life that was like nothing he had ever seen bloomed everywhere.

But the fine view was badly marred by the smashed machinery and broken-up pieces of ship that were scattered everywhere.

And the view was ruined even more by the two men and one woman standing just downhill from him, pointing guns at his head.

Ahna and Roberto carried the inducer across the deck to the airlock, and Ahna set to work figuring out the controls. It seemed to be a fairly straightforward rig, obviously designed to be easy to use in an emergency. She pulled the inner door open with her free hand, and the two of them staggered into the lock with the inducer between them. They set it down on the deck, and Ahna opened up the inducer's control panel. There was a simple visual menu system, and it only took a minute to get the thing switched on and set up for the proper activation sequence. She left the inducer in standby mode, rigging it so all they had to do was hit the start button, shut the airlock's inner door, and open the outer door. The inducer would take over from there. It would automatically fly to a safe distance, and then commence the sally port induction sequence, linking back to Edge Station Three, and the Solar System—and their job would be over.

Once Adam came back through the *Roanoke* t-port, it could all happen.

Ahna had a great many reasons for hoping they wouldn't have to wait too long for him to get back—but it was hard not to worry that he'd never come back at all.

"Keep your hands in plain sight," the bearded man said to Adam. "Come down here slowly. Slowly."

Adam was too astonished, too confused, to say much of anything. "But—but—I'm not Least—I'm—"

"You sure aren't, buddy. Or if you *are* Least, you sure have changed since last night."

"What's a Human doing coming through a Devlin t-port?" the woman demanded.

"Looking—looking for you!" Adam said as he moved slowly down the hill. "It took a lot of doing to find you."

"You sure took your sweet time about it," said the clean-shaven man. "We've been stuck here for close to fifteen years." He gestured with his handgun. "Sit down there, take that backpack off, and slide it over to me."

Adam did as he was told, and decided to try and keep the conversation going. If they were talking to him, they weren't going to shoot him. "No one even knew you were still alive until a couple of weeks ago," he said. "They started doing everything they could, the second they had the slightest clue at all."

"What do you mean 'they'?" the woman asked. "Aren't you one of them, whoever they are?"

Adam winced. How in the world could he ever explain

it all? "Not exactly," he said. "It's really complicated. There isn't time to tell it all."

"Why not?" asked the bearded man.

"Because sooner or later Least and his friends are going to notice we've broken into their sally port network and come looking for me."

"So you've come, just in the nick of time, to save us?" the clean-shaven one asked. "Whisk us all away through the Devlin sally ports to freedom?"

Adam shook his head sadly. "No," he said. "I'm sorry. If you went through the sally port, it would almost certainly kill you. Going through sally ports doesn't hurt Devlin, or Humans younger than about fifteen, but it'd kill any Human much over about sixteen or seventeen. Even I'm old enough so it's pretty hard on me."

The three of them exchanged glances with each other. "We thought that might be it," the woman said. "Or something like that. We've spent the last fifteen years wondering what killed our parents and all of the crew. We came up with lots of answers. Poison gas, radiation, alien weapons." She gestured toward the debris field. "There wasn't much evidence left to go by, after the crash—and we were only kids, anyway."

"And you had the younger ones to take care of," Adam suggested. "Just staying alive must have been hard."

"It was," the woman said, and the two words spoke volumes. "Ethan—anything interesting in the backpack?"

"Tools, what looks like a camera, rope—no death rays or hunter-trackers."

The woman looked thoughtfully at Adam. "You're no Devlin stooge, are you?"

"No, ma'am, I'm not."

She nodded and tucked her pistol into her tunic. "We were expecting Least again," she said. "We were going to hold our guns to his head, and make *him* start answering *our* questions."

"And maybe force him to let us escape through his t-port," said Ethan, holstering his own gun. Adam watched with relief as the other man lowered his gun as well. Ethan laughed bitterly. "If what you're saying is true, then maybe Least would have said yes. He'd go through safe, and all of us would die."

Adam shook his head. "I don't think so. Prime might try a trick like that, but somehow I don't think Least would. Or could."

"No," Ethan said thoughtfully, "I don't suppose he could. Least has a decent streak to him." He looked at Adam. "My name's Ethan Dushan, if you didn't catch it. That's my wife Maurha, and her brother Markus."

"My name's Adam. Adam O'Connor."

"Glad to meet you, son," said Ethan.

"Ah, you too, sir." Adam glanced back up toward the Devlin t-port bunker. "But I'm running out of time. I've got to get back."

Ethan looked annoyed. "That's it?" he asked. "You risk life and limb and war with the Devlin, just to poke your head out of a hole and tell us we're stranded forever?"

"What? Oh! No, sir. Even if you can't go through a sally port, they—we—are going to set up a sally port—a Human-controlled one—to get you back in contact with Earth. Send you new supplies, equipment, robots. All sorts of things. But I have to get back fast with proof that you're here, or there might not be a chance to set up the port in time."

Proof. Not just proof to show Ahna and Johan. They did not need it. But proof to put before the Devlin and the K'lugu. Proof that could be put before the whole universe.

"I see."

Adam looked around the landscape. "Ah, excuse me

230

for asking—but are you three the only survivors?"

It was Maurha's turn to be surprised. "Goodness! We forgot to give them the all-clear." She put her two index fingers to her mouth and let out a piercing whistle.

From out of nowhere, it seemed, from behind rocks, behind crevices, teenagers and young adults popped up into view. "A lot more than three of us made it," Markus said with obvious pride. "And my sister and her husband have even managed a new addition."

A little girl, no older than two or three, came hurtling toward Maurha, and leapt into her arms. Maurha caught her and hoisted her up onto her hip. "Adam O'Connor," she said, "I'd like you to meet Virginia Dare Dushan. Ginny, this is Adam."

The little girl stared solemnly at him. "Hello, Adam."

"Hello, Virginia," Adam said. He looked at Maurha. "Her name," he said. "Virginia Dare. The first child of English settlers born in North America. Born in Roanoke, in what's now North Carolina, in 1587."

"You know the story," said Maurha.

"Yes," he said. "My family lives just a few hours away from Roanoke. I've been there."

"Maybe our story will end up a bit differently," said Markus. "They never did find any trace of the first Roanoke. We were beginning to think it would be the same way with us."

Suddenly Maurha stepped toward Adam, holding her child. "Proof," she said. "You wanted proof." She lifted Ginny off her hip and offered her to Adam. "Take her. Take her with you."

"What!" Ethan shouted. "Have you gone crazy?"

Adam took Ginny in his arms automatically, without thinking. "But, ma'am—it's dangerous out there."

"It's dangerous here, too!" said Maurha, her eyes flashing. "Shall I show you our graveyard? There's a whole hillside of proof there if you want it. If what you're saying is true, then everyone else on this planet is too old to survive a trip through the sally port, but it won't hurt *her*. And—and if something goes wrong, and you *can't* get back here—she'll be safer out there than she ever could be in this place.''

Tears came to Maurha's eyes. ''But nothing *will* go wrong,'' she said. ''And they'll see a little girl—and they'll *know*. They'll know we're here, and we're still alive. And then you'll bring her back—and they'll send medicine, and books, and all the other things she's never had. They'll *have* to send them—because they'll see her, and they'll *know*.''

Adam looked to the little girl's father, and her uncle. ''What—what should I do?'' he asked, totally confused. ''I'm running out of time.''

Markus looked at Ethan. ''Think of last winter,'' he said gently. ''Think of how close it was then.''

Ethan's eyes teared up, and he looked at his daughter, at his wife. ''Maurha's right,'' he said. ''Take her with you. Don't let this Virginia Dare vanish without a trace the way the first one did. And don't send her back, unless you send help with her.'' Ethan looked at all the other survivors. Just about all of them had to be older than Adam, but Adam was taller, heavier, stronger, than any of them. They were, all of them, thin, bordering on gaunt. ''And send *lots* of help,'' he said.

''Hey!'' Aaron shouted. ''Something's happening.'' Ahna looked up, and saw that the t-port frame had come back to life. But who had turned it on? All three of them backed away from it as it powered up. Ahna tried to figure out what in the cargo bay would provide the best cover.

But then the t-port resolved. It was Adam, after all. Adam with a three-year-old girl riding on his shoulders. He was ashen-faced, unsteady on his feet. The passage through the t-port could not have been easy on him.

''Hello,'' said the little girl. ''We're going on a trip.''

"We sure are," Adam said. "We sure are." He turned to Ahna as soon as he was through the frame. "Ahna! We're in the right place. The *Roanoke* crashed here. Is the inducer ready to go?"

"Yes, but how in the world—"

"Later," he said, the weariness plain in his voice. "There's no time. Least could show up any second. Get the inducer going, *now*." He scooped the little girl off his shoulders and set her down on her feet. "Stay with me, Ginny," he said.

"Least might be waiting for us," said Aaron. "The t-port turned itself off. Ahna thinks Least might have done it."

"Then he's waiting for us," Adam snapped. "Where else have we got to go? The longer we wait, the more chance he has to get reinforcements together. Let's *go*."

Ahna sprinted for the airlock. She knelt by the inducer, and punched in the final commands. She jumped through the inner door of the airlock, sealed it, and pulled the lever she hoped would start the lock working.

It did. Powerful air pumps whirred and thumped, and then grew silent as the last of the air was sucked away. Ahna watched through a porthole as the outer door swung open.

The inducer came to life. It floated up off the deck-plates and out through the outer airlock door. Without any fuss, it eased itself out into space, and boosted away from the Devlin ship.

That was it. The end of the job they had come to do. She watched, fascinated, as the inducer pulled away, shrank to a tiny dot of light, and vanished. Soon it would be far enough away to activate itself. The ships from Earth would come—and the Roanoke castaways would be castaways no more.

And a whole new world, a lovely, blue-green world, would be added to Humanity's domain. They'd have won the game of worlds. Or at least this round of it.

Mission accomplished, she thought. *At least, if the inducer didn't break when we dropped it.*

"Ahna, let's go!" Aaron shouted.

She turned her back on the airlock, and ran back toward the sally port frame. Aaron urged her through, and followed after her, the last to leave the Devlin ship.

Aaron felt his feet about to go out from under him again, even as he crossed through the gate. His transit headache was bad, maybe even worse than it had been going the other way. But as bad as he was, the others were all struck down worse. All three of them passed out cold, dropping like stones as soon as they passed through the sally port frame.

Ginny, the little girl Adam had brought back, didn't seem to be suffering, but she could see all the other people hurting. "Will they be all right?" she asked Aaron in a very serious voice.

"In a minute," said Aaron. "The trip through that doorway made their heads hurt. That's all." *I hope.* The cumulative effect of all those sally port and t-port jumps couldn't be healthy for any of them.

"Put your hands up," said a low, growly voice from behind them. A jolt of fear shot through Aaron, but he forced it back down. He would not let them see he was afraid. Never again would he let them.

They turned around—and there he was. Least, with a big ugly gun pointing right at them.

"Hello, Least," said Ginny. "My friends don't feel good."

"Quiet now, Ginny," said Least.

Aaron looked down at the little girl, and then back up at the Devlin. All right, they knew each other. Why not?

Least waved his gun at Aaron. "You. Let go of her, and put all—both—of your hands in the air. Now."

Aaron was not a bit surprised that Least was there, waiting for them. But somehow, just the sight of one of those four-armed bullies pointing a gun at him was enough to stiffen Aaron's spine, push the pain away. "Or else?" he asked.

"Or else I shoot you," said Least.

Surrender, Ahna had told them. If they catch you, give up without a fight. It made sense. Besides, hadn't their side already won? The inducer was probably starting to activate already. They had found the *Roanoke*, and a whole new planet besides.

But winning didn't make Aaron feel the least little bit like surrendering to a race of bullies. And he knew, all too well, just how far giving in would get them.

"Wait a second," he said to Least. "I'll be right with you." Aaron let go of Ginny's hand. "See that big stack of boxes over there?" he asked. "I bet you can't climb them."

"Sure I can!" Ginny said.

"Show me!" he said.

The little girl raced away.

"There," Aaron said. "Now you've got a nice clean field of fire. So go ahead."

"What do you mean?" Least demanded.

"I mean shoot," he said, barely controlling the anger in his voice. "You have to shoot us all anyway. Why waste time? Why not get started?" He gestured toward Roberto, Adam, and Ahna. "They're all out cold," he said. "Nice easy targets. Why not shoot them all now and save yourself the trouble later?"

"Quiet!" Least shouted. "Quiet or—"

"Or what?" Aaron demanded. "Or you'll shoot me? Tell me, please—what I can do so you *won't* shoot me? Is there anything? You need us dead to keep the secret, right? The *Roanoke* secret? Fine. Shoot us all you like— but it won't be enough. You'll have to shoot everybody who knows. Like all the *Roanoke* castaways. Including that one." He pointed at Ginny, who was just scrambling to the top of a stack of boxes. "How good is your aim. Think you can hit her from here?"

Aaron moved forward a step. "Then there are the other four members of our team, back on Bogwater. They know all about it. But if you kill *them*, then you'll have to get rid of the witnesses—the K'lugu who were at the meeting. Nightcurrent, Waveripple, all of them. And any other K'lugu *they* might have talked to. And there's a whole bunch of other Humans. People back at Edge Station Three who know all about it. The ones who sent us. I can give you their names, if that would help you track them down. And then there are all kinds of robots who know all about it, but I bet you won't care about blasting *them*."

Aaron stalked closer and closer to Least, until the Devlin started backing away.

"But supposing one out of all those Humans and K'lugu and robots and artificial persons and whatever told someone I forgot to mention? No problem. Shoot 'em. Problem solved. Unless there was a Devlin somewhere. A really weird one. One with a conscience, maybe with a *guilty* conscience, and maybe a shred of decency and a sense of shame who—"

"Quiet!" Least bellowed. "Quiet! Silence!"

"Least!" It was Ginny, calling to him from on top of a stack of packing cases. "Least!" she called again, waving her arms and grinning from ear to ear. "Look at me! Lookit!"

"There she is, Least," Aaron said. "Perfect target. Want to see if you can pick her off from this range?"

Least raised his upper right arm, the one without the weapon, and slapped Aaron hard across the face. "Quiet!" he said.

Aaron staggered back under the blow, but then drew himself up to his full height. "Give me a reason to be quiet," he said, "or make me quiet forevermore." He could hear low moaning behind him. The others were waking up. The moment was ending. "Decide fast, Least," he said. "Once they wake up, some of them might escape before you can get them all. Start killing us all, *right now*—or throw the gun away."

Aaron stared at Least's face, forcing the Devlin to look at him. There was no sound in the cargo hold for the space of a dozen heartbeats. Absolute silence. Not a moan from the three Humans just waking up, not a shout of glee from the little girl on the packing cases. Nothing.

And then, at last, there was a noise, made all the louder by the silence that surrounded it.

With a crash and a clatter, Least's assault blaster dropped to the deck of the ship.

FADE AWAY

Adam walked the hallways of the C.O.B. for the last time, heading for the medical center. From there, he'd head for the Yank chamber—and from there—home.

As he walked, his mind reached back, straining to catch, to hold, to cherish, to say farewell, to the memories that he knew had to vanish. There was a lot to be proud of, a lot they had accomplished.

Least had not only escorted them through the last of the t-ports, he had flown them from Blackback Island to the Parley Pavilion. Their arrival there, with Ginny in tow, had caused a most satisfactory uproar, with the K'lugu there as a neutral party to witness it all.

Ginny had made most of it happen. She proved the castaway story, just by being there. But the photos Adam had taken of the *Roanoke* castaways, and the wreckage of the ship—and the Devlin t-port bunker—all made a significant impression on the K'lugu. The upshot of it was that the Devlin, mere hours after agreeing that continuous occupation conferred ownership, were forced to concede the Human claim to a brand-new world—a world that would be named for the lost ship, and the lost colony it honored, as soon as everyone could get organized for a formal naming ceremony. But, of course, everyone was calling the place "Roanoke" already.

The incident had produced a major scandal for the Devlin. As best intelligence could gather, The Contact-with-Humans Group was suddenly in need of a new Prime—and Least had been transferred as well, to another group, and was Least no more, but had moved up quite a bit in the ranks. It was good to know. It told Humans that there were Devlin around who would rebel against immoral orders—and higher-ranking Devlin who had the sense to reward, and not punish, subordinates who showed moral courage.

And, needless to say, humbling the Devlin just a bit was going to make the job easier for Dr. Halshaw and Thompson. The planning for Meeting Two, on Earth, was already under way. Both sides expected it to be quite a bit more orderly than Meeting One—if perhaps a bit less exciting.

The new sally port link between Edge Station Three and the planet Roanoke was already up and running. Virginia Dare Dushan had already gone home aboard the first ship to travel across the new sally port. A good half dozen ships had followed, piloted by skilled Human teens. No one on Roanoke would starve next winter.

Adam understood why he had to forget it all before he went back. But he would have traded all the rest of it for the chance to remember his new friends. He reached the med center, and the door slid open for him.

Ahna was already there in the waiting room. So were Roberto and Aaron. Strange to see them in their own clothes, instead of Operation Hourglass s-suits. For that matter, it felt odd to be wearing his own twentieth-century clothes. They felt baggy, clumsy, awkward.

He looked from one to the other. Ahna. Roberto. Aaron. And he had been there too, doing his part. It had taken all four of them to get through it all. Take any one of them out of the mix, and no one would have made it.

"Well," said Aaron with a smile, "they're taking Roberto and me first for the memory-fader gadget. You come after—so I guess this is good-bye."

"I guess so," said Adam. They shook hands. "Good luck to you," he said. He knew, even if Aaron did not, just how much luck Aaron would need in the years that lay ahead of him. "Take care of yourself back there."

"Oh, I will," said Aaron. "I learned a few lessons about that up this way."

"But you're about to forget all your lessons," Roberto objected.

Aaron smiled gently. "The mind might forget," he said. "But the soul remembers." He looked to Ahna, and smiled. "*Auf wiedersehen, Fräulein Ahna.* Until we meet again."

"When are you two ever going to meet again?" Roberto asked with a laugh.

Aaron shrugged. "Stranger things have happened," he said. "Most of them in the last couple of weeks."

"Good-bye, Aaron," said Ahna. "Thank you. And thank *you*, Roberto. You won our people a whole new planet, and perhaps helped stop an interstellar war. We wouldn't have been able to do it without both of you."

"*De nada*," said Roberto. "It was nothing. It was our great pleasure to serve with you, *Senhorita* Ahna. I know I will miss reading—in my soul—even if I cannot remember it. Thank you for such a precious gift, even if it was only mine for a short time. And thanks as well to you, *Senhor* Adam. You did well. Very well indeed. *Ate logo.*"

The door to the main med unit slid open. Their heads held high, the ghetto boy from 1930s Berlin, and the nineteenth-century Brazilian slave turned and walked inside. The door slid shut behind them.

Ahna and Adam stood there, simply staring at the

door, for a time. At last Adam turned to Ahna. "Did you bring them?" he asked.

"I don't know why you want to bother," said Ahna, handing him a datareader. She nodded at the med unit. "You'll forget it all yourself, as soon as you go in there."

"Wouldn't you want to know, if you were me?" asked Adam. "Besides. Maybe Aaron is right. Maybe the soul remembers."

Ahna smiled. "Maybe," she said. "I hope so."

"I know this must be hard for you," he said. "You don't have to wait and keep an eye on me. When the door opens again, I'll go through it."

"I know you will," said Ahna, tears in her eyes. "And, for what it's worth, *I'll* always remember *you*." She stepped in close to him, just for a moment, and kissed him. "Bye," she said, and hurried out into the hall.

Adam sat down on the couch, and switched on the datareader. He wanted, he *had* to know. He wanted the knowledge in his head, if only for a few minutes. What happened to them? How did they turn out?

Galvão, Roberto. Born 1868, Fortelaza, Brazil. Born into slavery, freed by abolition of slavery in state of Ceará, 1884. Taught self to read and write. Established a school for ex-slaves, 1891, despite strong opposition. Wrote extensively in later years, mainly essays on political subjects, urging social and political reform (many of which writings were suppressed) and a series of adventure stories popular in the region . . .

Schwartz, Aaron. Born 1923, Berlin, Germany. Escaped with family to England, January 1939 by use of false papers. Joined British Army on eighteenth birthday, 1941.

Served with distinction, North Africa campaign. Gained promotion to sergeant, 1943. Landed in Normandy on D day plus 4, 1944. Wounded twice. Emigrated illegally to Palestine, 1946. Active in movement to found Israel. Enlisted in Israeli army, and promoted through ranks to colonel . . .

Adam set the datareader to one side. No doubt, somewhere in this building, there was a computer file with a little pocket biography that began

O'Connor, Adam. Born 1984, North Carolina, U.S.A. . . .

But what did it say after that?

Aaron. Roberto. As best he could tell, both of them had spent their lives breaking the rules—but it seemed to Adam they had both broken *bad* rules, and broken them for good reasons, and had been willing to risk the consequences. They had fought for worthwhile things—and won.

So what worthwhile thing had *he* ever fought for? And what direction, exactly, had his life been moving in, right at the moment he dropped down that weird blue manhole cover?

He was still trying to answer that question when the inner door to the med lab slid open again.

Adam came to sprawled out on the sidewalk, tangled up in his bicycle. He could feel a bump rising over his left temple, and he had a splitting headache.

He sat up slowly and shook his head to clear it. He must have tripped somehow while walking his bike and banged his skull against the pavement.

He got to his feet, and was surprised at how stiff and sore he felt. He could feel a good half dozen tender spots on his arms and legs. He ran his hand over his head, and winced to find two or three other good-sized knots up there. That must have been some spill.

In fact, he must have been out for quite a while—long enough to hallucinate his way through the strangest dream he had ever—

He struggled to remember it, to remember *any* of it, but the memories flitted away as he strained to retrieve them. *Could* you have dreams when you were knocked out cold? Adam wasn't sure, but it didn't sound right.

Never mind. It was over and done with now. He leaned his bike up against a parking meter, dusted himself off, and climbed back on. He checked his watch as he pedaled, and realized he couldn't have been out more than a couple of seconds. Odd. He still couldn't remember any of it, but he had the distinct impression that his dream had gone on for days and days.

It didn't matter. The main thing was, he still had plenty of time to get to Mrs. Meredith's house and—

And do what? He frowned to himself as he rolled on through the quiet streets and the cool fall night. What had he been *thinking* of? Somehow, the closer he got to Mrs. Meredith's house, the crazier the whole idea was. Why take such risks, why chance getting into more trouble? And why do something so *dumb*? There were a dozen ways he was likely to get caught.

But getting caught was suddenly the least of it. Somehow the trouble he was in, the trouble that seemed so big and serious, and scary, seemed like nothing to be afraid of, nothing he couldn't handle. He had done something really dumb, and he had gotten caught. So? He had faced lots of things that were worse—though he couldn't quite remember when.

Adam slowed down as he turned onto Mrs. Meredith's street. He had been going at this thing all wrong. Tying it up into knots, lying and trying to weasel out of it. All he was doing was making things worse for himself—

worse, probably, than the original trouble itself.

No. The best way through a problem was . . . straight through it. It was like—like a tunnel, a tunnel through the sky, one of those spacewarp things from science fiction, making a shortcut between where you were and where you needed to be. The image was strange, not the sort of thing Adam usually came up with, but that didn't matter. The point was you could go up and down and around in circles—or you could go straight ahead. Face the problem. Deal with it. Move on.

He came to a halt in front of Mrs. Meredith's house. It was small, and not real fancy. The front yard was tiny, but the lawn was neatly mowed. And there was her car, that crazy old '73 Dodge, parked in the driveway. There was a lot of work that could be done on that car. With a little time and effort, Adam had a feeling he could really make something out of it.

But there was one other little job he would have to do first. He pushed the kickstand down on his bike, and parked on the sidewalk in front of her house. There was a light on in the living room. It looked like she was sitting up reading.

It was late, very late. He knew he shouldn't be there bothering her at this hour. But it was better to do it at once, and not risk the chance of losing his nerve. Better to get it over with. Right now.

Adam walked up the front steps of Mrs. Meredith's house, reached to ring the bell—and hesitated. His heart was pounding so loud it was a wonder Mrs. Meredith couldn't hear it. Somewhere, in the back of his mind, he had the fleeting memory of facing some other door, some really weird door, that had scared him almost as much as this one. And there had been a button there, too. Not a doorbell, exactly. More like an elevator button, but that wasn't quite right either.

Whatever it was, he couldn't bring it to mind. Probably just part of that same crazy dream. But wherever the memory came from, he was sure that he had gone ahead and *pushed* the button. He had gone *through* that door. Somehow, it had hurt, a lot. But he had come out all right on the other side.

He reached out and pushed the button hard. The bell rang, echoing in the small, well-kept house.

Adam heard footsteps. The door opened. And there was Mrs. Meredith, holding her book, her thumb marking the page she had been reading.

"Adam!" she said in surprise. "What in the world are you doing here?"

"Hi, Mrs. Meredith," he began. "Um, it's about your car. And that business with the cherry bomb."

"What about it?" she asked suspiciously.

Adam O'Connor looked his teacher straight in the eye and forced himself to speak calmly. It wouldn't end here—but it had to start somewhere. Take the punishment and then move on. There were a lot of things he ought to be doing with his life. But none of them could happen until he dealt with this.

"The cherry bomb was *me*," said Adam. "I'm the one who did it."

Two books mentioned in the text—*The Mansions and The Shanties* and *The Masters and the Slaves*, by Gilberto Freyre, are big, serious texts on Brazil's history and its struggle with slavery. *The Brazilians* by Joseph Page provides an excellent snapshot of modern-day Brazil. The following web sites have a good deal of information, in both English and Portuguese, concerning the huge and fascinating country of Brazil:

- Brazil Online—**http://brazilonline.com**
- The Brazilian Embassy in Washington D.C.—**http://brasil.emb.nw.dc.us**
- Meu Brasil—**http://darkwing.uoregon/edu/~sergiok/brasil.html**

Go to the web site of the United States Holocaust Memorial Museum at **www.ushmm.org** to learn more about Nazi oppression—and worse—of the Jewish people. William Shirer's excellent books, *Berlin Diary*, *The Nightmare Years*, and *The Rise and Fall of the Third Reich* are not light reading, but paint a vivid picture of the evil and violence of Nazi Germany, often providing a special focus on the Nazis's treatment of the Jews.

Go to **www.thelostcolony.org** to learn about the play about Roanoke that has been running for 60 years—near the site of the colony. For background on the lost colony of Roanoke itself, see Trackstar: The Lost Colony of Roanoke at **http://scrtec.org/track/tracks/s00428.html**.

FREE! FREE! FREE!
DAVID BRIN'S
OUT OF TIME
P O S T E R   O F F E R

Avon Books is pleased you've chosen the exciting new **OUT OF TIME** series by *New York Times* bestselling author DAVID BRIN and a team of highly acclaimed science fiction writers. As our welcome gift to you, we'd like to send you a dynamic full color poster illustrating this original science fiction adventure series—absolutely FREE! Just fill out the coupon below, and send it to us with proof of purchase (sales receipts) of: *Yanked* (on sale in June 1999), *Tiger in the Sky* (on sale in July 1999), and *The Game of Worlds* (on sale in August 1999) and we'll rush a poster your way.

Void where prohibited by law.

Mail to:
Avon Books, Dept. BP, P.O. Box 767, Dresden, TN 38225

Name_____

Address_____

City_____

State/Zip_____

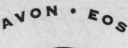